Divine Intervention

"Please!" the old woman begged pitifully when she regained consciousness.

With one hand raised to protect her bloodied face, she scrambled along the floor of the shed, searching for escape, clawing at the rough cedar planks below her.

"Please, let me go! I've done nothing!"

Crouching down with a piece of yellow rope grasped firmly between my hands, I stared at her. She reminded me of a deer, caught in the headlights of an oncoming car.

Removing the hood from my head, I smiled.

Her eyes widened with recognition and terror.

I carefully tied her feet together and pushed her to a sitting position. Then I wrapped the stiff rope around her neck. Yanking her toward the wooden workbench, I heard her gasping for air, her short legs jerking spasmodically beneath her.

I leaned down and asked her one important question.

With a glimmer of hope in her terrified eyes, she whispered the answer in a small voice.

"No...man. No...man wash—"

"Nana?" a child's voice called from outside the utility shed.

I held my breath and prayed that the child would go away, but when the door opened and a small face peered inside, I knew that I had no other choice.

Grubbing the little girl's arm, I hauled her into the shed.

"You should have stayed inside the house. Now look what you're making me do, you naughty girl."

The child whimpered softly while I tied her tightly to the semi-conscious woman. And then I left them, trussed up like animals, while I made the final preparations.

Reviews of Divine Intervention

"An action-packed book for summer readers. As with all well-written mysteries, the perpetrator turns out to be the person who the reader least expects. The many entangled relationships between the characters ensure that the story will keep readers turning pages."
~ Bruce Atchison, freelance writer

"*Divine Intervention* was a hugely pleasant surprise. Cheryl Kaye Tardif has definitely found her genre with this new crime novel set in the not-so-far future. Believable characters, and scorching plot twists. Anyone who is a fan of JD Robb will thoroughly enjoy this one—especially any who have been waiting for an excellent voice to bring alive a genuinely Canadian crime novel. *Divine Intervention* will undeniably leave you smoldering—and dying for more."
~ Kelly Christian, WGA member and DF (Devout Fan)

"WONDERFUL! Riveting, with imagery almost agonizingly clear. Tardif's characters and story have an integrity that makes it nearly impossible to stop reading!"
~ Kate Leighton, Canadian editor and writer

Reviews of Whale Song

"Moving...sweet and sad...Tardif, already a big hit in Canada...a name to reckon with south of the border."
~ Booklist

"A wise, enchanting story..."
~ The Edmonton Examiner

"Poignant and compelling, a coming-of-age story that addresses important societal issues within a contemporary backdrop. Ms. Tardif has a writing style which is appealing and meaningful."
~ Ian Anthony, Award Winning Author,
www.secretbookcase.com

"Great new voice in Cheryl Kaye Tardif! A wonderful story. This book is absolutely worth picking up...because one cannot help but fall in love with these characters. The book is written so passionately, with stunning conviction."
~ Kelly, Amazon.ca reviewer

"A beautiful, heart-warming story...it is truly beautiful. From the first page to the last, I was captivated. Cheryl's storytelling ability is phenomenal, and real. I felt every emotion, every triumph and defeat. I have given this book to several of my friends as a gift, and they all love it as much as I."
~ Amazon.ca reviewer

Novels by Cheryl Kaye Tardif

Whale Song

Divine series:

Divine Intervention
Divine Justice *

* not yet published

Divine

intervention

Cheryl Kaye Tardif

www.cherylktardif.com
cherylktardif@shaw.ca
Cover design by Imajin Creations

ISBN: 978-1-4120-3591-0

 www.trafford.com

North America & international
toll-free: 1 888 232 4444 (USA & Canada)
phone: 250 383 6864 ♦ fax: 250 383 6804 ♦ email: info@trafford.com

The United Kingdom & Europe
phone: +44 (0)1865 722 113 ♦ local rate: 0845 230 9601
facsimile: +44 (0)1865 722 868 ♦ email: info.uk@trafford.com

10 9 8 7 6 5 4 3

ACKNOWLEDGEMENTS

This book is dedicated to the courageous, persistent firefighters who fought one of British Columbia's largest fires—the Okanagan Mountain forest fire in 2003. These men and women are the heroes to those whose homes were saved and the heroes to those who lost everything—except hope. Firefighters' lives are always on the line and we pray they remain vigilant and fireproof.
We thank you and salute you!

It is also dedicated to my husband, Marc, who was a volunteer firefighter in BC for a couple of years. He always 'lights my fire'! *Thank you for encouraging me to be who I am.*

Special thanks to my good friend, Carolyn Shinbine—a *RN* at University of Alberta Hospital—for her medical expertise, and for giving me clarity. *Your input makes Jasi's world a realistic one.*

To my editors, Mary Kaye, Francine Tardif and Marc Tardif, thank you for keeping the story tight. *Your hard work is much appreciated!*

Thanks also to Kelly Christian for allowing me to borrow "Eric Jefferson". *I may not be done with him yet!*

And a final thanks to my daughter, Jessica; my Japanese daughter, Ayumi; and my Japanese son, Yuki, for their support and self-reliance while my mind has been elsewhere! *I love you!*

Any mistakes, or impossibilities, are my own.

There is surely a piece of divinity in us,
something that was before the elements,
and owes no homage unto the sun.
~ Sir Thomas Browne

Intervention – to occur or lie between two things
~ *Webster's Collegiate Dictionary*

Prologue

It always began with the dead girl in her closet.

Every night when little Jasmine opened that closet door she expected to see lovely dresses and hangers—not a child her age strung up by a pink skipping rope, her body dangling above the floor…unmoving.

The dead girl had long blond hair. Her blue eyes stared blindly and were surrounded by large black circles. Her mouth hung open in a soundless scream. The pink rope was tied tightly around her neck, a thick pink necklace of death. A purplish-black bruise was visible and ugly.

The most unusual thing about the girl, other than the fact that she was swinging from a rope in Jasmine's closet, was that her skin and clothing were scorched.

Gagging, little Jasmine stepped back in horror.

When the girl's lifeless body swayed gently from a sudden breeze Jasmine let loose a cry of terror and raced down the stairs, searching anxiously for her parents.

"Daddy?"

Her throat was constricted and dry.

"Mommy?"

Then she screamed. "Mommy, I need you! Help me!"
In the lower hallway, the shadows quickly surrounded her.
Then she saw them.
Red eyes flashing angrily at the end of the hall.
Jasmine took a hesitant step backward. She tried to run but her feet would not cooperate. Her small body began to shake while the eyes followed her.
Glancing over her shoulder, she noticed a listless form moving toward her, arms outstretched—pleading.
The girl from the closet wasn't dead anymore.
Blistered hands reached for Jasmine.
The girl's mouth yawned and a horrendous shriek emerged.
Trapped and terrified, Jasmine began to scream…

1

Agent Jasi McLellan awoke from her nightmare screaming and drenched in sweat. Irritated by a piercing sound, she turned her pounding head and glanced at the wall beside her.

A technologically advanced video-screened wall, or *vid-wall*, had recently been added to her daunting security system. The wall was divided into four monitors—each coded for different activities.

The message screen flashed brightly.

Someone was trying to contact her.

"Receive message," she croaked.

She was rewarded with silence.

Jasi eyed the clock. *5:30 in the goddamn morning.* Who the hell would be calling her this early on her day off?

Glaring words flashed across the monitor followed by a voice, deep and urgent. *"Jasi, we need you! Ben."*

She was suddenly wide awake.

"Message for Ben."

When the system connected with Ben's data-communicator, she said, "Give me fifteen minutes. End message."

She glanced at the words on the screen and realized her *holiday* was over. She wondered for a moment what was so important that Ben had to interrupt her downtime. With two days left, she had hoped to catch up on some much-needed rest.

Crawling from beneath the sweat-soaked sheets, she crouched on the edge of the bed and reached for her portable data-com.

She checked the calendar.

A black *X* was scribbled over the date.

"Oh God," she moaned.

Today was her twenty-sixth birthday.

Jasi hated birthdays.

She pushed herself off her bed. In the dark, her toe connected sharply with the corner of the dresser and she let out a startled yelp.

"Ensuite lights on, low!"

Her *Home Security & Environmental Control System* immediately raised the lighting to a soft muted glow. Some days she was very thankful she had allowed Ben to install *H-SECS* in her new apartment. Of course, on the days when she couldn't remember a command or the security code to her weapons safe, Ben would get an earful.

Limping to the bathroom, Jasi shook her head.

Could this day possibly get any worse? Maybe I should go back to bed...wake up tomorrow.

She hugged her arms close to her chest and stepped into the ensuite bathroom. Parking her butt on the toilet, she stared at her throbbing toe. Scowling, she stood up, leaned tiredly against the sink and examined her reflection.

That's when she remembered her recurring nightmare.

"Why can't you leave me alone?" she whispered to a dead girl who wasn't there.

Frowning at her puffy, shadowed green eyes, Jasi splashed cool water on her face and rested her elbows on the edge of the sink. She traced a finger over the small scar that ran down the left side of her chin. It was barely noticeable, except to her.

Spurring herself into action, she cast a self-deprecating glance at her hazy image and then headed for the shower.

"Shower on, massage, 110 degrees," she commanded as she removed her panties and nightshirt. "Radio on, volume 7."

Music from her favorite rock station pounded in through the ceiling speakers as she stumbled into the large shower stall. Stretching hesitantly, she relaxed her tense muscles and breathed a sigh of relief when the steamy water sent thoughts of a dead girl swirling down the drain.

Jasi lathered her long auburn hair and stood under the spray, allowing the water to massage her scalp. Grimacing, she slid a wide-toothed comb through the tangled mess of wavy locks. Her hair had a mind of its own. More than once Jasi had threatened to chop it off but she was afraid she'd end up with a 'fro.

Couldn't have that. No one would take her seriously.

Her central data-com beeped suddenly.

Her fifteen minutes were up.

Cursing under her breath, she spit toothpaste into the sink, barely missing the soap dispenser.

"Data-com on!"

"Hey there, sunshine!" a male voice boomed. "You miss us?" Benjamin Roberts, her friend and partner, didn't wait for a response. "Divine has issued a Command Meet. He says he's sorry to cut your downtime short but we need you."

His voice followed Jasi as she returned to her bedroom and ordered the lights on full.

She sighed loudly. "It's not like I have anything better to do today. Like relax, go to a movie, or hook up with a handsome stranger for a night of passion."

She eyed the closet nervously, then whipped the door open and stepped back, unsure of what or who might emerge.

No one was there.

"Hey, *am* I interrupting something?"

She grabbed some clothes, slamming the door quickly.

"I *wish*! What's up, Ben?"

Stepping into a pair of casual slacks and a light blouse, she waited for her partner's answer.

"You still in the shower, Jasi? Maybe you should put up the vid-wall." She heard him snicker.

"Yeah right!"

"We caught a case near Kelowna—a fire." Ben's voice grew serious. "One victim, Dr. Norman Washburn, ER doc at Kelowna General."

Jasi frowned, and strapped on a shoulder harness.

Kelowna.

She hadn't been there in years. Not since the disastrous Okanagan Mountain forest fires of 2003. Now, nine years later, she would be returning. She'd have to take some precautions, prepare herself.

"Why'd they call us?"

"Sorry, Jasi. I know you're still officially on downtime, but this one is bad. They found a link to another fire. Two victims—a mother and child in Victoria. Unsolved."

There was a long silence.

"Ben?"

She heard a soft chuckle on the other end. "By the way, Jasi, Happy Birthday."

"How'd they link that one to the doctor?" she asked, ignoring the reference to her birthday.

When he told her what the crime scene investigators had found at the scene, Jasi grabbed her 9-millimeter

Beretta, checked the safety and jammed it into the holster. Then she dashed from the apartment—a shadow hot on her heels.

A cab dropped her off at an isolated address in the West End. On the roof of a seedy-looking warehouse, a helicopter waited, its engine camouflaged by the busy drone of the streets below. Vancouver was a city in perpetual motion. A city that never slept.

Hiking her handbag over one shoulder, Jasi keyed in her security access code and spoke her name into the VR box. The Voice Recognition program was the latest addition to security.

When the door opened, she stepped inside a small airlock. A man in army greens and a brush-cut greeted her. He was loosely carrying a rifle in one hand.

"Hey, Thomas," she waved.

The weapons tech was tall and muscular, with a face like a pit-bull. Recognizing her, he cracked what was his idea of a smile. "Agent McLellan. Good to see you back."

Jasi removed the Beretta from her pocket and laid it in a clear plastic tray. The tray was carried on a conveyor into a hole in the wall where the gun was scanned and the registration was recorded.

Thomas buzzed her through.

She followed a short hallway that opened to a large room filled with computers and electronic equipment. Another guard escorted her through a body scan, metal and powder detector and a fingerprint analyzer.

The last stage was the Retinal Scanner Device.

"I spy with my little eye," the RSD tech, Vanda, greeted her cheerfully.

"Eyes that are puffy and bagged…and belong to a sixty-year-old," Jasi muttered when the RSD clicked off and Vanda waved her on.

"For a sixty-year-old, you're lookin' pretty damned good, girl," the woman teased.

"Yeah? Well, next time Divine calls me out on my downtime, I'll roll over and play dead!"

Jasi neared the final scanning gate.

It examined the small tracking device that had been surgically implanted in her navel. The tracker was used when an agent went missing—and for identification purposes. Especially if an agent's body was recovered in an unrecognizable state.

Benjamin Roberts greeted her from the other side of the gate. "Pass on through, oh Queen of Darkness." He made a sweeping motion with his black-gloved hand.

Thomas slid the tray with her gun toward Ben.

Examining it, Ben said, "You know, Jasi, we do have better weapons than this old thing."

She shrugged. "I know. But it has sentimental value."

He handed her the gun.

"Happy Birthday, Agent McLellan," Thomas called out.

Jasi glared at Ben, her eyes shooting daggers. "What'd you do? Take out an ad in the newspaper?"

"Naw, just a vid-wall ad on Hastings," he said, laughing. "Ouch! Watch that elbow!"

Jasi examined her co-worker, taking in his broad shoulders and gray eyes. Benjamin Roberts was in his mid-thirties. He was a tall striking man who wore Armani suits like a second skin fitted to every contour of his muscular body.

"New ones?" she asked, indicating his gloved hands.

"I needed a better lining."

She thought of how challenging it must be for him.

Ben was a Psychometric Empath.

If he touched someone, he often sensed flashes of thought or emotion. He wore specially designed gloves when he was out in public. Inside the black leather gloves, a protective coating blocked his empathic abilities. It was essential that he keep his mind fresh, so that he could focus on each case without unnecessary interruptions.

Ben was also an expert in various martial arts and the best profiler the CFBI had. He had been with the Canadian Federal Bureau of Investigators for over fifteen years, before it was ever known as the CFBI.

Back in the late 1990's, the Canadian government requested a more 'open-door' policy with the United States—and the sharing of information. It started with computer programs designed to be accessed from either country so that information on every criminal perpetrator, rapist, pedophile, kidnapper, or serial killer was available at the touch of a keyboard. CSIS was still dedicated to protecting Canada's national security and focussed primarily on international terrorist activities.

Then in 2003, the CFBI was formally introduced as a Canadian counterpart to the previously established FBI organization in the US. Eventually the CFBI took over CSIS and integrated a variety of divisions. Agents were employed and deployed from either side of the border, anywhere they were needed.

Some agents were Psychic Skills Investigators—*PSI's.*

Of course, the public was naively unaware that both governments were implementing the use of psychics. Even now, in 2012, it was a closely guarded secret.

"Hey, Jasi! Ben! Over here!" a woman called.

Jasi's other partner, Natassia Prushenko, was tall and leggy—and had breasts Jasi would kill for. Her black hair was razor-cut in a short wispy style. Her sapphire eyes twinkled mysteriously. It had been almost two weeks since they had seen each other but Jasi immediately sensed that something was different about Natassia. Something other than the copper streaks in her jet-black hair.

Natassia passed her a sealed manila envelope.

Then she gave a similar envelope to Ben, saluting him cockily. "Agent Prushenko, reporting for duty, sir."

"Aw, cut it out, Natassia," Ben growled, rolling his gray eyes before pulling himself into the helicopter.

The woman smirked, then climbed in beside him. "Aye, aye, *mon capitaine.*"

Jasi curiously eyed Natassia.

Why, she wondered, was her friend grinning like a Cheshire cat?

When Ben leaned forward to talk to the pilot, Jasi nudged Natassia's leg.

"You'd better tell me what's going on."

"Later."

Jasi shrugged, then stared out the window. They were flying low under the canopy of clouds. As always, the beautiful British Columbia scenery with its lush forests and majestic snowcapped mountains entranced her.

When the flight ended, they landed safely on the heliport in the center of a gated complex. Perched high on the electric wall, numerous cameras zoomed in on their arrival. A sterile concrete field surrounded two large buildings in the center of the complex. Both held a reception area and countless offices.

Most were empty—a front.

To civilians, the complex was known as Enviro-Safe Research Facility. To Jasi and the rest of the CFBI, it was Divine Operations. Or *Divine Ops*, as most agents referred to it. But the real Divine Ops was not visible. It was actually a maze of underground tunnels and offices more than fifty feet below the surface.

"Well, now I *know* this is a big one," Natassia mouthed, her eyes glittering darkly while she followed Jasi from the heliport.

On the tarmac ahead of them, a man paced restlessly.

"Yeah," Jasi agreed. "A power-figure must be involved. I think this fire has someone hot under the collar."

She nudged Natassia and they hurried toward the creator of Divine Ops.

Matthew Divine's investigation of psychic phenomenon had initiated the construction of the first PSI training facility in Canada. The Federal government had listed the building as nothing more than a laboratory—one that researched the environment and its effect on people, animals, plant life and weather patterns.

The locals knew nothing of the CFBI's presence. They were unaware that a web of offices existed underground, stocked with high tech computer equipment. They had no idea that the people they saw flying in and out of Enviro-Safe were highly trained government agents with specialized psychic skills.

They *did* know that Matthew Divine and Enviro-Safe had brought prosperity to the area. When Enviro-Safe was first built, there was one existing town nearby. Originally called Mont Blanc, the town's name was changed in 2005.

Through a unanimous town council vote, it was renamed *Divine*.

Jasi straightened to her full five feet, eight inches as she reached Matthew Divine. He was a man of average height, average looks but above average intelligence. His long gray hair was tied back with a strip of leather. Intense brown eyes were framed with outdated tortoise-shell glasses. No one dared ask him why he hadn't gone for the ever-popular SEE—sectional eye enhancement—to restore his vision.

Divine's arms were crossed.

The grim expression on his clean-shaven face made Jasi gasp.

A serial killer was on the prowl.

2

Jasi followed Divine while he led the PSI team into the primary operations station—Ops One. An assortment of security scanners recorded each agent's various stats before admitting them to a small corridor. The same programmers that designed *H-SECS* created the Divine Ops security system. Ever since the kidnapping and murder of the Prime Minister in 2008, security programmers had been rallying to design a system that was impenetrable and virtually flawless.

Jasi allowed a technician to scan her with the paranormal electroencephalograph unit, an apparatus that recorded brain waves and psychic residue. This security precaution safeguarded PSI agents against overuse of their skills.

Heaving a sigh of relief, she smiled when the PEU flashed green. She was clear.

"Welcome back, Agent McLellan," Divine finally said with a curt nod. "I hope you enjoyed your well-deserved holiday. Sorry I had to cut it short. Have you been given details of the case?"

Jasi held up the envelope. "Ben told me that the killer left something behind...a lighter?"

Divine pulled her aside. "A *Gemini* lighter. Same as the one you received in the mail two months ago, Agent McLellan. The same brand found at a fire in Victoria last month."

They waited for Ben and Natassia to clear security, and then the four of them crowded into an elevator. When the elevator doors opened, an electronic voice informed them that they had reached the PSI floor where an expansive maze of halls and pale mauve cubicles lay before them.

"Happy Birthday, Agent McLellan," a co-worker greeted her.

Jasi whacked Ben in the arm, hard.

They wove through the maze of hallways, passing agents and technicians engrossed in their work. Artificial light hovered over occupied cubicles while the empty ones remained in darkness.

Abstract paintings lined the wall—someone's attempt at personalizing the underground lair. One painting showed a window opening onto a garden. Beside it, a photograph of a wooden maze tempted two rats to find their way out.

We're all just a bunch of lab rats, Jasi mused. *We live underground, running through this insane maze every day.*

Part of her wished that her downtime hadn't ended. On the other hand, two weeks of pretending to be normal, living in her empty apartment in North Van, had been about as much as she could take of herself. Even her plants couldn't live with her. The last ivy had died a slow, torturous death, its neglected soil shrinking from lack of water.

"Why didn't we hear about the Victoria fire a month ago?" she asked Divine.

"Victoria PD thought they had an isolated case last month so it didn't show up on our radar. Until this morning's case, just outside of Kelowna. The current victim is Dr. Norman Washburn. He was the head of Surgery at Kelowna General Hospital. He's also the father of Premier Allan Baker."

There's the higher influence.

Divine escorted them to the Command Office.

As they sat down around the conference table, Jasi opened the manila envelope and slid one picture from the stack of photographs.

A blond-haired man smiled confidently into the camera.

Premier Allan Baker.

Allan Baker was the youngest Premier ever voted in by any Province in Canada. Now, at thirty-two years old, he had set the precedent for bringing in young blood. Baker was now a front runner for Prime Minister of Canada.

She passed the photo to Ben, then carefully examined a surveillance photograph taken the year before, in which the Premier of British Columbia and Dr. Washburn were engaged in an intense argument.

Jasi recalled that the newspapers had created a frenzy when it was discovered that Baker's mother had given birth to the son of a prominent, *married* doctor. The scandal had almost cost Baker the position. It had cost Washburn his marriage.

Divine flipped a switch on the box embedded into the table in front of him. Two oak panels in the wall parted slowly, revealing a large vid-wall. He pressed the remote and a photograph of a lake appeared.

"Dr. Washburn's remains were found at Loon Lake early this morning. Loon Lake is less than an hour's drive from Kelowna."

The photo zoomed in to reveal a smoldering mass that was once someone's holiday home.

"Who reported it?" Jasi asked.

Without missing a beat, Divine answered, "Shortly after four o'clock this morning an anonymous caller reported a cabin fire near the lake. Fire fighters were sent to the area, and ten minutes later, the Kelowna PD arrived and secured the scene."

Jasi's eyes locked on Divine's. "How secure?"

Divine flipped to an aerial photo, revealing neon orange perimeter beacons that surrounded the crime scene.

"Kelowna PD has guaranteed that there has been no contamination of evidence—other than water, of course. The fire was almost out by the time the trucks got there."

Ben cleared his throat loudly. "We've heard *that* before. How'd they know there was a body?"

"Kelowna PD used an X-Disc," Divine explained. "As you are all aware, very few departments outside of Vancouver and the major cities have access to X-Discs. And our PSI division is the only unit to have the Pro version. Kelowna PD has one of the original prototypes."

"What's the estimated time of death?" Ben asked.

"TOD is between one and two this morning."

The wall photo switched to a black and white of the esteemed Dr. Washburn. The man had posed for the hospital staff photo as if it were a painful experience, his brow pinched in a wrinkled scowl. His receding white hair looked wiry and stubborn.

Like the man himself, Jasi thought.

She had met Dr. Washburn a couple of years ago during a symposium on children's health. The man had not impressed her. There was something about him she didn't like, something she couldn't quite put her finger on.

Divine turned to Natassia. "Forensics came back as a positive on Washburn. His dental scans matched. I'll need you to dig deep on this one, Agent Prushenko."

Jasi saw Natassia's head dip in agreement.

"We need any information pertaining to the victim. His life, his career—everything," Divine said.

Jasi rubbed her chin. "If this is his second fire, then what's the connection between the victims? What can you tell us about the Victoria fire?"

Divine's data-com beeped suddenly.

He examined it, then shook his head. "I'm sorry, Agent McLellan. I have a meeting with the Premier in half an hour. You'll have to upload that info into your data-communicators." He walked to the door, then paused. "The sooner you pick up your supplies, the sooner you can get your team moving. I need you at the Kelowna crime scene A-SAP. Allan Baker's going to want some answers—fast."

Divine held her gaze. "Get me some."

Then he left.

Jasi plugged her data-com into the Ops mainframe and began reading aloud while the computer uploaded to her portable. "Case H081A. Two victim's. Charlotte Foreman, sixty-three, and Samantha Davis…four years old."

Poor baby.

Her voice faltered slightly. "TOD is 9:05 p.m. on Charlotte Foreman. She was pronounced in the hospital. The child died shortly before. Smoke inhalation."

"Who called it in?" Ben asked.

"A neighbor. When the fire department got there the rain had already extinguished the fire. Victoria PD exhausted their leads. The case was cold. Until now."

Her eyes gleamed with determination.

"So we have jurisdiction over *both* fires, now that it's a serial arson case."

For the next half-hour, Jasi examined the evidence, including the fire investigator's statements and forensic reports on the two bodies found at the scene in Victoria. There wasn't much to go on. A cable truck would warrant investigating but other than that, no one in the neighborhood remembered seeing anything remotely suspicious.

"Let's start with Washburn and work backward," Ben suggested. "I'll call ahead, Jasi, and make sure that everything's ready for you in Kelowna."

He disappeared down the hall.

Meanwhile, Natassia continued flicking through the wall photos of the Washburn murder.

"See anything?" Jasi asked her, moving beside the dark-haired woman for a closer look.

Natassia pointed to the close-up of a strange melted mass of plastic. "There's a few possibilities. The X-Disc found IV tubing. Washburn was secured to his recliner with it. Funny thing, though. The recliner was fully extended."

Jasi chewed on her bottom lip, wondering why someone would bother to recline the chair...or use plastic IV tubing.

Wouldn't a rope have been better? And how did the arsonist get possession of the tubing?

"Back in a sec, Natassia. I have to get my pack."

She walked down a narrow corridor to a door marked *PSI Prep Room*. Swiping her ID card, she was buzzed inside. The room held a row of lockers lined against one wall.

She inserted her card into the slot on locker *J12*.

It beeped, then opened.

Removing a hefty black backpack, she silently cursed its necessary weight. She placed the bag on a metal table in the middle of the room and kicked the door to her locker shut. The zipper to the main compartment of the bag jammed. Frustrated, she tugged at it until it finally opened, revealing two thin flashlights, evidence markers, a piece of florescent chalk and other field supplies.

From a shelf above the lockers, she grabbed the last can of *OxyBlast* and shoved it inside the bag. Satisfied, she closed the backpack, heaving it over her shoulder.

Then she returned to Command.

"Okay, ladies, we better get moving," Ben suggested, poking his head through the doorway.

"Ladies?" Natassia asked with a laugh. "Jasi, did Agent Roberts just call us *'ladies'*?"

"Well, one of you certainly doesn't fit that description," Ben grumbled under his breath.

"Come on, Natassia," Jasi said with a snort. "Focus."

"I *am* focussing."

Watching her, Jasi chuckled. She couldn't help but admire Natassia Prushenko. Not only was the woman gorgeous, she had self-confidence up the ying-yang.

Natassia was a Russian immigrant. In some ways, she was a trade from the Russian government in return for favors from the PSI division. She spoke five languages and was the best VE Jasi had ever worked with.

And Jasi had worked with a number of Victim Empaths over the years.

Natassia had joined her team just over two months ago, during the Parliament Murders. Jasi had seen firsthand what her partner's skills could take out of her. A VE sometimes assimilated the emotions of the victim, to the point that it was almost impossible to separate—to come back to reality.

"Happy Birthday, Jasi. Great way to be spending it, huh?" Natassia's grinning mouth snapped firmly shut when Jasi whipped her head around.

"Okay, the chopper is ready," Ben announced.

Covering their ears, they dashed across the tarmac. The four-blade rotor of an Ops helicopter sliced through the air, droning and choppy. The sound was deafening until the pilot handed each of them a headset.

A few minutes later, they were onboard and gliding across the treetops.

"We'll do the scene first," Jasi said, plugging her data-com into the outlet in front of her.

Natassia nodded. "Okay. After that, I'll see if I can get a read off Washburn's remains. Maybe I'll get a hit. There's a good chance Washburn knew the perp."

"I'll get the reports for both fires and make some calls to set up interviews," Ben said, removing his gloves. "Then I'll start my profile. So far, what do we have?"

"A sick bastard who likes to set fires," Jasi murmured.

"Yeah, we have that. Hey, are you going to be okay in Kelowna? Do you need anything special?"

She handed him a short list. "Just this. I have everything else."

Ben read the list quickly, then keyed in the request on his data-com.

A few minutes later, his unit beeped a response.

"Everything will be waiting for you, Jasi. Just see the Chief of Arson Investigation on-scene."

She knew that her day would be long and grueling. She recalled the disaster that occurred years ago. A raging forest fire had swept over Okanagan Mountain, burning almost three hundred homes to the ground and destroying over twenty-five thousand hectares of natural forest.

As the private helicopter soared closer to the dreary crime scene, Jasi settled into the seat, pulled her long auburn hair up into a quick ponytail and closed her eyes. She would need to be alert and rested.

Agent Jasi McLellan could already taste the bitter smoke in the air.

And something more—death.

3

~ *Loon Lake near Kelowna, BC*

The helicopter deployed Jasi and her PSI team one mile from the fire. A fog of gray smoke greeted them. It hung in the air over the crime scene like a smothering electric blanket set on *high*. The scorching sun smiled down upon them, adding to the heat.

Fire trucks were parked on the side of a grassy field surrounded by thick trees and weedy underbrush. An oversized khaki-colored army tent had been pitched in the center of the field while an exhausted group of firefighters slept nearby in the shade. A variety of police vehicles slanted across the gravel road, blocking off public access.

A tired, sooty police officer strolled toward them. "Hey, Ben."

Ben grinned and introduced the man. "This is Sgt. Eric Jefferson, Kelowna PD."

"How's it hangin', Ben?" Jefferson asked, after introductions were complete. "Are you supervising this case?"

"Actually, *I* am," Jasi said, only slightly offended.

Ben grimaced apologetically. "Eric and I trained at the VPA range together."

The Vancouver Police Academy was highly regarded worldwide for its superior training of police officers. The academy owned acres of land outside the city limits. The rough terrain had been converted to a firearm training facility used by CFBI agents and police officers.

There was also a separate area for the bomb squad.

"A van's coming to get you," Jefferson said. "And someone'll be here any minute with the supplies you requested."

"Where's the Chief of AI?" Jasi asked him.

"Over by the tents, I think."

Jefferson glanced over his shoulder at an approaching truck. "Your supplies are here."

A police officer in his mid-forties, dressed in a fresh uniform, jumped from the truck. When he spotted them standing by the edge of the road his eyes narrowed. A firefighter wearing fire gear, minus the hat and mask, climbed from the passenger side carrying a bright red equipment bag. He had a stocky build and blond hair that was cut in a surfer style, long on the sides.

The man reminded Jasi of an advertisement for steroids.

She caught his eye and he aimed a withering look in her direction. Uh oh, she thought. *Steroid-man* wasn't happy to see them.

"Detective Randall," Jefferson murmured, indicating the officer. "He's the lead on the Victoria case."

"He *was* the lead," Jasi corrected him.

She watched while Randall and the stocky firefighter lumbered closer. When the two men reached her, she held out a hand.

"Agent McLellan, CFBI."

The detective winced at her words. Then his hand crushed her fingers, challenging her to back down.

Jasi squeezed harder until Randall let go.

After introducing her team, she caught Randall fighting with Ben for *alpha male* status. Detective Randall lost. Tension sliced through the air, thick with male testosterone. She saw Ben wave Eric Jefferson aside.

Jasi stole a glance at the firefighter.

The man's head was turned slightly away. On the shoulder of his jacket, a blue firefighter's patch flapped loosely in the breeze. *R. J. Scott, KFD*, the patch read.

"Have you got the supplies?" she asked him, feeling a shudder of pain behind her eyes.

Scott dropped the red bag on the ground, crouched down and jerked the zipper open. "Right here."

Her head began to pound. The smoke was invading her pores. She reached into her black backpack and extracted the can of *OxyBlast*. For half a minute, she sucked on the mouthpiece, inhaling pure oxygen and clearing her lungs.

"The oxy-mask is in the bag," Scott muttered in a voice that was hoarse from breathing in too much smoke.

When he brushed the hair from his eyes, she sucked in a puff of air. The left side of the man's face was scarred—a motley web of spidery burns.

"Hazard of the job," he shrugged when he noticed her shocked expression.

Detective Randall joined them. "You done here, Scott?"

"Yeah," the firefighter grunted.

Randall stared at Jasi and laughed rudely. "I don't know why she needs the mask."

Scott scowled at her. "Yeah, it's as useless as tits on a bull—unless she's gonna go into a live fire."

The men grinned at each other, then caught her eye.

"Detective Randall," she said coldly. "There are *many* things that are useless on a bull."

She allowed her eyes to slowly drift down past Randall's waist, locking in on his groin area. The man's face grew pinched, and then he muttered something indistinctly.

She turned her back and reached into the bag, removing the familiar navy-blue mask. It had a built-in filtration system that eliminated air contamination, giving the wearer a clean source of oxygenated air. Small and lightweight, the oxy-mask fit securely over the nose and mouth.

She drew it snugly over her head and adjusted her ponytail. Fighting back a feeling of claustrophobia, she took a deep breath.

"I'm fine," she assured Natassia who was watching her intently. "The residue is bad out here."

The oxy-mask muffled her voice.

"It wasn't *that* big a fire," Scott huffed.

"Not *this* fire. The Kelowna fire."

The firefighter eyed her suspiciously.

"What? That fire was years ago." The scarred side of his face stretched tautly and barely moved when he spoke.

"Agent McLellan?" Ben called out, hurrying to her side with Sgt. Jefferson in tow. "Everything all right here?"

"Everything's fine," she assured him.

Her head swiveled and her eyes latched onto Detective Randall's. "Right?"

The man flashed her a dangerous smile. "We don't need your help. Victoria PD is more than capable of handling—"

Jasi threw the man a frigid glare.

"This isn't a pissing contest, detective. The CFBI was called in and it's our case now. Both of them. And if you have a problem with that, then take it up with *your* supervisor."

Outraged, Randall tipped his head toward Scott, then stomped back to the truck and sped away in an angry cloud of dust. Scott watched him go. A second later, he rasped a quick goodbye and headed for the field. Joining a small group of firefighters, he pointed in Jasi's direction and circled one finger beside his head.

Crazy.

Cursing under her breath, she spun around and looked Eric Jefferson directly in the eye.

"What about you, Sgt. Jefferson? You have a problem with us being here?"

The police officer smiled. "Whatever gets the job done, Agent McLellan. That's my motto. With a serial arsonist on the loose we can use all the help we can get."

"Too bad those two don't feel the same way," Jasi growled, casting a shadowed look in Scott's direction.

Jefferson glanced toward the field. "Scott's just a rookie with a big mouth. Randall, on the other hand, he's a hotshot. He needs the collar." He nudged his head in Detective Randall's direction. "It's guys like *him* you need to worry about...and maybe Chief Walsh."

"I'll take care of the chief," she muttered. "As soon as I find the man."

Jefferson elbowed Ben. "If Scott or Randall get in your way, you let me know. I'm the CS Supervisor."

Jasi caught a brief nod then the man headed for a patrol car.

"Good luck with the chief," Jefferson called over his shoulder.

When the officer was gone, Ben removed two mini-cans of OxyBlast from the equipment bag and passed them to Natassia. Natassia tucked the cans into Jasi's backpack and pulled out a small protective nosepiece. She handed it to Jasi who carefully tucked it away in the top pocket of her black PSI jacket.

"Thanks," Jasi smiled beneath the oxy-mask.

She shoved her arms through the straps of her pack, shifting it slightly so the weight was balanced on her back.

Natassia nudged her. "Let's find the AI Chief. He's supposed to be here somewhere. Then we can get a ride to the scene. Man, I'm starved! I could go for lunch right about now—maybe a nice marinated steak."

Jasi grinned. "Yeah, with sautéed mushrooms."

"Excuse me for interrupting your culinary exchange," Ben nudged dryly. "I'm going to talk to the police. You gonna move or stand there swapping recipes all day?"

Laughing, Jasi adjusted her backpack while Natassia picked up the red bag. Then they headed toward a group of firefighters.

Jasi noted their smoke-covered faces and sooty yellow fire jackets. The men were in the middle of a serious discussion and no one noticed their approach.

"Excuse me, gentlemen," Natassia called out.

The men stopped talking.

Oh Jesus! They're gonna start drooling any minute.

Jasi rolled her eyes when she saw the firefighters focus in on Natassia like a swarm of bees. One of the firefighters stepped forward, grinning unabashedly. The man's eyes slowly perused Natassia's body, then his ice blue eyes turned and rested on hers. One eyebrow lifted when he registered the mask she wore.

She stiffened slightly, registering his obvious contempt.

"Well, well. What have we here?" the man drawled sarcastically. "Uh, ma'am? The fire is out now. There's no need for that mask."

The firefighter was over six feet tall—a lumbering, magnificent personification of man. He had eyelashes that most women would die for, and eyes that were such an unusual pale shade of blue that she wondered if he had visited a SEE office. A jagged scar intercepted his right brow, narrowly missing his eye. A slight cleft in his chin gave him an air of stubbornness. Dark wavy hair clung to his head and she couldn't help but wonder what it would feel like to run her fingers through those curls.

Jasi held his gaze while she examined him like a lab specimen in a jar. Built like a tank, she thought.

"I think maybe you're a bit lost, ma'am," he said, his lip curling disdainfully.

He turned toward the men, brushing her off like an annoying wasp at a barbecue.

She stared at the back of his head and then flipped her badge. "That's Agent McLellan, not *ma'am*. Where's the chief?" Her voice was cool, her eyes unwavering.

"Whoo-eee!" the man whistled when he caught sight of her ID. "An agent with an attitude. How rare!"

He shifted so that he was standing in front of her. Behind him, some of the men snickered loudly.

Jasi's smile was deadly sweet. "Listen, you arrogant asshole. When I find the chief and report you I'll have you on desk duty for a month. Now where is he?"

The man's eyes snared hers, turning her knees to mush.

Suddenly he reached for her arm, gripped it firmly and led her away from the laughing eyes of the firefighters. She felt the heat of his fingers through her jacket, branding her as his possession.

Natassia nudged her sharply. *"Jas—"*

"Shh!" Jasi interrupted her, glaring up at the man whose tanned fingers still curled around her upper arm. "I could have you up on charg—"

"Check out his shoulder patch!" Natassia hissed.

Jasi glanced down. Then her eyes found the patch.

Walsh, Chief of Arson Investigations.

Her eyes traveled back to the man's face. His expression was dark and smug. For a second her composure flickered. There was something annoyingly attractive about the man.

But damned if she would let *that* cloud her judgement.

"Brandon Walsh, at your service," he said blandly, interrupting her thoughts. "AI *Chief* Walsh, that is."

Jasi ignored his outstretched hand and felt her temper rising when his eyes scoped Natassia's hip-hugging jeans and tight blouse. *Men!*

When he turned to issue a command to the firefighters, Jasi couldn't restrain the snicker that erupted from her throat. The back of the man's fire jacket was well worn.

The lettering in some places was covered with black scorch marks.

Walsh, Chief of Ars In stig tions.

"Arse, all right," she muttered under her breath.

Abruptly, Walsh turned, piercing her with a frigid stare. Then he frowned and jerked his head.

"This way, *Agent* McLellan."

"Now isn't he a fabulous piece of work?" Natassia mumbled in her ear. "Check out the size of those hands."

"Natassia!"

Although Jasi had to admit, his hands were well shaped—like the rest of him.

Beside her, Natassia giggled beneath her breath. "You know what they say about large hands—"

"Shhh! Wouldn't want him to hear you. It might go to his head."

And that's big enough already!

She followed Walsh to a table standing beneath the shade of a tent.

He pulled out a chair beside his, offering it to her.

"You gonna tell me why you're wearing that mask?"

Jasi's eyes fastened on his and she took the chair across from him instead. "Allergies."

Walsh watched her for a long moment. "As the AI Chief, I've been informed of your…uh, special team. I wasn't given much info though."

"What have you got so far on the victim?"

"We've only received a few of the reports. Dr. Norman Washburn, age fifty-eight. He's the only victim. The fire originated in his livingroom where Washburn was tied to his recliner with IV tubing."

"Time of death?"

"Estimated TOD, one to two a.m.," Walsh replied. "We believe he died from smoke inhalation. We'll know for sure when the autopsy's in."

"What about neighbors? Anyone see anything?"

Walsh shook his head. "The cabins are separated by trees and bushes. He had no immediate neighbors."

"Did you ask around?" she asked impatiently.

"Listen," he said glibly. "I'm well aware that we've been ordered by the CFBI to cooperate with your team, but personally, I think AI is capable of handling this ourselves. And I don't really buy into the whole psychic thing."

She detected a trace of bitterness in his voice.

Jasi bit back her reply, frustrated.

She was sick and tired of having to defend herself—and her team. This wasn't the first time that someone had questioned the PSI's value.

"Chief Walsh, we've got two fires, three murder victims and few leads to go on. We're here to aid this investigation, not hamper it. You're not too macho to take help wherever you can get it, are you?"

Walsh laughed. "Macho? Now there's an outdated term."

Jasi refitted her oxy-mask.

She desperately wished she could tear it off her face and rip into the man before her. His attitude grated on her and left her feeling uneasy.

Walsh pointed to a Qwazi laptop and touched the screen with a stylus.

"Here's the data from the X-Disc. Have a seat and read through it. And yes, we asked around. No one saw anything. I'll go check on the other agent. Where'd he go, anyway?"

"Agent Roberts is busy drafting up a rough profile and arranging for transport to the scene," Natassia spoke up for the first time.

"Upload the data, Natassia," Jasi ordered. "*I'll* go check on Ben."

She cast a warning look in the AI Chief's direction. "I'm counting on your support. Don't get in my way, Walsh."

The man raised a well-shaped eyebrow. "I have no intention of getting in *your* way. Just stay out of mine."

She clenched her teeth. "Trust me, I'd be happy to stay away from you."

"Jesus, thanks. I think. And here I thought I was irresistible."

Jasi huffed in exasperation.

The man was insufferable. The sooner she finished her job here, the sooner she could put Brandon Walsh out of her mind.

Walsh accompanied her outside, and slipped on a pair of dark sunglasses.

"Need anything else?" she asked tightly.

"Yeah. What's Agent Prushenko's role?"

"She's a Victim Empath."

The man stared blankly, his lip curling in disbelief.

"She picks up vibrations—pictures from the victims," she explained. "Usually she sees their final moments."

"Yeah, right," he scoffed.

Jasi gripped Walsh's arm, her eyes flashing angrily.

"Agent Prushenko has empathic abilities, whether you believe in them or not. She's been a PSI for eight years, traveled worldwide and is recognized as one of the best VE's in the CFBI."

She wanted to slug the man.

Walsh grinned. "What about you?"

"I've been with PSI for almost six years. That's all you need to know."

"What do *you* do?"

"She reads fires," Natassia interjected, poking her head from the tent.

Wordlessly, Jasi glared at her partner.

"He needs to know, Jasi. Otherwise he's useless."

Brandon Walsh—useless?

Jasi hid a sly grin. "I can usually tell you where and how a fire started. Sometimes I pick up the perp's last thoughts or the last thing he saw."

"She's a Pyro-Psychic," Natassia bragged. "Jasi is the best there is."

"Jasi?" Walsh smirked.

"That's *Agent* McLellan to you!" Jasi snapped.

She'd make Natassia pay for that slip-up.

Oops, Natassia mouthed silently, raising her open hands in the air.

"Time for you to leave, Walsh," Jasi said rudely. "I'm sure there's something out there for the Chief of AI to do. Just remember we're running the show here."

Walsh's breath blew warm against her ear. "We'll see about that."

Then he hurried from the tent. "See ya later...*Jasi*."

With her eyes glued to his back, Jasi cursed aloud.

"Not if I can help it!"

Brandon Walsh walked away from the tent, unsure about the PSI's role. He had heard of the Psychic Skills Investigators in his dealings with various police departments, but his cases rarely required CFBI intervention. Or interference, as he thought of it.

As the AI Chief, he was compelled to assist the CFBI in any investigation involving serial arsonists. And that didn't sit too well with him—not one bit.

He'd show Agent Jasi McLellan who was boss.

After all, wasn't he the one responsible for capturing the arsonist involved in the Okanagan Mountain forest fires of 2003? He had led the AI team that had tracked down the arsonist and the accelerant used to set the blaze.

The press had blamed an unattended campfire for the raging fires that consumed a massive portion of the BC forest. Then a week later, it was rumored that a single cigarette had ignited the blaze. That was before the public ban on smoking became official—before people were restricted to smoking in the privacy of their homes, in well-ventilated smoking rooms.

Brandon had never believed the fire had started from a cigarette. He personally sifted through acres of destroyed forest, searching for a clue. He had explored the land until he discovered an abandoned cabin deep in the mountains.

There, he found remnants of liquid methylyte and zymene, highly flammable chemicals used in the underground production of Z-Lyte. Z-Lyte, with its sweet musky scent, had become the hallucinogenic drug of the new generation.

Public homeowner records listed Edwin Bruchmann as the owner of the cabin. An hour later, Bruchmann was in custody. When the old man was escorted into an interview room by his caregiver, Brandon was disappointed to discover that Bruchmann suffered from Alzheimer's.

Brandon's leads were slowly disintegrating—until his suspicions turned to the caregiver. Gregory Lawrence, thirty-nine, had been employed by Bruchmann for the past two years and had access to all of the old man's documents. But Lawrence denied knowing anything about a cabin.

"When was the last time Mr. Bruchmann visited his lakeside cabin?" Brandon had asked the caregiver.

Lawrence's face had registered confusion.

Then, without thinking, he had blurted, "You idiots! Edwin Bruchmann's cabin is not by any lake. See? I told you, you have the wrong person. Mr. Bruchmann's cabin overlooks the *valley*."

Brandon had smiled then. "I thought you knew nothing about the cabin?"

"I, uh…" the man stuttered. "Well, I m-might have heard about it once. But that doesn't prove anything!"

A knock on the door halted the interrogation and a detective passed Brandon a toxicology report.

"Maybe not," Brandon had agreed. "But this sure does."

Earlier he had recognized the sweet-smelling body odor common with Z-Lyte users. Suspicious, he offered Lawrence a can of pop. When the man had finished it, Brandon dropped it into a plastic bag and handed it over to the lab for analysis.

It came back positive for Z-Lyte.

The case was immediately closed, Gregory Lawrence locked away, Bruchmann established in a care facility and Brandon promoted to AI Chief.

All accomplished without any outside help.

And Brandon certainly hadn't needed a PSI!

This new case was no different, he reasoned. What could Agent Jasi McLellan possibly offer?

Psychic mumbo-jumbo?

He laughed suddenly, adjusting his shades.

How could the woman expect him to believe she had the power to see into a killer's mind?

I'd have to see it to believe it.

4

Jasi fumed indignantly while she waited for Natassia.

"I've uploaded all pertinent info from Walsh's laptop," her partner grinned. "And a few extra files to boot."

"I don't want to hear it, Agent Prushenko," Jasi scolded, covering her ears with both hands. "You know better than to illegally hack into another investigator's computer."

Even if he is an ass!

"Hacking?" Natassia said with a grin. "Hey! Chief Walsh gave me permission to upload. Not my fault if some extra files found their way onto my data-com. It's not as if he'll know."

Jasi sighed. One day, her friend was going to hack into the wrong person's files. And then there'd be hell to pay.

A dark green van rolled up alongside them.

Ben sat in the driver's seat.

"The ME's already taken the remains to the coroner's office," he said as they climbed inside. "Natassia will have to get her reading later."

Jasi sat in front and cautiously peeked out the window toward the tent.

Brandon Walsh was insolently leaning against a wooden support post, his legs crossed at the ankles. His candid gaze caught her off guard.

If I'm lucky, the posts will come crashing down and knock him unconscious.

As they neared the crime scene, Jasi readied herself.

The unpaved road was a mess of mud and water. The van lurched forward into potholes, stopping suddenly every once in awhile to navigate carefully over the boggy ground. It ventured down a narrow lane and into the thick brush. Spruce and cedar trees surrounded the vehicle, long branches scraping restlessly against metal.

Ben drove cautiously down the road, cursing loudly when the tires spun rebelliously.

"This is the worst part of it. There's grass up ahead."

Sure enough, the marshy ground opened to a grassy field. The ground hardened and they parked a few yards from what was once a rustic summer cabin.

Stepping out of the van, Jasi surveyed the scene.

The emptiness hit her, assaulting her senses. The area was devoid of life—except for her PSI team.

Off to one side, charred wood and clumps of black mud covered a cement pad. Washburn's cabin. Perimeter beacons were spaced every twenty feet. The beacons emitted a six-foot-high screen of orange light that quarantined the area. Anyone stepping through the beam would automatically trigger an alarm that would then activate a GPS, pinpointing the intruder's location and identity.

Jasi stepped closer to the scene and surveyed the damage.

"Okay, *shake 'n bake* time."

This was her ritual—something she said before entering every crime scene.

"Natassia, you're on data. Remember, don't tell me anything that you've gotten from the X-Disc. The less I know the better."

Jasi turned to Ben. "While we're inside you can send in the X-Disc Pro. Maybe we'll get lucky—fingerprints, trace fibers. Hell, anything would be good right about now. We need a break, something."

Natassia brought out her data-com and programmed it for automatic voice recording. With a simple voice command, the data-com would pick up every word.

Jasi opened her backpack and pulled out the *OxyBlast*.

"Give me a sec."

She peeled back her mask and took a few quick puffs of oxygen. Then she grabbed the nosepiece from her pocket and slipped it over her nose. Once the mask was attached to a cord on the side of her jacket, she pocketed the *OxyBlast*.

Ben tugged on Natassia's arm. "She can't use a mask when she's reading so—"

"I know," Natassia said, cutting him off. "Keep an eye on her."

"Stop talking like I'm not here," Jasi groaned. "I'm not deaf, you know. And I don't need babysitters. Come on, Natassia."

When they reached the edge of the crime scene, Jasi entered the code on the main beacon to deactivate the perimeter alarm. The blackened ruin of the cabin beckoned her closer. Ashes fluttered in the breeze and she walked slowly, so as not to disturb them. Smoke from the extinguished fire teased a trail toward her. She could taste its acrid bitterness.

A man died here, she thought. Burned beyond recognition.

"Voice record on!" Natassia ordered.

Jasi closed her eyes, anxious to clear her thoughts. She stood at the edge of the crime scene, her hands stretched above her. Trying to relax, she brought her arms slowly to her sides.

Focus. Deep breaths...in, out.

The wind began to stir. She could hear birds in the distance. *Breathe.* The smoke clung to her skin and swirled around her body. It entered her mouth, assaulting her senses.

In her mind, she saw Washburn's cabin. She could visualize it as it once was. Smoke rising from a chimney, the curtains ruffling in the breeze.

A body strapped into a recliner, unmoving.

Jasi took a step forward, one step closer.

The darkness sucked her in, deeper...

The man muttered a curse. His fishing rod had disappeared again. Maybe he was just getting too old.

Maybe 'old timer's' had kicked in.

"Son-of-a-bitch! Where did I put it?"

I observed him from the bushes, and laughed scornfully at the old doctor's complete lack of attention. He was easy prey. I wrapped the IV tubing around my hands, testing its strength. I saw the moment the old man noticed the fishing pole I had leaned up against the railing. I crept forward and slipped behind a large screen that separated part of the deck.

Then I held my breath.

Dr. Washburn, with his snow-white hair and paunch belly, teetered through the doorway onto the deck.

Fate had delivered him to me.

I pulled a black ski mask over my face. Then I crept up behind him, reaching above his bent head and brought the tubing around his neck. I could feel him buckling and straining beneath my hands.

"Don't fight it, Doctor," I whispered in the man's ear.

His body slumped forward and I dragged him inside the cabin. Hoisting the unconscious man into an old leather recliner, I tugged his inert body until his head rested at the top. Leaning over, I gripped the lever and reclined the chair. I quickly wrapped the rope around his body, looping it around his neck.

And then I sat on the threadbare sofa.

And waited.

I heard the doctor groan a few minutes later. I laughed when he cried out in terror at finding himself tightly tied to the chair. A rope of tubing bound his legs, waist, shoulders and neck.

"I wouldn't try to move your legs too much. The more you move, the tighter the tubing will get around your neck. It's a neat trick I learned."

I reached for the gas can at my feet. The diesel was Super Clean. Only the best for the best. I poured it around the chair, savoring the horrified expression in the doctor's face. The fumes were strong and my eyes teared slightly.

"Why me?" he cried.

I stared at him for a moment, daring him to remember me.

"Because you burned me once."

I reached into the pocket of my jeans, pulled out a Gemini lighter. The gas can leaked diesel behind me as I carried it toward the door.

I peered deeply into the old man's eyes. He sobbed like a child and I watched a tear roll down his wrinkled cheek.

"Who are you?" he croaked, his eyes bulging with terror.

Without answering, I flicked the lighter in my hand. I lit a piece of newspaper, then heard the old doctor scream as I tossed it toward him.

"I don't know who you are!" the old man shrieked. "I don't know you!"

The fire licked the floorboards, searing the old cedar planks. It crawled voraciously up the chair, over his writhing body, and a low keening moan was the last sound Dr. Norman Washburn made.

Satisfied, I glared at the man engulfed in flames.

Strolling outside, I stood a safe distance away. I smiled when the cabin went up in a blazing inferno and a small explosion ripped through the wall. Tossing the lighter on the ground, I glanced back at the wreckage. Thick black puffs of smoke billowed from the roof.

I rolled up the ski mask so I could breathe.

Reaching into my pocket, I brought out my list and meticulously crossed off Dr. Washburn's name.

"You might not remember me, but I sure as hell remember you."

Then I began the long hike past the moonlit beach, listening to the wind and the occasional crackle of fire behind me.

A hollow darkness surrounded Jasi, blinding her.

"Ben! She's barely conscious," a woman's voice said apprehensively.

I sure as hell remember you!

Jasi fought to open her eyes.

"She's coming around," she heard Ben say. "She'll be okay."

"Here. Let me have a look at her." The voice was deep and arrogant.

Jasi opened her eyes slightly, squinting at the sudden sharp pain in her head. She hazily examined her surroundings. She was safe, inside the van.

Then Brandon Walsh leaned over her.

He grinned when he caught her gaze. Turning her head gently, he examined a small scrape on her forehead.

"You fainted," he said scornfully. "And landed on your head."

She knocked his hand away, ticked off by the man's attitude. "It's just a bump."

"Well, Agent McLellan, I guess it didn't knock any manners into you."

Walsh leaned forward, then dabbed the cut with peroxide.

"Ouch! Damn it, Walsh!" she hissed.

His expression was smug, insolent. "Oh, sorry. I forgot to warn you. This might sting a bit."

"Walsh," Ben growled softly. He leaned down and settled the oxy-mask over her face.

When Jasi noticed his bare hands, she said, "Shouldn't you be wearing your gloves?"

Ben threw her a warning look. "I'll put them on when I get out of the van."

Walsh glanced at them—puzzled, suspicious. Then he opened a bandage wrapper and gently covered the wound on her forehead.

Jasi endured Walsh's touch, mostly because of the raging headache that threatened to rip her eyeballs from their sockets. Her head felt like someone was shooting a nail gun into her skull.

She cautiously eased herself into a sitting position, watching the man suspiciously. "What are you doing here? Thought we left you back at the tent."

"Gee, thanks for the warm welcome," Walsh remarked sarcastically.

"Who said you're welcome?" she snapped.

Natassia grinned widely, her head bouncing back and forth as if watching a tennis match. By the expression on her face, it was a thoroughly enjoyable game.

"Agent Prushenko, haven't you got work to do?" Jasi growled. To Ben she said, "I'll be fine. Just give me a few minutes to recuperate."

Then she glared at Walsh.

"Alone!"

5

Benjamin Roberts gripped Walsh's arm firmly with a bare hand. Steering the man away from the van, he swore under his breath. The AI Chief wore too many layers. Ben couldn't get an accurate read but Walsh's intense frustration and skepticism wasn't difficult to pick up.

"Man, she's a feisty one," Walsh grinned, jerking his head toward the van.

Ben lifted his hand from the man's arm. "Agent McLellan is one of the best PSI's in Canada. Don't underestimate her, Walsh. She's very good at her job."

"So am I, Roberts."

Walsh strode across the field, making a beeline for Natassia. He cast a smirk over one shoulder, then steered Natassia under a tree.

Ben clenched his teeth in exasperation.

Walsh was becoming a pain in the ass. There was something about the man that Ben didn't like. Maybe it was Walsh's grating insolence. Or the way he deliberately flirted with both Jasi and Natassia.

Ben ventured a look at Natassia who was persuasively drilling Walsh for information. He almost laughed aloud at the man's clumsy attempts at withholding facts. Yeah, Chief Walsh wouldn't know what hit him—once Natassia was through with him.

Ben knocked hesitantly on the side of the van. He slid the door open and Jasi beckoned him inside. She was huddled on the bench seat, wrapped in a blanket. Her face was pale and it worried him.

"Are you ready?" he asked her.

"Let's do it."

"Agent Prushenko!" Ben hollered.

A minute later, Natassia's head appeared, a smirk lingering on her face. "You bellowed?"

Ben released a sigh. "Just get in."

"Let's play back the data recorder first," Natassia suggested.

"What about me?" Brandon Walsh inquired innocently, poking his head inside the van.

"Sorry," Ben said smugly. "CFBI only."

He closed the van door with a slight slam, barely hiding his satisfied grin.

Walsh was definitely a nuisance, he thought.

"Thanks, Ben," Jasi smiled.

His eyes flicked toward the closed door. "Any time."

Forcing Walsh from his mind, Ben listened while the data-com replayed Jasi's voice.

Her words were low and hoarse. *"Don't fight it, Doctor."*

When Jasi went under, she took on the perpetrator's emotions, thoughts and actions. She literally saw through the eyes of the arsonist. Jasi relived moments in time, as if she were there in body.

Ben, on the other hand, was a highly skilled profiler with the ability to touch someone and feel his or her thoughts. But his psychic abilities were unreliable and infrequent.

The data recorder played back Jasi's voice. *"You might not remember me but I sure as hell remember you!"*

Ben watched her carefully. He noticed the small shiver as she heard herself laughing insanely. Even after all these years, it was something that Jasi still had difficulty with.

Who could blame her?

"Previous knowledge of the victim is a positive," Natassia said, consulting her data-com. "I'd say we're looking for a male, based on the lower vocal tone in your voice."

"Anything on the accelerant?" Ben asked.

"It's Super Clean diesel fuel."

"What about our X-Disc?" Jasi interrupted suddenly.

Ben scrolled through his data-com and downloaded from the X-Disc Pro's data site. "We've got a partial boot print. About six yards from the house, behind the apple tree. Could be our perp. The Disc also took a soil sample from the tread. We'll have it analyzed back at Ops."

"You want a list of known contacts now, Jasi?" Natassia asked.

"Yeah," Jasi said. "Search all data regarding previous contacts of Dr. Washburn. All complaints issued against him, either personal or professional. Lawsuits, wrongful death, misdiagnoses. Someone had a hate-on for the doctor."

"Give me thirty minutes. Maybe an hour. I have a feeling it could be a very long list."

Jasi stood and reached for the door. "I'm going back to the crime scene."

Ben grabbed her arm. "Twice in a short time-frame might be too much. You've given us plenty to go on. Why don't you—"

"I'm fine, Ben. I won't go under again. I just want to see everything."

She adjusted her oxy-mask and climbed out of the van before he could say another word.

"Jesus Christ!" he heard her say.

Ben leaned out the door and followed her gaze.

Brandon Walsh was leaning against the bumper of the van. "Well, not quite."

Jasi ignored the man and doggedly headed toward Washburn's cabin.

Ben was furious. "Walsh!"

He led the fire chief away from the van, fuming under his breath. "Listen, don't mess with any of us. This town might be your territory, but Agent McLellan is *my* territory. She's gone through too much to be messed with by an egotistical redneck who—"

"Hey! I surrender!" Walsh managed, throwing his hands into the air. "Look, I just want to help. Trust me, your Agent McLellan has nothing to worry about with me."

Ben clenched his teeth. "Just keep your hands off her—and Agent Prushenko too, for that matter."

The tension between them mounted.

Then Walsh turned on his heel and walked back to a nearby police car. Walsh said something to the driver who immediately handed him the radio.

Ben watched, suspicious.

What are you up to, Walsh?

Glancing away, Ben held up a hand to shield his eyes from the sizzling sun. Jasi was moving closer to the crime scene. He saw her muscles tighten in response to the chaos. He prayed that the mask would keep out the toxic fumes that triggered her psychic abilities.

Jasmine McLellan was like a sister to him. A stubborn, self-reliant, younger sister who sometimes needed rescuing. There was an air of innocence about her, yet she exposed herself to evil every day. Ben guarded her, protected her and even loved her…as a brother would.

But most of all, he owed her.

Ever since the Parliament Murders…

He hopped inside the van and leaned over Natassia's shoulder to check the data-com screen.

"The good old doctor had enough enemies to fund his own political campaign," she smiled grimly.

"Anyone we know?"

"A few wrongful deaths. Remember the actress, Stacey Beranski? Her son filed a WD because she died on the operating table after what was supposed to be a routine appendectomy. Rumor is, Dr. Washburn was intoxicated while he performed the surgery and he botched the job."

Ben leaned closer to see the monitor. "What happened to Washburn? Did he get charged with wrongful death?"

Natassia wrinkled her nose. "He was reprimanded internally. It appears the alcohol was covered up, made to look like he had suffered from a mild stroke during the operation. He got off. Case closed."

"What's the son's name?"

"Jason Beranski, age twenty-nine. He's a pharmacist, works at Pharmacity Drugs in Kelowna." Natassia glanced up from her data-com. "Now, *he* would have access to medical supplies."

"You and Jasi want to check him out?"

Natassia gave him a smirk that said *Hell yeah!*

He was positive that somewhere in the list of names was a clue—the identity of a serial arsonist. It was only a matter of time before they found him. But time was running out.

Ben sensed that the arsonist would strike again...soon.

Twenty minutes later, he heard loud, angry voices coming from outside the van. Someone pounded insistently on the door. Natassia unlocked it and slid it open while he peered over her shoulder.

A well-dressed man in a pale maroon suit stood outside the van. The man's California-blond hair, previously broken nose and flashing brown eyes made his face one of the most recognizable in North America. He was none other than Allan Baker—the Premier of British Columbia…and the deceased Dr. Washburn's son.

"Where is he?" Baker demanded softly.

"Where is who?" Ben asked. He jumped from the van.

Resentment flared in Allan Baker's eyes. "My father."

Ben watched the man carefully, sizing him up. Baker didn't seem particularly heartbroken. Upset, yes, but not exactly the picture of the grieving son.

Baker peered down his nose. "Who's in charge here? I don't have all day."

Ben held out his hand. "I'm second in command. Agent Benjamin Roberts, CFBI."

Natassia stepped from the van, catching the Premier's eye. "Agent McLellan is the lead, but she's in the field."

Premier Baker glanced uneasily toward the charred ruins of the lakeside cabin. Then he tossed Ben a disdainful frown. "Okay, so where is he?"

Ben frowned. What exactly had the Premier been told?

"We're very sorry but your father is dead," Natassia said gently.

"Of course he's *dead*!" Baker snarled. "I wouldn't be here if that wasn't the case. I want to know where his body is. I need to make arrangements."

Subtly, Ben nudged his head at Natassia who gave a faint nod.

"Premier Baker, let's go some place more comfortable," she suggested.

As Natassia led Baker to a communications tent pitched near the road, Ben followed close behind. Allan Baker had just promoted himself to number one suspect on Ben's list. Everyone knew there was no love lost between father and son, and that Baker resented his father for not acknowledging him when he was a child.

Now if that's not motive enough, then what is?

Yeah, Allan Baker warranted a closer inspection.

And speaking of closer looks…

Ben caught Baker checking out Natassia's assets.

"Premier Baker," he growled. "Take a seat, please. We have some questions for you. Would you care for a coffee?"

"Please. Double cream and sugar." Baker leered openly in Natassia's direction. "I like sweet things."

Ben wanted to punch the man. Instead, he handed Baker a container of cream and their hands made contact. In an instant, he picked up a kaleidoscope of emotions and thoughts.

Anger, sorrow, secrets and lies.

"Premier Baker," Natassia said coolly. "Your father's remains were discovered in his cabin. How much of the details do you want to know?"

"Everything," the man remarked haughtily.

Ben shrugged.

Baker wanted all the details? That's what he'd get then.

"Premier Baker, your father was murdered. He was tied to his recliner and the cabin was doused in diesel. He either died of smoke inhalation or fatal burns. We'll know more once the coroner has completed the autopsy."

Baker's hands clenched. When he opened them, he rubbed the palms, scratching an unbearable itch.

Ben's eyes were drawn to a faint patchwork of tiny scars that covered the man's palms. The lines were refined and silvery, as though Baker had undergone laser dermal resurfacing to make them less noticeable.

"Can you tell us where you've been for the past twelve hours?" Natassia asked, breaking Ben's concentration.

Baker smiled—a politician's smile. "I've been touring British Columbia. We were in Kelowna yesterday for most of the day. Last night I entertained guests at the Paloma Springs Hotel in Penticton until maybe two this morning."

His gaze narrowed suddenly, realization crossing his face.

Standing abruptly, he exploded, "What, you think *I* killed him? Are you insane?"

Ben leaned forward, his hands gripping the table that separated him from Baker. "No, but someone certainly is."

"This is a goddamn outrage!" Baker uttered acidly. "For your information it's been almost a year since I've seen or spoken with my...father. I've been campaigning. It's been busier than hell. And regardless of my past issues with Doctor Norman Washburn, I'm running for Prime Minister. I don't need the negative publicity."

Ben folded his arms across his chest. "We'll need a copy of your itinerary for the past day, including a list of all contacts that can verify your whereabouts."

"You mean an *alibi*," Baker snapped hotly. "You know, that bastard got what was coming to him. Don't expect me to cry for him." He slumped into the chair, resting both arms on the table.

Natassia continued tapping on her data-com. "No one's expecting anything from you."

"What's that supposed to mean?" Baker growled.

She raised her head. "It simply means, Premier Baker, that how you grieve is up to you. We're here to deal with the facts and the evidence."

Ben curled his lips into a tight smile. "Once we confirm your whereabouts, Premier Baker, we'll be able to rule you out. No worries, right?"

Allan Baker glared bitterly, then rose to his feet.

Smoothing the front of his jacket, he said crisply, "I'll have my assistant fax you my itinerary and the list of contacts as soon as I return to my office."

Ben watched Baker climb into a sleek black sedan. The dust swirled behind when the car sped out of sight.

"I'll take Baker," he told Natassia. "While you and Jasi follow up on Beranski."

He brushed a hand through his thick hair, then released a deep breath. "I have a feeling Dr. Washburn made a lot of enemies. And I think his son is hiding something."

"I'll go get our fearless leader," Natassia murmured, finishing her coffee in one gulp.

When Natassia reached the unarmed perimeter beacons, she surveyed the wreckage. The bumpy ground was scorched and black. The ashes were now cool to the touch, but the odor of roasted human flesh still lingered in the humid air.

She could see her friend bent over a pile of rubble, gloved hands carefully pulling aside boards and melted plastic. Natassia had only worked with Jasmine McLellan for a short time, but she admired the woman's dedication. She was grateful for the opportunity to work with Jasi—and Ben.

Standing near the edge to avoid contaminating the scene, Natassia hollered at Jasi. "Got anything?"

Her partner glanced up briefly and waved. "Not yet. I'll have to wait until everything is collected and bagged."

Natassia watched Jasi carefully re-trace her footsteps back to the main beacon and reactivate the security code.

"We have a potential, Jasi."

"Who?"

"Jason Beranski, a pharmacist in Kelowna. And we already had a visit from our primary suspect."

Natassia witnessed the shock in Jasi's eyes.

"Premier Allan Baker," she told her before Jasi could ask.

"What? Baker was here and I missed it?"

"You sure didn't miss much. The man is a disgusting pig. I can't believe he's Premier of BC. All he seemed worried about was how fast he could get dear *Daddy* into the grave."

Maybe Baker even put him there!

Jasi snorted loudly. "Yeah, that's Baker. What'd he have for an alibi?"

"He said he was at a function at the Paloma Springs Hotel in Penticton. Ben wants to take Baker."

"Then we'll take the pharmacist."

Natassia flagged down a passing patrol car. As they climbed inside, she asked the officer to drop them off at the helicopter, then waited while Jasi connected to Ben.

"We're heading to Kelowna to interview Beranski," Jasi told him. "Meet us there when you're done."

While Jasi exchanged a few words with Ben, Natassia listened, tamping down the flicker of jealousy that erupted every time she thought of their close friendship. Ben and Jasi were just friends—she knew that.

"We could have Beranski brought in to Ops," she suggested when Jasi had ended the communication.

"No, we're going to pay Mr. Beranski a surprise visit."

Natassia pulled out her data-com and continued narrowing down the list of Washburn's potential enemies. As long as the press didn't get wind of Premier Baker's status on her list, the investigation would progress smoothly.

Aboard the helicopter, Natassia strapped herself into the seat while Jasi puffed on *OxyBlast* to clear her lungs. A few minutes later Jasi dozed off.

Awake and anxious, Natassia tried to calm the rumbling in her stomach.

After interrogating Jason Beranski, it would be time for her to take a trip to the Kelowna Coroner's Office.

In the bowels of the city morgue, a victim lay on a metal slab—a victim who had something to say.

Something only Natassia could hear.

6

~ Kelowna, BC

Jason Beranski smiled politely at an elderly woman while he filled her prescription of *Arthrotec.*

"One hundred m-milligram capsules. Make sure you take this with f-food so it won't upset your s-stomach, Mrs. Beaumont."

Pharmacity was one of Kelowna's busiest drugstores. Today there seemed to be an unusual amount of traffic. But Jason didn't care. Today was a great day and nothing was going to spoil his mood.

"I'm on b-break," he told his assistant, Doris.

He had missed his lunch and was dying for a cup of sludge that the day manager made instead of real coffee. Removing his orange striped apron, he left it on a stool and disappeared into the back room. The shelves were stacked with expired pharmaceuticals and new freight.

He nudged a box into one corner before grabbing some coffee. Then he slipped out the back door.

Outside, he straddled an empty crate and sniffed the blistering, humid air.

The alley was littered with trash. A large rusted Dumpster overflowed—a potpourri of ripe, spoiled food...and something else. Urine. Beside the Dumpster, a stray tabby cat meowed forlornly, anticipating a treat. Sensing danger, it remained a safe distance from the skinny man with the shaved head.

The alley was Jason's domain.

The other staff members remained inside during their breaks. They couldn't understand why he would choose to sit amidst the garbage and stench instead of in a clean, although cluttered, back room.

How could he possibly explain to them that he save his freedom? In the alley, no one judged him. N teased him about his speech impediment.

He watched the cat attack a piece of newspa blew across the pavement. Leaning forward, he p a squished pop can and hurled it at the stray.

"I guess *you're* not a cat lover," a voice said su

Jason turned and was shocked to see a w long auburn hair standing in the doorway.

"Jason Beranski?"

He nodded, sensing that his great day was

The woman fished a badge from a pocke toward him. "Agent Jasmine McLellan, CFB

"CFBI? W-what do you w-want w stammered uneasily. "I haven't d-done any

Agent McLellan eyed him strangely uncomfortably.

"We're conducting an investigatio questions. Do you mind?"

He hesitated before answering her if I d-did?"

The agent ignored him, then br computer device. Moving beside another crate, swept off the top an

I know what this is about, he thought. That bastard got what was coming to him.

He spared the woman a look, and was positive that she could see his guilt.

"Voice record on," the agent commanded.

Jason felt a shiver of apprehension race up his spine.

Inside the pharmacy, Natassia immediately headed for a petite young woman with short fire-red hair. The pharmacy assistant, Doris Richards, appeared to be ready to hurl when Natassia showed her a badge.

"We'd like to ask you a few questions."

The assistant's mouth quivered. "I haven't done anything wrong."

Natassia released an impatient sigh.

Why did people look so scared when she questioned em? Maybe she should try a gentler tactic.

"Ms. Richards, uh…may I call you Doris?"

he woman nodded hesitantly.

Ve're not investigating you, but we sure could use help." Natassia almost bit her tongue on the word

's eyes widened. "Of course. What can I do?"

tioned Natassia to follow her into the back room.

nvestigating an arson and Mr. Beranski's name

ow I'm not saying he's a suspect, just that we

shou all bases. You understand, Doris?"

Na ki?" The woman glanced nervously over her

Intervie back door. "He's a decent boss."

worker o out her data-com. "Voice record on!

understand is Richards, assistant pharmacist and co-

The woma eranski, case H085A. Ms. Richards, you

is simply an informal interview?"

d timidly and bobbed her head.

Natassia pointed impatiently to her data-com, to which Doris responded with a loud, "Yes!"

"How long have you worked with Mr. Beranski?"

"About eight months. I transferred from Shoppers when they bought out Pharmacity."

"What can you tell me about him?"

"He's an okay boss. I mean, he pretty much leaves me alone to do my job." Doris smiled tentatively. "He keeps to himself mostly. Ever since his mother died last Christmas, he does his job and goes home."

Natassia wondered how angry the man was over the death of his mother. How close was Beranski to her before she died? Maybe close enough to go after Washburn for revenge.

Doris tugged nervously on a strand of heavily gelled hair.

The woman probably kept the hair companies rolling in dough, Natassia mused.

The assistant interrupted her thoughts. "What do you think he's done? I mean, I work with the guy. I'd like to know."

"Sorry, Doris. We're still investigating."

Sensing the woman's disappointment, Natassia said, "I have a few more questions and then you can go. Has Mr. Beranski been acting unusual in the past two or three days?"

"He's *unusual* all the time!" The woman crossed her arms and blew out a long breath. "Well, he has been acting kind of strange today."

"What do you mean?"

Doris shrugged. "Usually he's quiet. He does his job but doesn't talk to anyone. He's not particularly happy most days. You know what I mean?"

Natassia knew exactly what the woman meant.

Beranski was a loner. Kept to himself, no real friends, no family. A prime candidate for someone out to prove himself. *A prime suspect.*

"So what's different today?" Natassia prodded.

"Jay—I mean, Mr. Beranski has been whistling and smiling all day. He's even been friendly to our customers, asking them how they feel. Every few minutes I hear him saying *'It's a great day today'*, like he's won the lottery or something."

"Doris, why do *you* think he's so happy?"

The assistant smirked. "I'll tell you exactly why I think he's so happy. This morning, on the radio? We all heard that some doctor in Kelowna was killed in a fire. The store went quiet—all except Jason. He was stocking the new shipment and dropped a case of *Amoxil*. Luckily it was bubble-wrapped."

"So he dropped the pills…and?"

Doris's eyes strayed toward the ceiling while she tried to remember the order of events.

"Yeah," she managed finally. "And then he smiled. It was weird. Here we all were, thinking about that poor doctor's family, and Mr. Beranski was smiling."

"Is that it?"

"No. When I asked him what was so funny? He just said *'It's a great day today. The bastard finally got what was coming to him.'* And since then, he's been smiling and friendly to everyone. Weird! That's all I can say."

Doris chewed on her fingernail, then blinked.

"Hey! Was that the same fire you're investigating?"

"Voice record off," Natassia replied, without answering the woman's question. "I'm sorry, but I can't tell you any more."

She thanked Doris for her time and watched the woman rush back to the pharmacy.

The gossip was going to be good today.

Natassia checked her watch.

Time to join Jasi and Beranski.

But first she would do a quick, although illegal, search of the back room. Perhaps one of the boxes contained IV tubing. And if a piece of it just happened to be on the floor then she would need no other reason to investigate. She knew that Jasi would keep Jason Beranski busy for at least fifteen minutes.

That would give Natassia plenty of time.

Outside in the back alley, Jasi fumed.

She had wasted her time trying to establish Beranski's background and his whereabouts during the early morning. The man was clueless and infuriating.

"Mr. Beranski, are you aware that Dr. Norman Washburn was murdered this morning?"

"Yeah, so what of it? You expect m-me to feel s-sorry for him?"

"We're fully informed about the charges you filed against Dr. Washburn. We also know that he was found not guilty in your mother's WD case."

Pacing in front of her, Beranski booted a rusted coffee can against the Dumpster.

"Not guilty? That d-d-drunken bastard killed my mother! He s-slaughtered her in the operating room so that no other surgeon could p-put her together again. And the h-hospital officials? Those assholes d-defended him. They m-made up some excuse that he b-blacked out. A stroke, they said."

Jasi clipped her data-com to her jacket and slid a photo toward him. "You hate him enough to do this?"

The X-Disc had taken the photograph on its fly-by. It showed Washburn's body, blistered and burned to a crisp. In fact, it was impossible to discern where the body ended and the chair began. It was an image of death, a macabre thing to show a suspect.

But Jasi wanted to see the man's reaction.

She wasn't expecting his face to turn green, though.

"The ME had to identify the body by dental records," she nudged. "Every inch of him was roasted, the flesh was peeled from his bones like an overcooked turkey."

The pharmacist stood up, knocking over his coffee mug. He reached for the back door, desperate for escape.

"S-stop it!"

"Look at the picture again, Mr. Beranski, and then try to remember what you were doing this morning around one o'clock." She could tell he was fighting not to gag.

When he grabbed the door handle, she shoved the photograph toward him.

There are certain moments when it seems as though time moves in slow motion. This was definitely one of those times, Jasi realized a little too late.

Just as Jason Beranski reached the door, it was pushed open from inside. Agent Natassia Prushenko had the misfortune of stepping into the alley at the same moment that the pharmacist tried to get to the washroom.

Beranski didn't make it.

Neither did Natassia's blouse.

"What did you get from Beranski the Barfer?" Natassia asked her when they reached the women's washroom.

"Not much," Jasi answered, handing her some paper towel. "Beranski the Barfer seemed confused. The guy can't remember whether he was home last night or at the movies. Changed his story a couple of times."

"I searched the back room," Natassia grinned. "Nothing."

Jasi watched her friend valiantly trying to plug her nose while cleaning vomit from her blouse. "Sorry about this. I guess I pushed him a bit too hard."

Natassia raised a dark eyebrow. "Who, you?"

Jasi let the comment ride. "We'll have to check out the movie alibi. He says he saw a remake of *Titanic* last night...midnight show. That would put him there until three."

She was frustrated with Beranski. Because he had changed his story twice, she'd have to spend valuable time determining exactly where the man had been.

"I have an appointment with the coroner *and* a corpse," Natassia reminded her.

Tossing the soiled paper towel in the garbage, Jasi said, "I should come with you, be your reality line."

"No, I'll ask the coroner to stay. All I need is a voice to pull me out if I go in too far. I'll be fine."

"Okay, I'll take the theatre then. You hear from Ben?"

"Yeah, he said he'll meet us for dinner." Natassia's eyes drifted down the front of her blouse. "Crap!" she pouted, plucking at her damp shirt. "Ben has my pack."

Jasi aimed an apologetic look in her partner's direction.

She didn't envy the coroner...or the corpse.

7

Entering the Kelowna Coroner's Office, Natassia held her head high, eyes front. Her blouse had dried but the stench of vomit trailed after her like cheap 'knock-off' cologne. People stared at her but she ignored them, heading straight for the information desk. She was buzzed through a security door while the receptionist sniffed the air trying to detect where the foul odor came from.

"Agent Prushenko?"

The security guard that greeted her sported a tattoo of a shark's head that was barely visible above the collar of his crisp white shirt. The man was long-limbed, dark-eyed and dark-skinned.

Ebonic, she reminded herself. That was now the politically correct term for people of African or 'black' origin. In 2006, the word had replaced *African American* and all other related descriptions because Ebonic people had protested being lumped into *African* or *American* phraseology. *Ebonic* was more general, like *Caucasian* or *Hispanic*.

"You sure you want to go to the morgue?" the guard asked. The shark's mouth pulsed menacingly.

Natassia waited, silent and impatient.

The man shrugged. "The coroner will meet you at the bottom."

He carefully scanned her badge and then escorted her down a long corridor. When they stepped inside the elevator he keyed in a code and hastily moved back into the hallway before the doors closed.

The elevator was quick and settled with a gentle lurch.

When the doors opened, Natassia took a few seconds to readjust her blouse, examining it in the dim light. The smell was dissipating. Or maybe it had killed off her olfactory senses. Perhaps no one else would notice.

A tall man with a close-shaved goatee lunged toward her and pulled her from the elevator.

"Agent Prushenko, we meet again."

Winded, her eyes locked on the face of the suave Marcel Desrocher, Quebec City coroner *extraordinaire*.

"Marcel! What in God's name are you doing here?"

The man loosened his death grip and kissed her firmly.

Natassia shrugged him off, then studied him.

They had met when she had been transferred to Quebec City after basic training. One of her first cases as a rookie VE pitted her against a skeptical and somewhat older coroner who had swept her off her feet.

"Ah, *mon Dieu!*" Marcel sniffed.

He wrinkled his nose in disgust when a waft of something rotten hit him. "What is that terrible *parfum* you are wearing?"

Pushing him away, she scowled. "*Eau ze vomi!*"

Vomit.

He backed away a few feet and frowned.

Then waving at the space between them, he grinned wickedly. "Ah, *mon chéri*, it has been too long."

"Not long enough," she muttered disdainfully.

Marcel Desrocher hadn't aged a bit, Natassia thought. His silver-tipped black hair was trimmed neatly, his moustache and goatee a bare shadow, and his dark eyes still gleamed like a wild child at an illicit rendezvous. Tall and thin, the man appeared unbelievably fit—for someone who was in his late forties.

She followed him down a short corridor. "How's the new girlfriend...uh, Maureen, is it?"

"Marilyn. She's in Cuba."

Natassia really didn't want to discuss his latest conquest, so she changed the subject. "Are you here permanently or just on loan?"

"Which would you prefer, *ma belle*?"

When she didn't answer, he chuckled. "On loan. The regular coroner is on holiday in Greece, probably sunbathing *tout nu*...naked." His dark eyes glimmered with desire as they rested on her breasts.

Natassia huffed indignantly, then firmly fastened the top button of her blouse.

Marcel leered at her, then stopped at a door marked *'City Morgue'*. He scanned his thumbprint and keyed in his password.

Then, with a sweep of his arms, he opened the heavy door. "*Voici, m..châte.u!*"

The morgue gleamed with brushed stainless steel cabinetry, tables and counters. The concrete walls were beige—what little wall space there was. On the ceiling, small track lights were aimed in various directions. One light illuminated an older model forensics body scanner that hovered over a polyurethane table in a far corner of the room. Beside this, a low dividing wall separated an area of desks that held computers, printers and a fax machine. Two walls housed a variety of shelving, filing cabinets and six sinks. Steel tables extended from each of the sinks, with drainage hoses attached.

The tables were clean.

And all were unoccupied—except one.

Marcel indicated the fully clothed man lying on the table. "Nathan Watts. My assistant. We've had a long night and Nathan is *trés fatigué*."

Natassia suspiciously eyed the man on the table. She searched his chest for signs of life. The man's eyes were closed and his hands were folded across his chest. His pristine white lab coat was the only indication that he didn't really belong on a slab of dead cold metal.

"Over here," Marcel beckoned.

He led her to the third wall—the one lined with sliding drawers each labeled meticulously with the name of the deceased.

"Dr. Norman Washburn, case H085A. *Prête?*"

"Ready," Natassia nodded.

Marcel pressed a red button.

A noise issued from the wall. The humming sound was high-pitched and intermittent. The sound stopped abruptly when a bottom drawer slid fully open, revealing the black body bag that preserved Washburn's remains.

"Jesus!" Natassia muttered under her breath.

The stench of death oozed from the bag.

A waft of pungent air was released when she eased the zipper down, and she swallowed hard.

Don't lose it, Natassia!

Removing a tube of *Mentho* from her pocket, she sprayed it into both nostrils and inhaled deeply. The heavy menthol base coated her olfactory nerves. For thirty minutes, she would have no sense of smell.

Now why hadn't she used it after Beranski unloaded his breakfast on her?

Forcing the bald-headed pharmacist from her mind, Natassia focused on the corpse in front of her. Norman Washburn's face was a contorted mass of blackened and blistered flesh. Both eyes had literally melted into the sockets, his mouth was frozen in a tortured scream, and the scalp had been burned to the bone. Not a trace of the thick white hair that had once covered it remained.

She pushed the bag aside, examining the rest of Washburn's body. The left arm revealed seared tendons, and three of his fingers were missing—burned completely and converted to ash.

A loud rumbling sound erupted from the far end of the room, and Natassia raised her head.

Nathan Watts, the live stiff, was snoring.

"Anything you'd like me to do for you, *mon chéri?*" Marcel murmured softly, hovering over her shoulder.

"Yeah. Leave me alone with my corpse."

Marcel was getting on her nerves. Now she remembered another reason why she had ended their brief affair. The man was overconfident and overbearing.

And he was nothing like Ben.

Natassia sat bolt upright in a chair next to the drawer and stared at the lifeless cadaver. Then she reached into the bag and with closed eyes, gently traced her fingers across what was once the doctor's face. Hardened skin and smooth bone. Most people cringed when they touched the dead but for Natassia, it was an intimate act of necessity.

She perceived her mind floating—hovering above the black bag. She felt her own body invading the empty corpse.

Unresisting, Natassia slipped inside...

Into darkness, despair and loneliness.

These were the first emotions that Natassia recognized. She fought to open her eyes but they remained closed. She allowed herself to be lured in...deeper into Washburn's soul.

"I don't remember you!" she heard him scream.

Time traveled erratically in flashbacks.

"I can function just fine, Nurse Landers. Who are you to tell me I'm incompetent?"

Natassia absorbed Washburn's hostility. How dare they persecute him! He was the head of Surgery, God-damn-it! Now Washburn was losing everything he valued. His marriage, his son, his career. What was there to live for?

The despondency in Washburn was so strong that Natassia was slipping, her identity drifting away. Her empathy grew and Washburn's emotions became hers.

Life was unfair! Even Allan hated him.

"I'm sorry, Allan. What can I say? Your mother practically threw herself at me. She knew I was already married but she still wanted me. Yeah, Sarah Baker was a great lay."

A hazy image of Washburn's wife, Freda, floated nearby.

"Other women? Yes, there were a few, Freda. But I wouldn't have turned to them if you had given me what I needed—what I deserved."

Did she know about the prostitute in Vancouver—the one he saw during the conventions he frequently attended?

"Freda, don't leave me! Those other women meant nothing to me."

He needed another drink. He was empty. Lost…

"What do you mean, that son-of-a-bitch Beranski is filing charges? Stacey Beranski died because she waited too long for the surgery. Against my orders, I might add. By the time I got hold of her, her appendix had already burst and poisoned her system."

Washburn was outraged. How could the hospital administrators question his competency?

"You want what? A blood test? Jesus Christ!"

He could feel a panic attack coming on. They were slaughtering him. His career would be over! And he was the best surgeon in Canada…when he wasn't drinking.

"I don't understand how the results could come back positive for drugs or alcohol. I haven't taken either in over a month! I swear!" The lie came easily, persuasively.

"Marty, you better get me out of this mess. We wouldn't want the others to know what we've been doing…now would we? Tell the press whatever you want. Tell them I had a stroke, for all I care."

He knew he had the administrators in his pocket, or at least one of them. They couldn't afford to replace him and they certainly could not afford the scandal.

"Thank you," he said when facing the board members' stern faces. "You won't regret your decision."

He deserved a drink after this. Maybe two, to celebrate.

Natassia struggled to regain control of Washburn's memories. Backing off a bit and inhaling deeply, she tried to steer Washburn toward his last painful moments.

"I better put my fishing gear away. Tomorrow's another day," Washburn murmured to himself, alone in his cabin by the lake.

Events flashed quickly—too quickly.

A hospital room, a woman crying.

A dark shadow standing in a doorway.

The shadow shifted, revealing a young man wearing a neon yellow jacket that was too big for him. His arm was wrapped in a plaster cast and suspended in a blue sling. He was smoking a cigarette and blowing circles in the air. All around him were rows of incubators, some containing sleeping babies.

At the opposite side of the room, Natassia saw Washburn hovering over a bed. Lying motionless on blood-soaked sheets, a woman screamed with fear. Her swollen belly contracted powerfully when the doctor reached between her legs.

Washburn was performing a delivery□ or an abortion.

Natassia looked down and was surprised to see several hundred-dollar bills clenched in her hands.

Then a female voice whispered, *"Give me the money, doctor. I'll take care of everything."*

Suddenly the incubators exploded.

Litter from the blast filled the room until it resembled the city dump. A tiny hand, detached from its owner, lay on the floor at Natassia's feet. Raising her head, she ga□ed into the open eyes of the woman on the bed.

When Natassia looked back toward the doorway, the young man had disappeared and she knew it was time to return. To stay *any longer might be dangerous. Especially since she had no reality line—no one to help bring her back.*

Retreating into safety, Natassia's body floated toward her while Washburn disappeared slowly, fading into death and debris.

Like the piece of garbage he was, Jasi thought when Natassia finished telling them what she had seen. Jasi realized she felt little sympathy for Norman Washburn.

They were seated on plump embroidered cushions on the floor of *Ayumi's Japanese Restaurant* in Kelowna. Hand-painted paper lanterns decorated with cherry blossoms were suspended from the ceiling by brass chains. The lanterns illuminated the small private room with a warm golden light. Two traditional Japanese sliding doors, *fusuma*, separated them from the other rooms in the restaurant.

Jasi made a face while Natassia tried to coax her into eating a seaweed-wrapped rice ball stuffed with raw shrimp. How could her friend eat that stuff?

"No, thanks," she grimaced. "I prefer my food cooked to extinction." To prove her point, Jasi piled steaming chicken teriyaki on her plate and doused it in Soya sauce.

Natassia glanced at Ben who was sipping sake from a small cup. "Want to try some sushi?"

Apprehensively, Ben scrutinized the food, then shook his head. "I have to agree with Jasi. Give me a salmon steak on the barbecue any day."

Natassia pouted, then promptly deposited the roll into her mouth, watching Ben as she did so. "You don't know what you're missing."

Jasi snickered at her partner's blatant innuendo.

"I'm missing real food." Ben threw Natassia a warning look then quickly finished the rest of his sake. "I've finished profiling our arsonist, by the way. It's uploaded to your 'coms."

Jasi looked up, her mouth full of chicken. "What can you tell us?"

Ben heaped a beef noodle concoction onto his plate. "Basically we're searching for a male—primarily a white male between twenty-five and forty. Physically strong enough to lift or drag a three hundred pound man." He took a sip of sake before continuing.

"His crimes are premeditated. Emotionally, he harbors feelings of inferiority, low self-esteem and rage toward those who have hurt him in the past. There's a high probability that our man was abused as a child—sexually, physically or psychologically."

Jasi knew that a serial killer usually had unresolved issues in his past. He would continue killing until those issues were worked out...or until he ended up dead.

"I've made reservations at the hotel next door to give us time to finish with these leads," Ben continued. "Were you able to confirm Jason Beranski's alibi?"

Jasi's trip to the theatre had been inconclusive, but she told them what she had found out so far. The ticket booth attendant had remembered Beranski. A tall skinny man with a pale shaved head would stand out in most places nowadays.

"He took a cab to the Pyramid Theatre and purchased his ticket to *Titanic* shortly before midnight. The guy taking the tickets recognized the photo of Beranski but like he says, Beranski could have slipped out the back door anytime."

"What time was the movie over?" Natassia asked her.

"3:10 in the morning. It was about twenty minutes late because they had some trouble with the first reel."

"Twenty minutes is nothing," Natassia huffed. "Compared to ten years ago. Remember when they used to show previews for over half an hour right before the movie?"

"Yeah," Ben replied. "Then they finally got smart and started showing them in between movies. It's better than those damn trivia questions they showed."

"Why didn't they think of that sooner? I mean, it takes them almost an hour to clean up after a movie and then seat people for the next one. That's the perfect time to be showing previews."

Jasi cleared her throat loudly. "Okay, you two. We've got work to do. The movie finished just after three. If he stayed there, then Beranski has a clean alibi."

"So we can cross him off the list," Natassia suggested.

Jasi shook her head. "For now, he stays on the list. Until I know for sure he didn't leave the theatre."

She stared at Jason Beranski's face on her data-com screen. He would have had plenty of time to get to Loon Lake. And back *before* the movie ended.

Natassia reached for another shrimp roll. "The coroner should be sending us the autopsy report tomorrow."

A soft knock on the fusuma ended their discussion.

A tiny Japanese girl wearing a yellow and red yukata slid the door open and presented them with a new bottle of sake. She bowed, then trailed from the room, her feet whispering across the floor.

"What about Premier Baker?" Jasi asked Ben.

"Baker checked into the Paloma Springs Hotel at noon yesterday." Ben consulted his notes. "He held a private dinner party in one of the Ballrooms from eight until past two. Around midnight, he went up to his room to take a personal phone call and was gone for about half an hour. At least that's what he said."

Natassia placed her chopsticks on the table. "Alone?"

Ben studied her oddly. "Why? What difference does it make if he was alone?"

"Just curious. Perhaps he was taking a different kind of personal message. I'll check his phone records."

"Maybe Baker hired someone to do his dirty work," Jasi suggested.

The idea that Allan Baker had contracted out had flickered through Jasi's mind ever since the man showed up at the scene of the crime. Baker had the resources to hire a hit man—and the motive. His father was a disgrace. Dr. Washburn had embarrassed the Premier of BC, maybe one too many times. And with Baker running for Prime Minister, he couldn't afford another family scandal.

"Maybe *that* was the phone call?" Ben said.

Natassia suddenly waved a hand in the air. "Got it! Paloma phone records show one incoming call at 11:53 p.m. lasting about ten minutes. Number belongs to a Martin L. Gibney of 103 Dremner Boulevard, here in Kelowna. Should I check him out?"

"No," Jasi said pensively. "I think Ben should take Gibney. You contact the people on Baker's list of attendees. Make sure he was seen at the hotel between midnight and two. Loon Lake isn't very far, especially for a man with his resources."

"If you're taking Beranski, then you'd better bring a barf bag," Natassia cautioned.

"Yeah, I'll pack an extra shirt too," Jasi grinned. "First thing tomorrow, I'll check the cab companies. Maybe Jason Beranski ditched the movie once it started."

She yawned.

The trip to the crime scene had exhausted her. A good night's sleep was what she needed. Then she could get an early start in the morning. Thank God, she wouldn't have to deal with that tiring Brandon Walsh anymore.

After Ben paid their bill, the three of them walked across the empty street toward the Prestige Inn. The hotel lobby glistened with pearlescent floors and matching oak trim.

Jasi checked for messages, then they headed for the elevators. A group of boisterous, intoxicated politicians rudely pushed past them and confiscated the only vacant car.

"If people only knew what these guys were *really* doing with taxpayers' money," Natassia muttered.

"Then we wouldn't have to worry about voting," Jasi scoffed. "There'd be no election."

In the elevator one of the men shifted nervously. Jasi curled her lip, her eyes fastening on him, threateningly. As the doors slowly closed, the man sagged against the wall.

Whether it was from relief or too much alcohol, Jasi didn't know. She didn't care either way.

The second elevator announced its arrival with a brief melody. Then the doors opened, depositing a frazzled mother with five screaming children, all obviously headed for the swimming pool.

Jasi followed Ben and Natassia inside and pushed the button to their floor. When they reached the third floor, she strode down the hall, eager for her bed and sleep.

"Here's your suite," Ben said, swiping a room card across the scanner.

When the door buzzed open, he handed her the card.

"I'll keep in touch tomorrow," he told her, then strolled across the hall to his own room. "Goodnight, Natassia."

Jasi saw her partner's eyes trail after him, disappointment and longing engraved on her face.

"Hey, Natassia. Look on the bright side," she smirked when they entered their room. "At least you've got me for a roommate."

Natassia scowled grumpily. "Yeah, but you're not as much fun."

"Hey!" She ducked as Natassia chucked a pillow at her head.

"And you snore!"

8

The following morning Jasi called the taxi companies and narrowed down three that had serviced the theatre the night before. Each company stated that they could not release information over the phone. Hailing a Speedy taxi, she gave the driver the address for Kel-Cabs.

The driver's ID read _Ahmed_.

In the rear view mirror, Ahmed's black eyes bore holes into her face. Resisting the urge to scowl at him, Jasi curled up in the seat and stared at the gloomy morning sky. Rain was headed their way and that was not good. If the crime scene hadn't been cleared of all evidence, the rain would obliterate it.

Without warning the taxi screeched to an abrupt halt next to a bookstore. Jasi peered out the window, noting that the vehicles in front had slowed to a snail's crawl while anxious drivers _rubbernecked_ the area, eager for signs of catastrophe. At first, she thought there had been an accident. Then she noticed that a crowd had gathered across the street in front of City Hall. Two television station vans were parked nearby while camera operators forced their way to the center of the crowd, each vying for prime position.

A tall blond-haired woman seemed vaguely familiar.

Jasi realized that the blond was a new reporter for *CTBC News*. She groaned when she saw who stood beside the woman, basking and primping in front of the camera.

Premier Allan Baker.

Great! What the hell is he up to now?

"Wait for me here!" she ordered, handing Ahmed a twenty-dollar bill. "I won't be gone long."

Jasi jumped from the taxi and darted between the slowing vehicles until she reached the sidewalk. She pushed her way through the crowd just in time to hear the news reporter introduce Baker.

"Because of the unfortunate death of your father, you have been wrenched away from your regular duties as Premier of BC," the woman announced in a low, raspy voice. "Has his death been ruled an accident?"

Baker hesitated for a moment. "I'm sorry. I can't comment on the investigation. When the coroner releases that information I'm sure you'll be the first to know."

"Jesus!" Jasi muttered when she caught the Premier eyeing the reporter's skirt-clad hips.

The man was insufferable.

"Premier Baker, is it true that your father's employment with Kelowna General Hospital was going to be terminated?" The reporter innocently tucked a stray wisp of hair behind her ear.

Baker shifted uncomfortably, then gazed into the camera. "Miss Prescott, my father was fifty-eight years old and getting ready to retire. I have no idea what the hospital administration had in mind."

Prescott's hazel eyes flashed stubbornly. "But what about his alcohol problem? It's been reported that Dr. Washburn was drinking on the job."

"My father was a top-notch doctor—the best in his field," Baker replied coolly. "Any claims regarding alcohol consumption while working have been unfounded and all charges have been dismissed. I'm sure you can check the hospital records."

Baker eyed his watch, then peered into the crowd.

His eyes targeted Jasi's, and he smiled.

The reporter nudged the microphone closer. "Premier Baker, do you think your father's death will have any affect on the public support you receive, especially now that you've stated your intentions to run for Prime Minister?"

Baker's shoulders slumped noticeably and he emitted a long sigh.

Probably an act, Jasi thought.

"How my father's death will affect the public, I can only guess. Dr. Norman Washburn was my father and mentor. He supported my campaigns one hundred percent. I'll miss the old man, regardless of what anyone may think. As for public support? I'm very thankful that BC judges a man by his own acts, his own abilities—not by someone else's actions."

Jasi stifled a snicker. *Great act!*

Baker strode toward her, determination evident on his face. He elbowed his way closer while Prescott followed behind, motioning the camera operator to keep up.

"Now if you have additional questions, Miss Prescott, you can ask Agent McLellan here. She's with the CFBI, investigating my father's death."

A cluster of microphones collided in front of Jasi. She observed the eager, hungry faces of the news hounds that begged for a juicy treat.

She wasn't giving them any—not even one little bone.

Stepping forward, she said firmly, "No comment."

Prodding Baker past the cameras, Jasi swore under her breath. "Don't say another word to the press about the investigation. The information we gave you was strictly confidential."

She started to walk away but Baker caught her arm.

"Whoa! He was my father, Agent McLellan."

Jasi turned slowly to face him, her eyes narrowing.

"How did you know I was assigned to this investigation?"

Baker shrugged. "Your associates told me."

Lowering his head, he whispered in her ear. "I'd be very happy to help you...*investigate*."

"I don't need help. Especially from you. Just keep away from the press, *Premier* Baker. And stay away from me—and my team."

Jasi elbowed her way past a group of gawking spectators. Baker's laughter trailed behind her, a low threatening sound. She would need a hot shower after dealing with him.

"Agent McLellan?"

What now?

The blond reporter stepped from the crowd, self-consciously smoothing her navy-colored suit with her hands.

"Can I help you?" Jasi asked curtly, scouring the street for Ahmed and the taxi.

"Probably not. But I can help you."

The reporter smiled and held out a hand "Cameron Prescott, *CTBC News*."

Begrudgingly, Jasi shook it. "I'm familiar with you, Miss Prescott."

"Please, call me Cameron."

"How do you think you can help me?"

Jasi examined Cameron Prescott for signs of deception.

Although the woman had left both her microphone and camera operator behind, she might still be concealing a recording device. The last thing Jasi wanted to be responsible for was a press leak.

"This is completely off record," Prescott assured her, opening her jacket to prove she wasn't recording their conversation.

"I want an exclusive interview with you once the CFBI has reached its conclusion. In return, I'll let you in on a little secret and research anything you want."

"Look, Miss—uh, Cameron. I know what it's like to be the new kid on the block but I can't possibly discuss this case with you."

Cameron handed her a business card.

On the back, the name and address of a coffee shop was scribbled in pen.

"Meet me there at one," the reporter pleaded in a husky voice. "I've been assigned to the Premier during his campaign and I've got something on him that you're going to want."

Then Cameron Prescott vanished into the back of the *CTBC News* van.

As Jasi crossed the busy street, oblivious to the blaring horns and swerving vehicles, she wondered what the woman had on Baker. Whatever it was, Jasi thought, it had better be good.

Approaching the bookstore, she swore.

Ahmed, you bastard! Where the hell are you?

There was no sign of the Speedy taxi. Or its beady-eyed driver. The parking lot was empty except for a Mitsubishi Zen, one of 2012's newest model sports cars.

Jasi recognized the car.

Allan Baker didn't travel cheaply.

Locating Kel-Cabs on the data-com's city map, she discovered it was two blocks away. Oh well, walking was good exercise. And it would give her time to think.

She glanced at her watch. The morning was half over and she still had two other taxi companies to investigate. After that, she would have to check in with Ben and Natassia.

There was also Cameron Prescott's invitation to consider. And Jasi was very curious what the reporter had to say about Premier Allan Baker.

Kel-Cabs was located in an old brick building that backed onto a busy parking lot. It even housed its own car wash facilities. Three freshly washed cabs were parked inside a bay, their drivers standing impatiently nearby while a cleaning crew scoured the tires.

Situated on the ground floor, the main dispatch office was chaotic and noisy. A row of bored dispatchers wearing headsets was positioned along one wall. Each dispatcher had a computer terminal on his or her desk.

Jasi could see route maps on some of the monitors—the odd Solitaire game on others.

A cacophony of voices and bad frequencies delivered her a blinding headache. She massaged her forehead while notifying the secretary at the reception desk that she had an appointment to see the manager.

The secretary ignored her, as if she hadn't heard a word Jasi had said. Instead, the young girl continued talking on a cell phone. The girl's neon orange nails tapped the wooden desk nervously, betraying her knowledge of Jasi's presence.

"Excuse me!" Jasi grabbed the phone from the startled girl. Putting it to her ear, she snarled, "She'll call ya back later!"

Then Jasi flicked the cell phone shut and hurled it toward the secretary. A flash of her badge obtained a quick apology from the girl, and then Jasi was personally escorted upstairs to the manager's office.

"Uh, Mr. Hawkins will be right in. He's just finishing a…uh, meeting."

The secretary gawked at the empty office before she nervously scurried away.

Alone in the stale-smelling office, Jasi stood by a grimy window and thought about Cameron Prescott. She didn't know much about her, other than she was one of Vancouver's new top reporters. She must be good to have been sent all the way to Kelowna for a story.

There was no question in Jasi's mind about showing up at the coffee shop. If Cameron Prescott had dirt on Baker, then Jasi would definitely start digging. Maybe if she dug deep enough, perhaps the Premier would bury himself.

She knew Baker was guilty of something.

But was it murder?

"Can I help you?"

"Well that remains to be seen," Jasi replied, examining the manager from a distance.

The man was probably in his sixties. He wore a monk's fringe of gray, oily hair and sported a bulbous nose with enlarged pores—a drinker's nose. Grossly overweight, the man's belly bulged over a silver buckle fastened to a worn leather belt that was stretched to its limits. He wore jeans and a stained denim shirt with tacky rhinestone buttons.

The Rhinestone Cowboy, Jasi thought, positive that somewhere in the building a lone Stetson was perched haphazardly on a rack.

I wonder where the rest of the Village People are.

The man gasped nervously for air—like a fish out of water. Nervously he wiped his forehead, leaving a smear of sweat across the sleeve of his shirt.

A musky odor wafted toward Jasi, sweet and familiar.

The man was higher than a kite.

"Albert Hawkins, manager," the man coughed, holding out a shaking, grease-stained palm.

She peered down her nose at his hand, ignored it, and then showed him her ID. She explained that CFBI computers had traced his company to two pick-ups at the Pyramid Theatre after midnight the night before.

"I need to see those records."

Hawkins huffed indignantly. "We respect our clients confidentiality."

"I can subpoena them," she threatened softly, watching his bloodshot eyes.

Jasi knew she had him by the balls. There was no way Albert Hawkins wanted the CFBI snooping through his records—or his place of business.

She watched as he lowered himself into a torn leather chair. He pushed aside a half-filled coffee mug. It left a pale ring of dampness on the wooden desk. Shoving a pile of food-stained receipts and invoices to one side, he awkwardly fingered the keyboard of his computer.

"There."

He rotated the monitor in her direction and pointed a stubby finger at the screen. "Two pick-ups in that area after midnight. One at 12:15 paid by credit card and another at 12:39 paid in cash. The credit card we can track, but the other…"

Cash customers were the bane of Jasi's existence. There was no way to trace any kind of transaction if cash was involved.

"The credit card is registered to Gayle McDermid. Was signed by her too." Hawkins glanced up with a hopeful expression in his drugged eyes.

Jasi shook her head. Dead end.

Hawkins checked the screen again. "The driver with the cash payment indicated 'male passenger' in his logbook. The driver's name is Ian Vandermeer. You have a picture of the guy you're looking for?"

Jasi slapped the photo of Jason Beranski on the desk.

Hawkins squinted at the picture, then waved his arm.

"Show it to Ian. He might remember picking him up. There's nothing more I can tell you. We done, Agent McEwan?"

"McLellan."

"Wha—"

"The name's *McLellan*," Jasi snarled.

The man stumbled to his feet. "Is that all?"

Hesitating at the door, she turned back and gave him a penetrating stare. "No, that's not all, Mr. Hawkins."

Her eyes narrowed dangerously. "You might want to keep in mind that the next time the CFBI makes an appointment to see you, you better not stagger in here smelling like a Z-Lyte factory."

Without saying another word, Jasi made her way out of the office, leaving the door ajar. From the corner of her eye, she saw Hawkins slump thankfully into his chair. She was tempted to confront the man about his earlier *meeting*. Using Z-Lyte was one thing but the man could be dealing. A taxi company would be the perfect place to operate from. Unlimited contacts.

Today Albert Hawkins was safe though. Jasi had more important predators to bait. But one day…

In the back lot, Jasi was pointed in the direction of the driver who had been paid in cash. Ian Vandermeer was just a pimply-faced kid. He didn't appear old enough to be finished high school—much less to drive a taxi.

She was tempted to ask the kid for his ID, but instead she clenched her teeth and showed him the photo of Beranski. Vandermeer smiled slightly, revealing bright multi-colored braces. He told her that the man who had gotten into his cab two nights ago had been wearing a hooded jacket.

"Maybe it's him," Vandermeer shrugged. "I can't say for sure. All I know is the dude paid with cash. Lousy tipper, though."

She thanked the kid, her eyes following him while he responded to a message from dispatch. He climbed into his designated taxi and peeled away from the curb.

What is the world coming to when pimply-faced kids are driving city cabs?

9

Benjamin Roberts unfolded himself from the back seat of the taxi after it stopped at 103 Dremner Boulevard.

Martin L. Gibney lived in an impressive Victorian mansion. The house was located in an exclusive, posh Kelowna neighborhood known as *The Heights*. The white siding was trimmed with dusty rose shutters and brick pillars. A large turret rose on the right side of the massive home, its windows staring down onto the street.

The front yard was professionally landscaped and immaculately groomed with tall pine trees. A granite retaining wall sectioned off a three-tiered rose garden on the left. A meandering creek flowed through delicately scented flowers and poured between the rocks. At the bottom, a small waterfall emptied into a pond.

Ben followed a hedge-lined sidewalk until he came to a door. Just as he was about to push the intercom button, the door opened and a tiny elderly woman of Asian heritage jumped back in alarm.

"I have an appointment with Mr. Gibney," he explained to the startled maid. "Agent Benjamin Roberts."

The woman pointed to the mailbox outside the door. "I checking mail." Her voice was soft and lilting.

She pushed past him, opened the mailbox and retrieved a handful of letters and bills.

"Come!" she smiled, waving him inside and leading him to a spacious sitting room. "I get Mr. Gi-ney for you. You sit." Then she disappeared.

While he waited, Ben casually examined the room.

A portrait of a young black-haired woman with dark eyes and golden skin hung above the gas fireplace. She was lying on a chaise lounge in a candlelit bedroom. A sheer piece of lavender silk was draped lightly across her naked body. The fabric left nothing to the imagination.

Throwing a vigilant look toward the open door, Ben walked over to a cherrywood table. Arranged on it were a variety of professional photographs of the woman in the portrait. He cautiously picked one up, admiring the youthful innocence of its model. She was mesmerizing—exotic, alluring and inviting.

"Beautiful, isn't she?"

Ben jumped, then peered over his shoulder at the man standing behind him.

Martin Gibney had expensive taste. He wore an Italian designer suit. *Natazzi*, Ben realized. The gray of the fabric reflected the distinguished silver lights in Gibney's short black hair. He had to be in his late forties.

Ben placed the photo back on the table.

"Your daughter?"

Gibney gasped in amusement. "Not quite, Agent Roberts. Try *wife*." His laughter sliced the air, like a double-edged sword.

Startled by the man's admission, Ben's eyes drifted back to the portrait on the wall.

Damn! Gibney was one lucky man! His wife couldn't be more than twenty-five.

"She's from Brazil, my wife," the man said, as if that was an explanation for why he was married to someone at least twenty years younger.

"How'd you two meet?"

"I met her father when I was in Brazil on business, about five years ago. Her father was Orlando Santiago—the leader of the Brazilian Labor Party. Last year Orlando was assassinated. I had promised him years ago that I would take care of his daughter if anything happened to him. So when he was killed I brought Lydia back...as my wife."

Ben followed Gibney toward a plush leather sofa and sat down.

"So Agent Roberts. What can I do for you? I have to admit I was a bit surprised to receive a call from the CFBI."

Ben flipped open his data-com. "Do you mind?"

When Gibney shrugged, he turned the recorder on.

"Are you aware that Premier Baker's father died yesterday?"

Gibney heaved an enormous sigh. "Oh yes, I heard about it on the radio. A sad, sad situation." His head twitched slowly, back and forth.

The Asian woman entered the room, halting all conversation. She poured two tall glasses of fresh-squeezed orange juice, then left.

"I understand you called the Premier that night, just before midnight," Ben said after the door closed after her.

"Yes, I did call Allan."

"Was the call related to Baker's political campaign?"

The man laughed derisively and leaned forward.

"Agent Roberts, you do know what I do for a living?"

Ben realized that he had assumed that Gibney was connected to Baker in a political field. He hadn't checked fully into Martin Gibney's background.

"No, I'm afraid I don't."

"I'm on the Board of Administration at the Kelowna General Hospital. I worked with Allan's father." Gibney took a swig of his juice before continuing. "In fact, Dr. Washburn and I go back a long way. I met him when he first became an ER doctor. Back when I was a GP."

Ben recalled Natassia's vision.

Natassia had seen a hospital room. She had also recalled angry words exchanged between Washburn and at least one of the hospital administrators.

*Marty...*Martin Gibney.

Ben reached for his glass and knocked back the juice in one gulp. "Why'd you call the Premier?"

Gibney opened his mouth, about to say something, then closed it again.

After a moment, he said, "I'm not sure I should be discussing—"

"We can go downtown, if you like, Dr. Gibney."

"Mister," the man corrected, shifting uncomfortably in his chair. "I gave up the title of doctor a long time ago."

He gave Ben a resigned look. "We were going to fire Dr. Washburn—no pun intended."

The wheels turned quickly in Ben's mind. If the hospital was about to fire Washburn, perhaps Baker figured out a way to avoid the scandal. The call could have been innocent.

Or Gibney and Baker could have been discussing a hit. *Murder.*

"How did Premier Baker take this news?"

"How do you think?" Gibney asked blandly. "Allan can't afford another scandal. When the public found out his mother had slept with a married man they were outraged. How do you think Allan's supporters would feel if they knew that his father was about to be fired for alcohol and drug misconduct?"

They'd question Baker's suitability as Prime Minister of Canada, Ben thought.

And Allan Baker? He'd feel cornered.

"Why were you the bearer of bad news?"

"The Premier has made some significant contributions to the hospital and I thought he was worth some consideration. Better to hear it from me than on TV."

Gibney's manner was indifferent.

Ben mulled over the information. "Why didn't you attend his campaign party at the Paloma Springs? Your name was on his guest list."

"We held an emergency Board meeting to discuss Dr. Washburn. It didn't finish until eleven. By the time it was over I realized it was too late to go to Allan Baker's party."

Gibney peered at his watch.

A solid gold Rolex, Ben noted. The hospital administrator must be pulling in a hefty salary. So much for government cutbacks.

"Anyway, my wife represented us both. She was at his gala until maybe three in the morning."

The man rose to his feet, a blunt indication that their meeting was terminated. "Su-Lin will see you to the door, Agent Roberts. I have another Board meeting this afternoon."

"Is your wife home. I'd like to speak to her."

"I'm afraid she's out—shopping. You know women."

"Yeah," Ben agreed, holding out a bare hand. "Thank you for your time."

As he shook hands with the man, Ben sensed that Martin Gibney was hiding something—and he was terrified that someone would find out.

When Ben pulled his hand away, he was startled to see that his palm was covered with a sticky reddish-brown substance.

Blood.

Then the vision faded, leaving Ben feeling uneasy.

Martin Gibney had blood on his hands. But whose?

Ben ordered the voice record off.

Then he filed a mental note to talk to the wife at a later date. Perhaps Mrs. Gibney had noticed something at the party. Maybe someone who should have been there...but wasn't.

Following Su-Lin, he made his way past the fireplace and hesitantly studied the portrait of Gibney's wife. Yeah, she was the kind of woman a man would do almost anything for.

Outside in the warm sunlight, Ben thought of Natassia Prushenko.

Natassia was sexy, intelligent *and* beautiful. Although they had only worked together for a short time, he admired her immensely. Admiration wasn't the only thing he felt for her. But it was against CFBI policy for agents to mix business with pleasure.

Lately, however, the beautiful blue-eyed Russian was on his mind...more than he cared to admit.

Damn you, Ben!

Benjamin Roberts was on Natassia's mind too.

Trapped in a musty taxi with no air conditioning, she wondered why Ben had been assigned to Gibney while she was stuck with the lecherous old men and snobbish society women on Baker's party list.

Jasi would certainly get a piece of her mind too, Natassia thought.

Frickin' politicians!

If they weren't staring at her cleavage, they were winking at her. Most of the Premier's male supporters and political cohorts were men in their seventies and eighties.

Playing hooky from a graveyard.

The men were members of a pretentious group—one that believed in their own importance. The wives were no different with their polished acrylic nails, double-D-cup breast implants and 'extreme makeover' liposuctions and face-lifts.

The taxi took a corner and steered closer to her destination. Every now and then, Natassia eyed the streets—and the meter.

She pursed her lips in disgust.

If she had to interview one more pair of fake grape-colored eyes, compliments of SEE, she'd gag. She couldn't understand why women went for the fake look when they could get a more natural sectional eye enhancement.

Like her own.

Everyone believed the dark blue color of her eyes was natural, but she had taken a trip to a SEE office before transferring to Vancouver. Three thousand dollars and an hour later she went from brown eyes to blue.

Natassia surveyed her schedule.

Fifty-three people on Baker's list lived all over BC and had already given their statements via phone or data-com. Eight couples had lived nearby so Natassia had arranged a taxi to drive her for the day. She was now down to the last three people.

That's when she noticed that Martin and Lydia Gibney's names were at the bottom.

Oh well, Ben would take care of them.

Consulting her notes from the other interviews, she exhaled in disappointment.

Not one solid lead. Crap!

In fact, the only thing she could confirm was that the Premier had left the party before midnight to take a phone call. Every guest was positive they had seen Baker during the evening. The problem was no one was sure what time he had returned to the ballroom. His guests thought they had seen him off and on throughout the party and the hotel staff could only confirm that at around 2:20 a.m. Baker had notified the front desk that the ballroom had been vacated.

Natassia rolled down the window. She needed air.

Scrolling to the last name on her data-com, she let out a breath. She was almost finished.

Alyssa Bines was the final person on her list.

The taxi dropped Natassia off at *Tim Horton's*. The restaurant was peaceful and cheery. The scent of freshly made donuts and strong coffee lingered in the air. Thankfully, the morning rush of executives and homemakers was over.

She selected a table near a window.

Glancing around the room, Natassia noticed a young man slumped in a far corner booth. His long bangs hung in his eyes while he read college crib notes—cramming for an exam, by the look of the coffee cup graveyard on his table.

Other than the kid, she was alone.

Natassia was pouring over her field notes when a hesitant voice interrupted her.

"Agent Prushenko? Sorry I'm late."

She peered up to see a woman in her twenties standing beside the table.

Alyssa Bines was a natural beauty. Her long strawberry-blond hair was secured with a silver clasp at the nape of her neck. She wore a two-piece Vera Wang creation in a pale shade of coral. Her makeup was fresh and light.

The most noticeable thing about her, though, was her infectious grin.

"No problem, Miss Bines. I needed a few cups of caffeine anyway."

"Alyssa," the woman stated firmly before sitting. "*Miss Bines* sounds so…uppity."

Raising one eyebrow in surprise, Natassia grinned and activated her data-com.

This one was different from the other society *queens*.

A waitress brought them two vanilla lattes while Alyssa made herself comfortable.

"I've never been questioned by the CFBI before," the woman giggled.

Natassia nudged the data-com closer to the woman.

"Can you repeat your name, address and phone number, Alyssa?"

The young woman gave the information, then asked, "Is this about Premier Baker's father?"

"How'd you guess?"

Alyssa glanced excitably over her shoulder.

Then she hunched forward, chewing her bottom lip.

"Have you talked to Lydia Gibney yet? She could tell you a thing or two."

"My partner is handling the Gibneys."

Alyssa responded with a loud snort. "That husband of hers—Martin? He hasn't got a clue."

"What do you mean?"

Alyssa peered over the rim of her coffee cup.

"I don't like to gossip but…"

She paused for effect, then shrugged and laughed.

"Okay, so I *do* like to gossip. Anyway, the night of the party at the hotel I saw Lydia and Premier Baker *together*."

Natassia's head snapped to attention. "What do you mean, *together*?"

Alyssa smiled suggestively. "You know…*together*, together."

She took a long drag of her latte.

"I was invited to the party because my father is a major contributor to the Premier's campaign. I've been to tons of these things. Most of the time they're a bore. Stuffy old people."

Natassia could certainly understand how Alyssa felt.

Baker's followers would put most people to sleep.

"Once in a while I get lucky," the woman said mischievously.

Natassia's eyebrow winged. "Really?"

"I don't mean *that* way. It's just that sometimes I meet someone younger. Someone single and interesting."

"Are you talking about Allan Baker?"

"The Premier? No way! Not that he hasn't tried. Anyway, he's infatuated with Mrs. Martin Gibney right now."

Natassia watched Alyssa carefully, wondering if the woman was telling the truth.

"How long has that been going on?"

"About six months maybe. I first spotted them sneaking out to the gardens at the New Years Eve party in Vancouver. I've seen the two of them flirting with each other at a couple of other events too. Then, at the hotel, I happened to see Lydia duck into the Premier's room."

Natassia double-checked her data-com.

It was essential that she get Alyssa's statement on record. If the Premier of British Columbia was having an affair with a married woman then she needed solid proof.

Alyssa frowned suddenly. "The night of the party my father hooked me up with a son of a friend. The man was so obnoxious that I developed a terrible headache."

Natassia grinned.

She had dated a couple of men where a nasty headache—real or imagined—had come in handy.

"So you left?"

Alyssa nodded. "I went back to my room. Premier Baker's suite was a couple of doors down from mine, on the opposite side of the hall. That's when I saw them. Allan Baker and Lydia Gibney. They went into his room and I didn't hear anyone in the hallway until maybe half an hour later."

Half an hour was a long time for a ten-minute phone call. Natassia wondered what else Baker had been up to.

Alyssa lowered her voice. "Later, I heard them arguing in the hall. Lydia sounded almost frightened. I heard Martin Gibney's name mentioned a few times. Then I heard her run down the hall—crying. A few minutes later, Premier Baker walked past my door. He was talking to someone."

Natassia carefully sipped her latte, thinking about the ramifications of Alyssa's story.

Baker would have had time to talk to Martin Gibney on the phone, and then take Gibney's wife for a *ride*—albeit a short one. Maybe Lydia got off on pounding Baker while he talked to her husband on the phone.

But who was he talking to in the hallway? And where did he go?

It was only about eighty kilometers from downtown Kelowna to Washburn's cabin. If Baker had hopped in his car after his romp with Mrs. Gibney, he could have easily made it by one o'clock. At that time of night, he would have had no traffic to fight against.

Baker was definitely looking good for the murder of his father.

Natassia carefully studied Alyssa Bines. The woman had a certain freshness about her, an almost child-like quality. Yet, she was one hell of an observer—unlike the other wealthy socialites Natassia had talked to. The ones who had peered down their noses at her.

Alyssa withdrew some money from her purse and tucked it under her coffee cup. Then she rose gracefully from the booth.

"Coffee's on me, Agent Prushenko. My life is usually quite mundane, so this bit of excitement will keep me going for awhile."

"Thank you for talking to me."

Alyssa hovered near the table. "Tell me, Agent Prushenko. What exactly is it that you do in the CFBI, other than listen to bored women with nothing but time on their hands?"

"I listen to the victims," Natassia answered. "When no one else hears them."

The young woman nodded slowly. "They are very fortunate to have you."

When Alyssa Bines was gone, Natassia pondered the woman's parting remark. There were days when she would agree. Especially if she touched a live victim and correctly identified the perpetrator. But sometimes the live cases were the most difficult to handle.

At least a dead victim's pain and suffering was over.

Her data-com beeped suddenly.

"What's up?"

"I'm done with Gibney," Ben replied. "I talked to the staff at the Paloma and checked with hotel security. If Baker left the hotel that night, he didn't drive his vehicle. The parking attendant confirmed that Baker's Mitsubishi Zen was parked all night long."

To Natassia, it was like someone had knocked the wind out of her. The excitement she experienced earlier left her suddenly and completely pissed off.

But there were still inconsistencies in Baker's alibi.

And there *was* the affair.

"Meet me for lunch back at the hotel," Ben said.

"Okay, but I'm bringing dessert," she joked, thinking of her conversation with Alyssa Bines.

She heard a sharp intake of breath on Ben's end.

It wasn't until she hung up that Natassia realized how suggestive her comment had sounded.

10

The two remaining taxi companies on Jasi's list had begrudgingly shown her their credit card records. Both companies indicated customers who had been picked up at or near the theatre. Jason Beranski's name wasn't on any of them. So unless the man had sprouted wings, there was no possible way that Beranski could have left the theatre and made it to Washburn's cabin.

Unless he had been the man who had paid Ian Vandermeer in cash, Jasi mused.

Entering *Bits & Bytes*, a popular Internet café chain, she ordered a Chai latte and slowly scanned the room. There were eight data terminals with dividers between them for privacy. The terminals formed an oval in the center of the café. Small tables with hammered silver chairs surrounded the oval and lined the windows.

Bits & Bytes was a refuge to computer junkies and teenagers. Jasi was not surprised to see both, although it was a school day.

Walking past the terminals, she glanced at a computer monitor and caught two teenaged boys trying to override the café's porn-blocker. A quick show of her badge sent them scurrying out of the place—red-faced and terrified.

A teenaged girl led her to a table in the back corner.

Dropping thankfully into a chair, Jasi sipped her tea and pushed her sleeve back to check her watch. She had a few minutes before her scheduled meeting with Cameron Prescott. Reviewing her data-com message system, she found two messages. One was from Ben. He was wondering how her side of the investigation was going. She made a note to check back with him after the meeting with the reporter—if the woman ever showed up.

The second message was from Matthew Divine.

A CS report had been uploaded to Jasi's data-com.

Opening the attachment, she read it thoroughly. A boot print from the ground around Washburn's cabin had been analyzed. A man's boot, size 11, deep treaded and marked. The CFBI database cross-checked the tread and identified it as a Thermogard Cruiser with steel toe. A popular and common boot used by a variety of laborers.

Damn!

"Am I interrupting you, Agent McLellan?"

Cameron Prescott hesitated at the edge of Jasi's table. She carried a cappuccino in her hand.

"No, not at all."

Jasi indicated the chair across from her. "Just a reminder though, everything we talk about here is off the record. Agreed?"

The reporter nodded, and there was an awkward silence as they sized each other up.

"So, what can you tell me about Premier Allan Baker?"

The reporter snorted. "Other than he's a womanizing, arrogant asshole?"

Jasi couldn't hold back the grin that spread across her face. She immediately sensed that she and Cameron Prescott were about to become the best of friends.

During the next twenty minutes, Jasi listened while Cameron told her how she had begged her boss for the opportunity to research Allan Baker, and had begrudgingly been given a transfer to Kelowna.

"There's more to Allan Baker than simply being the illegitimate son of Dr. Washburn." Cameron smiled as if she had eaten something rotten. "Dr. Washburn lived in Victoria during his affair with Sarah Baker. A couple of years later, he requested a transfer to Kelowna General."

"Probably so he could shirk his responsibility," Jasi muttered.

The reporter eagerly leaned forward, her hazel eyes full of excitement.

"Ten days ago I got hold of Allan Baker's school records. Did you know that his mother put him into Child Protective Services when he was eight?"

Jasi shook her head slowly, an alarm ringing in her brain. *Victoria. CPS. Foster care…*

"The school he was attending had to be notified," Cameron continued. "Sarah Baker was sent to a rehab program for drug addiction. Allan was placed in a temporary foster home. Two months later his mother got him back."

"Do you know where he was placed when he was in foster care?"

"Records show he lived with a Charlotte and Ernest Foreman."

Bingo!

Jasi felt a surge of excitement race through her body.

Baker *was* connected to the Victoria fire.

Cameron took a long gulp from her cup, then looked at Jasi. "I traveled to Victoria last week to talk to them. I found out the husband died back in 2001. Guess what else I discovered, Agent McLellan?"

"That Charlotte Foreman died in a suspicious fire three weeks ago."

Jasi's thoughts raced.

If the Foreman woman had fostered Allan Baker, then Washburn must have known about her. He had to have known that his son was dumped into the system. And the bastard hadn't even had the heart to take the boy in.

"Have you printed any of this yet?"

"No," the reporter admitted, shaking her head.

"Can you keep this quiet, buy me some time?"

Cameron grinned. "As long as you give me the exclusive."

Jasi would give her the Premier's head on a platter. What a story *that* would make on the front page! Cameron Prescott was holding onto the story that could make her career. Allan Baker wouldn't know what hit him!

The only thing Jasi and her team had to do now was place Baker at either one of the crime scenes. It was purely a matter of time before she would have enough evidence to charge him.

"You'll get your exclusive."

Baker had now moved into the category of prime suspect. He could have killed his foster mother for a million reasons. And it was more than possible that he had killed his father to stop a pre-election scandal that could end his political career.

"Agent McLellan, can I ask you a personal question?"

Jasi shrugged. "Ask away…as long as it doesn't end up in the newspaper."

"What is it like to work for the CFBI? I mean, you're always on the move, hunting down criminals and putting your life on the line."

Jasi was unsure of how to reply. How could she explain the rush she experienced when she brought down a murderer? Or the look in a mother's eyes when told that the person responsible for her child's death had been caught?

"Most of the time it's a blessing," she admitted. "It's rewarding to find the answers, solve the puzzle. But, I'll admit—it's not always easy."

Jasi had been reading fires since she was a child. And then Divine had found her and brought her into the PSI division where she had floundered with her gift, uncomprehending its value. Matthew Divine had given her a safe place to practice and hone her skills, a place where she was accepted. A home.

Of course, she couldn't reveal all this to the woman sitting across from her. Studying Cameron, Jasi had the distinct impression that the reporter suspected that she was not simply a CFBI agent. She wondered if the reporter had heard anything about the PSI division.

Divine Ops wouldn't remain a secret forever.

"The worst thing about my job is that it doesn't leave much time for a normal life," Jasi admitted uncomfortably.

"Yeah, I hear ya," Cameron chuckled.

"Whatever *normal* is."

The reporter eyed her curiously. "What about family? Friends?"

Jasi laughed. "Man, I can sure tell you're in the right profession."

"Yup. My brother used to tell me all I did was ask questions. I irritated the hell out of him."

Cameron's eyes grew distant.

Jasi cleared her throat, curious why the reporter's mood had shifted. "I have a brother too. Brady. He's younger than me and a bit of a rebel."

"And your parents?"

Jasi felt a shiver trail up her spine. "Our mother was killed on Brady's birthday during a home robbery. I was eight."

"Oh my God! I'm so sorry."

"Yeah, so am I," Jasi said softly. "My mother was a wonderful person."

She peered beneath her lashes at the woman across from her. *Why on earth am I confiding in Cameron Prescott?*

There was a moment of awkward silence before Cameron murmured, "My brother died when I was a kid. It took me years to feel like a whole person again."

Jasi nodded.

Death could do that to a person. It could leave you feeling like a dark void had replaced your once-beating heart. Wondering if the emptiness would ever go away. Always wanting the impossible.

Banishing the dark thoughts from her mind, she said, "My father is still alive. He's retired. We don't really get along. Must be the Gemini-Capricorn thing. What about your folks?"

"I never knew my birth parents," Cameron murmured softly. "My brother and I were abandoned."

"That's awful!"

Jasi couldn't understand how anyone could walk away from his or her own flesh and blood.

"Did you ever search for them?"

There was a wistful expression in the reporter's eyes.

"No. After my brother died, I thought I might go looking for them but then I reminded myself that our parents had left us in a Dumpster—like trash."

"Someone found you in a Dumpster?"

"Most people think my low voice is sexy, husky. It's actually that way because my esophagus was damaged from exposure and infection."

Jasi was mortified. "And your parents?"

Cameron took a long sip of her cappuccino before answering. "The records are sealed—airtight. Our birth parents made sure we couldn't find them."

"How'd your brother die?"

"He drowned. Just before our twelfth birthday."

Jasi's curiosity was piqued. "You were twins?"

"Yeah. Fraternal twins, not identical. They separated us when we were about nine. But I was the lucky one. The Prescott's adopted me after I turned ten."

Cameron tugged at her sleeve in an effort to cover two small scars on her right arm. When she caught Jasi watching her, she shrugged. "Childhood injury."

An awkward silence announced the end of their meeting, but Jasi was reluctant to leave. Cameron had asked her about friendship. If Jasi had been honest, she would have told her that friends were very hard to keep in her line of business.

The reporter rose quickly. "Thanks for meeting me, Agent McLellan. I look forward to hearing from you. Especially if the Premier is involved."

"You'll be the first to know," Jasi promised, following Cameron to the street.

Overhead, dark clouds had taken the sun hostage. The wind was gathering and passers-by glanced uneasily at the ominous sky. A blast of air whipped down the street, scattering papers against the buildings.

Time to get back before the storm hit.

"Do you need a ride anywhere?" Cameron asked.

"No thanks. The hotel isn't far and I want to clear my head. Uh, Cameron…thanks for the info on Baker."

"Any time, Agent McLellan."

The reporter climbed into a metallic blue Daytona and gunned the engine.

On impulse, Jasi leaned into the passenger window.

"Cut the *Agent McLellan* crap and call me *Jasi*. After all, we're going to be working together on this Baker lead."

"Sure thing, Jasi."

Cameron Prescott waved goodbye, then slipped into the evening traffic and sped away in a cloud of dust.

Jasi released a weary sigh.

Didn't the woman know there were laws against speeding?

Jasi was across the street from the Prestige Inn when the storm clouds ripped open. The rain was torrential and bone-chilling. Scrambling for the glass door of the hotel, she drew a sigh of relief as the automated system kicked in. The door opened so slowly that if she had been running any faster, she would have slammed right into it.

In the elevator, she resisted the urge to make a face at a sales executive who peered down her nose in obvious disapproval of the soaked clothes and waterlogged hair. Instead, Jasi kept replaying her conversation with Cameron.

Baker's connection with Charlotte Foreman was impossible to ignore. But why would he have killed her? Getting rid of his drunken, incompetent father made perfect sense, but a past foster mother...and an innocent child?

Jasi thought about Cameron. Having a reporter along for the ride could make the investigation easier. Often they could get inside—where the CFBI couldn't go without search warrants and formal charges. Cameron had offered her services as a reporter but Jasi suspected that an offer of friendship had also been made. She somehow sensed that Cameron was in need of a friend...just as much as she was.

She sighed heavily, thinking of the few friends she had.

There was Natassia and Ben, of course. But other than that...

There was something very likeable about Cameron Prescott. Maybe her honesty—something rare in a reporter.

Whatever it was, Jasi liked her. And that led to two problems.

Making friends was not her forte.

And keeping them was next to impossible.

11

After a quick lunch, Natassia flopped on the bed and compared notes with Ben on Washburn, Gibney and Baker. She picked up the crime scene reports, eyeing them for a clue—a direction.

Maybe she had missed something.

"Do you think it's possible Martin Gibney killed Washburn so that Baker wouldn't have to get his hands dirty?"

"Anything's possible," Ben shrugged. "Gibney wanted Washburn out of that hospital as much as the rest of the board members. Yet he believed he owed it to Baker to tell him first."

"Maybe Baker's blackmailing Gibney."

Natassia had been playing with the idea ever since Ben had told her that Gibney had called Baker to warn the Premier that his father was being fired.

"Hmmm, blackmail," Ben said thoughtfully. "Baker was donating money to the hospital. He could have threatened to withdraw his financial support if Gibney didn't get rid of his father."

"I'll check the hospital financial statements and compare them to Baker's. If he paid Gibney for his *services*, there might be a corresponding donation to the hospital—or to Gibney personally."

Ben drummed his fingers on the table. "When I shook Gibney's hand I could see death all around him."

"Well, he is a doctor. I'm sure he's seen lots of death."

"I know," Ben sighed. "But I sensed he was holding back something."

Natassia wondered what Gibney could be hiding.

She flicked a glance in Ben's direction, admiring his persistence. Smiling to herself, Natassia admitted there wasn't much about Benjamin Roberts that she *didn't* admire.

"So this Alyssa Bines," he said pensively. "Is she a reliable witness? You think she's telling the truth about Baker and Lydia Gibney?"

"Yeah. Bines might be a bit of a gossip but she's attended every major campaign event in the past two months. She's seen them together more than once."

Ben tapped his data-com. "And she's positive she heard them fighting?"

"Uh-huh. Baker left his room shortly after Lydia had gone. None of the people on my list recall seeing him until close to the time the party ended. A couple of people said they thought they saw him between midnight and two, but nothing definite."

"So the Premier could have had time to slip out of the hotel, murder his father and get back in time to say goodbye to his guests."

She shook her head. "Baker couldn't have vanished into thin air. How could he have left the hotel? The staff never saw him leave—or return."

"Maybe a different pair of eyes caught him leaving."

Activating the huge vid-wall that lined one side of the executive suite, Ben pulled up the photo of the Paloma Springs lobby. Then he zoomed in on the half-hidden devices that monitored the hotel.

"Security cameras," Natassia mumbled ruefully. "Of course. I should have thought of that."

She mentally kicked herself. Hotel security had camera surveillance set up everywhere. If Baker had escaped through a back door then security would have it on disk.

"I'll get a warrant for those disks," Ben told her.

She listened while he connected with Divine and updated him on Baker. Divine assured them that getting a warrant for the security disks would not be a problem.

When Ben ended the transmission, Natassia jumped off the bed and plugged her data-com into the Prestige Inn's secure line.

"So what's Baker's motive," she asked. "Revenge for his father's abandonment?"

Ben examined the doctor's picture. "I think Baker was protecting his candidacy for Prime Minister. He was embarrassed by his father, couldn't stand the negative publicity. People would have looked at Baker twice if his father had been fired from the hospital."

"Baker needed to get him out of the way. Permanently."

Ben nodded. "So he killed him. He certainly fits the profile. His father abandoned him. He had a difficult childhood. Allan Baker is driven to succeed and be recognized, and he won't let anything or anyone stand in his way."

"But why would Baker go after the Foreman woman and Samantha Davis? It doesn't make sense."

She saw Ben shake his head. Then he stretched out on the bed, tired and frustrated.

"A *Gemini* lighter was found at both scenes, Natassia. The evidence doesn't lie. Foreman and Washburn were murdered by the same person."

"I still don't see a connection."

"There *is* a connection," Jasi confirmed, entering the room. "Allan Baker went to live with Charlotte Foreman when he was a boy. He stayed with her for about six weeks."

"Okay," Ben said. "But I still don't understand why Baker would kill Charlotte Foreman and Samantha Davis."

A long, tired groan escaped from Natassia's lips. She couldn't understand Baker's motive in murdering the Foreman woman either. It didn't make any sense. What did Baker have against her? Foreman had been a foster parent for more than twenty years.

"Time to take a trip to Victoria?" she asked Jasi.

Jasi flopped onto the bed beside Ben. "Yup."

Natassia turned to Ben and frowned. "What about the car rentals? We can't use them in Victoria."

"I'll get both cars delivered once you get back."

Passing Jasi a pop, Natassia asked, "Think we'll get much in Victoria?"

"There's not much left of the crime scene but I should pick up something. Too bad there's no body for you, Natassia."

Natassia knew that Charlotte Forman had been buried five days after her death. That had been almost a month ago. The only way Natassia would get a reading from her was if they exhumed the body. And that could take weeks to get authorization.

"I guess I'll live," she said, smiling at her own joke.

"I'll make the arrangements," Jasi told her. "You and I'll check out Victoria while Ben has a little talk with the Premier."

Natassia recalled Ben's profile of the serial arsonist. Baker definitely fit the criteria. Psychologically, he had been damaged by the lack of a father figure when he was a child. Perhaps Charlotte Foreman had the rest of the answers.

Her data-com chirped.

"The autopsy report from Mar—the coroner...is in," she announced, hoping no one had noticed the slip. "There was petechial hemorrhaging in Washburn's eyes and around his lips. And ligature marks around his neck, relating to the IV tubing found at the scene."

"Anything unusual?" Jasi asked her.

"Not really. Except cause of death is listed as asphyxia, not smoke inhalation. He probably struggled and tried to escape. The slip knot that was used would have tightened the noose around his neck when he moved his legs."

Jasi scooted to the edge of the bed. "So he literally strangled himself."

"Or his own son did," Natassia said candidly.

"But in my vision Washburn said he didn't remember his killer. How does that fit with Baker?"

"He could have been speaking figuratively. Maybe Baker was acting in such a rage that his father couldn't see the son he was familiar with."

Jasi glanced at Ben. "What about Beranski?"

Ben shook his head. "We have to cut him loose. One of the kids at the concession stand called in. Jason Beranski ordered popcorn and pop halfway through the movie. The guy might have had motive but he wouldn't have had time to drive to the lake, strangle the doctor and burn down the cabin."

At that moment, Matthew Divine's face appeared on the vid-wall.

"Voice on," Natassia ordered.

"The warrant for the security tapes is a go," Divine informed them. "The hotel manager is waiting for you. We also had enough to get a search warrant for Premier Baker's hotel room *and* his house in Vancouver. Who's taking the security disks, Agent McLellan?"

"Ben is," Jasi answered.

"Benjamin, keep in mind that the search needs to be handled delicately. If the Premier is innocent, we don't want this to come back on us. Keep it private, no press."

"Natassia and I are heading to Victoria tomorrow morning," Jasi said after telling Divine about Baker's connection to Charlotte Foreman.

"Sounds good, Agent McLellan. Just remember what I told you about keeping it quiet."

Natassia was about to end communication when Divine hesitated. "Oh, I almost forgot. We're working closely with Arson Investigations on this. They're sending someone over as a liaison. Take him to Victoria with you. And, for God's sake, don't let him out of your sight. I don't want some idiot from AI getting in the way."

Natassia caught Jasi's indignant, irritated expression. Babysitting some AI suit wasn't on Jasi's list of favorite things to do.

Divine also noticed Jasi's grim expression.

"Just put up with him for a couple of days. He should be at your hotel lobby any minute."

"Fine," Jasi moaned. "Whatever you want, sir. I'll work with the devil himself if it'll solve this case."

Natassia flinched at her partner's words, wondering if Jasi had just tempted Fate.

The devil himself...

12

The devil sat at the end of the gloomy bar.

The hotel manager had told Jasi that her *guest* was enjoying a rum and coke. That pissed her off. Perhaps he'd drink himself under the table and she could leave him behind. Whoever he was, he had his back to her so she couldn't see his sharpened horns.

But she was positive they were there—somewhere.

She hovered behind him, studying the man.

He wore a black leather jacket and tight black jeans. He filled out both just fine—and that irked her too. The man's face was hidden in the shadows yet she thought his voice sounded vaguely familiar when he ordered another drink.

The bartender noticed her but she waved him away.

"Excuse me," she growled, tapping the devil-man on the shoulder.

"Agent Jasi McLellan," the man said before turning to face her. "It's great to see you again."

Brandon Walsh's icy eyes made her blood freeze.

Staring at Walsh in disbelief, a million thoughts coursed through Jasi's mind. Not one of them was good. There was no way on earth that this man was going to be part of *her* team.

Walsh grinned. "What? Aren't you happy to see me?"

"Ecstatic," she spat acidly.

"Yeah, I was pretty ecstatic too, to find out I was assigned to be your partner."

"Partner?" she sputtered. "We have jurisdiction over this investigation, Walsh. You're here as a liaison...nothing more. Got it?"

"Sure thing—partner."

"You can shove the *partner* thing up your—"

"Okay, relax," he said, holding up one hand. "I come in peace."

"Chief Walsh—"

"The name is Brandon. We're going to be working closely so I think first names are in order...Jasmine. Or do you prefer Jasi?"

She glared at him, her eyes shooting daggers. "I prefer Agent McLellan. But if you insist on first names, then call me Jasmine. Only my friends call me Jasi."

Brandon Walsh hesitated. It was obvious he wanted to respond to her challenge.

Jasi pasted a false smile on her face.

"Walsh, let's get a few things straight. I don't like working with someone who doubts my abilities, or my gift. And I don't like working with a redneck who spends his time chasing skirts."

The man's eyes sauntered lazily down her body. "You aren't wearing a skirt, Jasi."

She gritted her teeth in frustration. Not only was he undressing her with his hot stare, he was using her nickname. Walsh was striking out—big time. Didn't he take anything seriously? How the hell could she work with him?

Jumping off the barstool, Walsh took a step closer.

"Jasi, regardless of what you think about me, I'm very good," he mocked. "At *everything* I do."

"All I care about is this case," she said coldly. "You let *us* handle it. You're an observer. Got it?"

"We'll see."

Walsh grabbed her arm and steered her toward a table in the far corner of the room. His grip was gentle but persistent.

"Okay, fill me in on what the CFBI has so far." A short pause preceded a soft, "Please."

It took Jasi fifteen minutes to get Brandon up to speed. She told him about Baker's connection to Charlotte Foreman—that the Premier had once been in the foster care system. Then she told him that Allan Baker was their prime suspect.

"AI checked out the diesel used in Washburn's murder," he offered. "The fire in Victoria used regular gasoline. We're not sure why he switched, but Super Clean diesel isn't cheap."

"Can you trace it?"

Brandon shook his head. "There are too many gas stations in the area that carry diesel. Whoever bought it probably paid cash. Credit cards would be too easy to trace."

"Did you run records and do a crosscheck on it anyway?"

He took a sip of his drink. "There were no purchases of diesel on Premier Baker's credit card."

Jasi released a long, tired breath.

There was still no direct link between Baker and the murder of his father. Maybe they should take a closer look at Martin Gibney, she mused. He and Dr. Washburn had worked together before. But why would Gibney go after Norman Washburn?

"Have you had supper yet?" Brandon asked, disturbing her thoughts.

Jasi practically salivated at the mention of food. "No."

"Come on, then. Let's go grab a bite."

He slapped down a twenty and rose from the table.

Noticing her hesitation, he bribed, "A girl's gotta eat. And we can talk corpses and death if you want."

"Fine," she said, exiting the bar with Walsh in tow. "But I need to take a shower first. I'll meet you in the restaurant in thirty minutes."

When Jasi stepped inside the lobby elevator, he winked at her. "See ya in half an hour then, Jasi."

She pursed her lips, biting back a nasty response.

When the doors closed, she heaved a sigh of defeat. Brandon Walsh grated on her nerves. The man was incorrigible. He provoked her like a small child poking a coiled snake with a stick.

But she was drawn to him—no mistaking that.

A minute later the elevator jerked to a halt. She stepped out into the hallway where warm, muggy air greeted her.

Jasi sensed that another storm was on its way.

Hurricane Walsh!

When she reached her room, Natassia and Ben were sitting at the table, sheets of paper spread out before them. Their heads shifted toward her in one fluid motion at hearing the door slam.

"Damn it all to hell!" Jasi moaned.

She stood with her hands on her hips while her eyes flashed dangerously. "You'll never guess who AI sent?"

"Who?" Ben asked warily.

"AI Chief Brandon Walsh," she replied sourly.

"I knew the man was up to something," Ben grunted. "He probably requested this assignment."

She gawked at him, shocked...speechless.

Ben shrugged. "I sensed he wasn't happy handing over control of this case to us. I knew he was up to something when I saw him talking to one of the police officers at the crime scene."

Jasi swore softly, then grabbed some clean clothes and stumbled toward the bathroom. "I'm taking a shower." She glanced back, a hopeful expression on her face. "I'm meeting Walsh downstairs for dinner. You two hungry?"

Natassia grimaced guiltily. "We already ate."

"Great then. Feed me to the wolves!"

Jasi closed the bathroom door and sneered at her reflection. "What the hell are you doing?"

When the other Jasi didn't reply, she growled and headed for the shower.

Apprehensive about meeting Walsh for dinner, Jasi dried her hair, deliberately prolonging the task. She was irritated that she had allowed Brandon Walsh to convince her to have dinner with him. When she finally stepped out of the bathroom, Jasi was ready to meet the devil.

Natassia was sitting on the bed, alone, buried in papers. "Where's Ben?"

Natassia sighed, disappointed. "He's back in his room."

"Are those Baker's financial records?"

"Yup. Nothing so far."

"You sure you don't want to join us for dinner?"

"Naw, you go. It's not every night you get to go on a date with a handsome man."

"It's not a date!" Jasi snapped. "It's strictly business."

Natassia chuckled softly. "Then why the makeup?"

Jasi's hand paused in midair, a tube of lipstick hovering near her mouth. Staring at her reflection, she made a face, then deliberately tossed the lipstick into her purse.

Ignoring Natassia, she stomped toward the door.

"Go get 'im, Jasi!" her friend snickered.

Jasi shivered with anticipation.

Yeah, but what do I do with him once I've got him?

13

The restaurant on the lower floor of the Prestige Inn had two small private dining rooms off to one side. Brandon waited inside one of them. Checking his watch for the third time in five minutes, he frowned.

An hour had gone by since he had seen Jasi.

Agent McLellan was late.

When she finally arrived, he took in her freshly washed hair and soft, glowing skin. Her face was lightly made up—although Jasmine McLellan didn't need artificial enhancements to make her beautiful. She wore a royal blue blouse.

And she had changed into another pair of slacks, he realized with disappointment.

"Hungry?" he asked her, taking in the dark shadows around her eyes.

"Starved," she admitted.

They chose a table close to the door.

"I thought it would be more appropriate to be in here if we're going to be discussing the case," he said when she examined the room.

After the waiter had taken their order, Brandon decided to seize control of the conversation.

"What's on the agenda for tomorrow?"

Jasi told him.

"Okay, I'll stick with you and Natassia," he suggested. "It'll be my first look at the Victoria fire too."

Jasi's eyes widened in surprise. "Weren't you in on that investigation?"

He shook his head. "The locals handled that one."

Toying nervously with a sharp steak knife, Jasi asked, "What's your take on all this?"

"I think it's possible Baker did it. He had motive enough, that's for sure."

Plus he's an asshole, Brandon thought.

He stared warily at the knife in Jasi's hand. When his eyes drifted back to hers, she grinned.

A discreet knock on the door announced the waiter's arrival. He placed their salads on the table. "Would you care for some wine?"

"Please," Brandon replied. "Two glasses of your best white."

"None for me, Walsh!" Jasi said sharply. "I don't drink on the job."

He reached across the table and plucked the knife from her hand. "You're not on the job right now."

When the waiter disappeared, Brandon raised his glass in the air and aimed an insolent smile in Jasi's direction.

"To our partnership."

He knew his words would annoy her, and he waited for her to explode. But then, without a word, she clanged her glass against his.

He smiled, enjoying the challenge in her eyes. "So what brings a nice girl like you to a crime scene like this?"

Jasi scowled. "Bad line, Walsh."

"Well?"

Her eyes latched onto his. "My father was a promoter of government agencies."

Brandon was surprised. "He was CFBI too?"

"No, Armed Forces. He's retired now."

Jasi told him about her parents. About her mother being killed in a home invasion. She didn't go into all the details but he could tell there was much more to the story than she let on.

"Were you close to your mother?"

Jasi nodded silently, reaching for her wineglass.

"My parents live in Europe now," he said, changing the topic. "I don't see them often. My sister lives back east…Ontario."

"Is she younger or older?"

"Younger. She's only seventeen."

"Ah," Jasi grinned. "An 'Oops!'"

"Yeah, an afterthought for my parents. Sierra's great."

He traced a pattern into the condensation on the wineglass. Then he watched her for a moment.

The wine was starting to kick in.

"So you get to play big brother," she said with a faint tinge of disdain in her voice.

He wasn't sure what Jasi meant by that comment.

"What about you?" he asked.

There was something about Jasmine McLellan that intrigued him.

Jasi stared at her salad. "I have a brother."

"Ever married?"

"Who? Me or my brother?" she asked mockingly.

He did a drum roll on the table and laughed.

She gave him a sheepish grin. "No, I've never been married. What about you?"

"Once," he shrugged. "A long time ago."

"What happened?"

Brandon smiled—a slow, knowing smile. Agent Jasmine McLellan *was* interested in him.

"We were both young, perhaps a bit foolish," he confessed. "In the end, Karmen couldn't handle being a firefighter's wife. It was an amicable divorce."

Brandon rarely thought about his ex-wife. Tonight, he only wanted to think about the intriguing but stubborn woman sitting across from him.

"Do you still see her?"

His lips paused at the edge of his wineglass, and he grinned wickedly. "Why? Would it bother you if I did?"

"Not likely, Walsh," she huffed. "I just want to know what baggage you're bringing to the case."

Grinning, he raised one brow. "See any baggage here?"

Brandon stretched back in his chair, flexed his arms and watched her eyes graze over him. When Jasi didn't say anything, he leaned forward, resting one hand on hers.

"Why don't you like me?" he asked in a low whisper.

"You don't believe in what I do."

She yanked her hand away from his and placed it in her lap.

"I really don't *know* what you can do."

Jasi's response was quiet, controlled. "Listen, Brandon. We're working on a case together and I have to know if I can count on you—if I can trust you."

Her eyes were serious pools of emerald lights, and he was drawn into their depths.

"You can trust me," he promised.

Sipping her wine slowly, she watched him, unsmiling.

"I need you to trust me too. Or else one of us could get hurt."

Brandon knew that she meant physically hurt. It was vital that they worked together as a team. They were, after all, hunting a serial killer, a person who had murdered three people—one, an innocent child.

"Okay, I get it," he said. "Tell me about your…uh, gift."

Jasi explained how the scent of fire would trigger something in her cerebral cortex, sending a flash of psychic energy to her brain. The rest was a bit of a mystery.

"Even to me," she added.

"Sounds complicated."

"I have visions," Jasi shrugged lightly. "It's that simple."

Part of Brandon's brain tried to rebel against the plausibility of her visions. Part of him tried to find a rational explanation. There was none. He had read her file—and those of Roberts and Prushenko. He couldn't argue with the fact that they had each solved a number of cases. Some cases had been dead cold. Other agents had given up on them after months of stagnation.

"How does it work?" he asked, staring into her eyes.

She had beautiful eyes—wounded eyes, he thought.

"When I do a reading I have to be very careful that I take certain precautions," she explained. "First I have to clear my mind and inhale pure oxygen. If it's a large fire with multiple victims I have to wear an oxy-mask."

Brandon recalled the first time he had seen Jasi.

She had been wearing an oxy-mask then. And he had laughed at her.

Feeling guilty, he bit his lip.

"How old were you when you started reading fires?"

"I-I've had visions since I was about six. Every time I'm near a fire, I pick up thoughts and pictures. It's actually very draining." Her eyes connected with his. "Emotionally *and* physically."

When the door opened suddenly, he cleared his throat, silently warning her that the waiter had returned with their meals. The man cleared their salad plates, placed two steak platters on the table and then left.

"How dangerous *is* your gift?" Brandon asked between bites. "To you, I mean."

"More controllable than Natassia's," Jasi admitted. "Natassia is a Victim Empath. With her job, she can lose herself in the victim's emotions and fears. Sometimes we have to pull her back. We use a reality line."

"A reality line?"

"We bring her back by holding one of her hands, talking to her. It's a form of hypnosis. We use keywords that mean something to her, to bring her out."

He felt a twinge of fear. "What about you?"

Jasi gave a shrug. "I seem to have better control. I don't get lost in a vision, but I can become very tired. That's all you need to know."

He knew he'd have to wait to learn more about her. Some other time. He was startled at the realization that he wanted there to be another time. The more he discovered about Jasmine McLellan, the more his interest grew.

Observing her across the table, Brandon realized that he wanted her in other ways. There was an undeniable chemistry between them.

Like a nuclear explosion waiting to happen, he mused.

He muffled a soft groan.

Ten minutes into their meal, Brandon saw Jasi stifle a yawn.

"You look exhausted."

His observation flustered her, rendered her speechless.

"What about Agent Roberts," he asked, changing the topic. "How does his gift work?"

Jasi tipped her head, and he could tell that she was trying to determine exactly what or how much to tell him.

"Ben's an excellent profiler."

"And?"

She eyed him warily. "He's a Psychometric Empath. He gets flashes if he touches someone. He can feel their emotions…thoughts."

"A-ha!" Brandon smiled mockingly. "That explains the gloves."

"Ben wears them most of the time, especially when we're around a large group of people. He takes them off when he wants to read someone."

Jasi's eyes narrowed, locking onto his.

"Like me?" Brandon guessed.

Jasi picked at the food on her plate. "Ben needs to know where everyone stands."

"Does he see anything if he touches objects?" Brandon wasn't sure he liked the softened expression in her eyes. He wanted Ben Roberts out of the way.

"No," Jasi answered, shaking her head. "Only when he touches people—live people."

He leaned forward, feeling bold and risqué.

"Are you and Roberts…?"

"A couple?" Jasi laughed. "No! We've worked together for a couple of years. We're friends—good friends."

Her voice lowered. "Don't get any ideas, Walsh."

"Hey!" he said, holding up a hand. "I just asked about the two of you. You know, team dynamics and all."

"Actually, Ben and Natassia have been getting chummy lately. They don't think I've noticed, but…"

Jasi's voice trailed away and she shifted restlessly in her chair.

Watching her, Brandon realized that she was fighting to stay awake. Her eyelids fluttered every now and then.

Must be my stimulating company, he thought dryly.

He emptied the last of the wine into their glasses. They had polished off two bottles during dinner. He credited the wine for the change in Jasi's demeanor. At first, she was suspicious, but then she relaxed.

Brandon caught her eyes and she smiled at him.

Jasi had a *drop-dead* gorgeous smile.

He passed her a glass. "Here, drink this. It'll help you sleep tonight."

Jasi eyed him suspiciously, then reached out.

When her fingers touched his, he gasped as heat radiated toward him. He experienced a spark, something unusual, pass from her hand to his. And the innocent touch left him craving more.

Brandon was attracted to her. There was no doubt about that. Shaking his head slowly, he reminded himself that she saw him as nothing more than a weight around her neck. But he couldn't stop the sudden need he had. It had been awhile since he had allowed himself to be even remotely interested in a woman, outside of a casual relationship.

Instinctively, Brandon knew that Jasi was not someone who would be satisfied with anything casual.

Nor would he.

Jasi McLellan had awakened something within him.

The next morning, Jasi awoke, groggy and displaced, while the sun beamed brightly outside. Sitting up suddenly, she moaned when a wave of dizziness overcame her.

What the hell is wrong with me?

Familiar sounds greeted her. A flock of sparrows chirped loudly on the balcony. Children shrieked in the hallway.

And Natassia snored softly in the other bed, oblivious to the commotion.

Jasi frowned.

How did she get to her room? The last thing she remembered was having dinner with Brandon Walsh.

Brandon…

The remnants of too much wine bathed her in confusion. She was weightless and lightheaded.

Damn you, Walsh!

She closed her eyes while a memory of strong arms around her came to mind. Pushing the bed covers to her knees, she gasped, horrified to discover that she wore her bra, panties, and...nothing else.

What have I done?

"Natassia?" she whispered anxiously, hiking the blanket to her chin.

The lump in the other bed grunted.

"Natassia!"

Her partner had a habit of sleeping like the dead. Once she fell asleep, Natassia barely moved. Often Jasi would sit beside her, waiting for a sign of life.

Jasi threw the covers aside, grabbed a t-shirt from a drawer and stomped over to the other bed.

She nudged Natassia roughly.

"Wake up! I need to ask you something."

Natassia groaned and tugged the covers over her head.

"What time did I get in last night?" Jasi asked fearfully.

She plopped herself down beside Natassia and yanked back the covers.

Her partner opened one eye and scowled.

"Around 11:30. Why?" Natassia's voice was hoarse from sleep.

"Was I...uh...alone?"

Natassia sat up grumpily. "You mean, was Walsh with you? Of course he was. He had to carry you here."

Jasi's face flushed with embarrassment. "What?"

"You fell asleep on him, Jasi."

On him?

Jasi was horrified.

Resting her pounding head in one hand, she tried to remember last night's dinner.

Did I go back to his room afterward?

"Tell me I didn't do anything foolish," she begged.

Natassia snickered.

"Oh no," Jasi moaned, hiding her head in her arms. "I *slept* with Brandon Walsh?"

"No, you didn't sleep with him," Natassia grinned, patting Jasi's arm. "You passed out in the middle of the chocolate cheesecake, so he had to carry you up here. But I don't think Brandon would have minded sleeping with you."

Smacking Natassia's hand away, Jasi laughed self-consciously. She was flooded with relief. Nothing had happened between her and Brandon. She should be elated.

So then, why was she ticked off—disappointed?

Natassia rolled over on her side and her mouth stretched into a slow smirk.

"Yup. You were all over him, kissing him. The poor guy."

Jasi groaned.

I kissed him? Oh my God!

She touched her lips lightly and instantly remembered Brandon's hot mouth on hers. She wanted to crawl back into bed and sleep the day away.

How could she possibly face Brandon Walsh now?

Victoria, here we come, Natassia thought.

She darted a quick glance in Jasi and Brandon's direction, and laughed softly. Walsh acted like he had eaten a sour lemon. Jasi, on the other hand, barely spared Walsh a look.

Watching Jasi when she was pissed off was like watching a storm roll in. You could never predict when the thunder would boom or the lightning would strike, but you knew it would happen.

Eventually.

Natassia felt a bit guilty that she had allowed Jasi to believe she had put the moves on Walsh. But it was just too much fun seeing Jasi squirm. Natassia had told her that she had been hanging all over the man, kissing him and rubbing against him—and that Walsh had just smiled and had enjoyed every minute of it.

The truth was a different story.

Last night, Brandon Walsh had knocked quietly on the door and had carried Jasi into the room with a quick explanation to Natassia. Her partner had had too much wine. With a chuckle, he even admitted that Jasi had kissed him...once.

"She doesn't drink much, does she?" he had asked.

Then he had deposited Jasi on the bed, and had left.

Natassia had debated leaving her friend fully clothed.

Then, with a mischievous change of heart, she had stripped the unconscious Jasi of her pants and shirt. She knew Jasi hated sleeping in her clothes.

Natassia also knew that it would drive her friend crazy when Jasi woke up and found herself dressed only in her underwear.

After all, what are friends for?

Now, eyeing Jasi and Walsh's discomfort, Natassia resisted telling her friend the truth.

Let Jasi think the worst.

At least it made for an interesting flight.

14

The Ops helicopter dropped them off in a field close to Charlotte Foreman's house. The house was located in the outskirts of Victoria in an upper-income neighborhood nestled next to a winding river. Far removed from the hustle and bustle of downtown Victoria.

As Jasi climbed from the helicopter, the humid air hit her like an overactive sauna. The temperature soared, making the back of her neck sticky with perspiration. Squinting toward the sun, she slid on a pair of dark sunglasses.

"It's gonna be another hot one."

She saw Brandon cast a quick glance in her direction.

Yeah, she shuddered. _Real hot._

From where they stood, they could see the green-shingled roof of the Foreman's house.

"The shed was completely destroyed," Natassia said, consulting her data-com.

"It's probably been cleared away by now," Brandon added.

Jasi nodded. "Which neighbor called it in?"

"A Jessica Marie Taranko, 1206 Waterton Lane," Natassia said, pointing down the road. "Two houses down from the Foremans. Taranko's backyard is on a curve so she can see into their yard."

Jasi studied the neighborhood. It was a quiet, remote area with a river tucked behind dense woods. Not a lot of traffic—in or out.

It's the perfect place…to commit a murder.

"What do you think, Natassia?"

Her partner scanned the neighborhood. "We'll need to canvas the street, see if anyone else saw anything."

"How about Jasi and I take the Taranko woman?" Brandon suggested to Natassia.

Standing behind him, Jasi shook her head emphatically.

Natassia ignored her, smiling slyly. "Okay. I'll knock on doors."

Jasi seethed indignantly.

How could her friend do this to her?

She glared in Natassia's direction and mouthed the words: *I'll get you!*

Then, resigned to her fate, she stomped off after Brandon.

"Hold on a minute, Walsh." When he didn't acknowledge her, Jasi shouted. "Brandon! Wait up!"

"Sorry," Brandon muttered when she caught up to him.

Sucking on a can of *OxyBlast*, Jasi strode briskly down the sidewalk, edging closer to Charlotte Foreman's house.

Brandon's eyes darkened. "How close can you get without that stuff?"

"It's hard to tell," she answered. "Every fire is different. I have to consider how many people have been injured or have died. It also depends on how strong their psychic energy is. Better to be safe than sorry."

Brandon reached out, one finger lightly tracing the scar on her chin.

She held her breath, nervous and afraid.

"How'd you get this?"

Jasi exhaled slowly and self-consciously touched the small jagged scar.

"It's a long story, Brandon. One I'm not prepared to tell right now."

"Okay," he said with a shrug. "We can swap scar stories later."

They rounded a corner and she pointed to an unpretentious two-story house on a small crescent-shaped lot. Jessica Taranko's house. From where she stood, Jasi could make out the Foreman's deck on the opposite side of the Taranko backyard. Only a fence separated the two.

Allowing Brandon to go first, she couldn't help but admire his well-shaped arms. That sudden thought reminded her of the night before. What the hell *had* she done? She couldn't very well ask him.

She followed him along a brick sidewalk until they came to the front door of Jessica Marie Taranko's house. Brandon raised a hand, but before he could knock, a girl's voice called out.

"Yeah?"

Surprised, they glanced around.

No one was there.

"Whatcha want?" the voice asked again, muffled and distorted.

Jasi pointed to a com-link box beside the door. "We tripped a security scanner. Probably hidden in the bushes along the sidewalk or set into the steps to the door."

She took out her badge and examined the side of the house. When she found what she was looking for, she held her ID in front of a camera lens.

"We just need to ask you a few questions about Charlotte Foreman."

"Okay, come on in. Door's open."

The door beeped softly and three locks disengaged.

"Wow!" Brandon whistled. "Some security system."

Jasi agreed.

This kind of security was uncommon, especially in a neighborhood like this one. Maybe the system was installed after the Foreman's shed was set on fire. After two people died a horrifying death.

A petite young girl with multi-colored streaks in her shoulder length hair made her way toward them. She wore hip-hugging cotton pajamas and her feet were bare. The pajama top was cropped, showing off a bronzed and *very* flat stomach.

Self-consciously, Jasi sucked in her abdomen, eyeing the small diamond that glittered in the girl's navel.

"We're looking for the home owner," she said. "Uh...Jessica Marie Taranko."

The girl laughed. "Yeah, that's me."

Jessica Taranko eyed Brandon with interest. The girl zeroed in on his lean body and chiseled jaw. Then she stretched languidly, like a wildcat comfortable in her own domain, and smiled at him.

Irritated by the girl's flirtatious manner, Jasi's brow grew pinched. She groaned in disgust when she noticed Brandon's eyes trailing after the girl as they were led through the house.

Scoping out the place, Jasi whistled in appreciation. The furnishings and electronic equipment must have cost over ten thousand dollars.

How could a girl Jessica's age afford to buy stuff like this? *Or her own home?*

Jessica showed them to a small living room. Black leather furniture framed with polished chrome and glass tables faced a huge vid-wall. The wall was activated and was playing a music video—heavy on the base and computer synthesizers.

Techno dance music, Jasi recognized.

Glancing from the singer on the screen to the young girl beside him, Brandon's eyes widened. "You're *that* Jessica Marie?"

Jasi studied the music video.

Brandon was right. The singer in the video was none other than Jessica Marie Taranko. *Jessica Marie*—to her fans. Now Jasi understood how a girl her age could afford to buy a house like this one.

Jessica Marie was a singing sensation in North America and Europe. At nineteen years old, she had gone further than any other pop star. She had taken off in 2007, replacing Britney Spears and Christina Aguilera.

"My sister, Sierra, loves your music," Brandon remarked. "I got her your *Good Girl* MD for her birthday. By the way, I'm Brandon Walsh. I'm with Arson Investigations."

The singer flopped onto the leather sofa, looked up at him and patted the space beside her. "Hope your sister liked *Good Girl*."

Jasi gritted her teeth when Brandon sat down beside the girl. Time to show him who's in charge, she thought angrily. Shaking her head in disdain, she activated her data-com, recorded a brief introduction and slapped it on the table between them.

"Miss…um, Jessica," she said, taking the seat across from the girl. "We're here about Charlotte Foreman's murder."

The singer nodded, pulling her legs up underneath her and leaning her knees against Brandon's thigh.

Jasi tried to curb her temper and waited for him to move away.

Instead, he shrugged as if to say, *What can I do?*

"Jessica, tell us what happened the night of the fire," Jasi said abruptly.

"I told the police everything I remember. Nothing's changed. I got home early that day. I just finished cutting a new single, *Living Dangerous,* and I was, like, exhausted. So I came home and started making supper. A few minutes later I smelled smoke. I thought I was, like, burning the chicken at first."

Jessica gave Brandon a wry smile. "Then I realized the smoke was coming from outside. When I went out onto my deck, I could see Mrs. Foreman's shed on fire."

"What'd you do?" Jasi asked.

Jessica briefly closed her eyes. "I called 911. Then I waited. I thought it was just her shed." The girl's voice filled with remorse and her eyes teared. "I had no idea that poor woman and that little girl were inside."

Brandon reached over and patted Jessica's arm. "There was no way for you to know. "

Resisting a tug of jealousy, Jasi pulled a clean tissue from her bag and pressed it into the girl's hand. "Even if you had known, Jessica, there's nothing you could have done to save them."

"I almost sold my house after that," the singer admitted hesitantly.

"Because you didn't feel safe?" Jasi asked.

"I thought that whoever had killed Mrs. Foreman might, like, come back here," the girl confessed. "You know, return to the scene of the crime?"

Jasi could understand the girl's fear. Jessica's theory of the killer returning wasn't *that* farfetched. It was a documented fact that most murderers returned to the scene so that they could relive the crime. Sometimes they slipped into the crowds of curious bystanders who watched while the crime scene was processed.

"That's why the press didn't mention me," Jessica murmured. "I offered them interviews in return for keeping my name out of the papers."

"So that whoever killed Charlotte Foreman wouldn't see you as a threat," Brandon guessed.

The girl stood up suddenly, hugging her arms close.

Then she flicked her head toward the backyard.

"I haven't been able to go out back. You know—that was, like, the second fire here in one month."

Jasi glanced at Brandon. "Two fires in May?"

"Uh-huh. Some kids set fire to a fence a couple of houses down."

"Did the police catch them?"

"Yeah, but then a couple of weeks later..." Jessica's voice trailed away as she nudged her head in the direction of the Foreman's backyard.

"We'll keep your name out of this," Jasi found herself promising.

She felt sorry for the young singer. Despite the sophisticated security system, the girl felt uneasy in her own home. Jessica Marie Taranko was as much a victim now as the three arson victims.

Collateral damage to a murderer.

"The night of the fire, when you looked outside," Brandon said. "Did you see anything suspicious? Someone in the yard...a car driving away?"

The girl shook her head. "Since that night I've tried to remember everything. The only thing I saw was the fire and the firefighters. That's it. Sorry."

Jasi leaned over and picked up her data-com.

"Voice record off."

She cleared her throat, indicating that it was time to leave and Brandon followed her. Jessica trailed behind them, humming softly.

"Hey!" the singer hollered. "Your sister—how old is she?"

"Seventeen," Brandon answered.

"Here, give her this." The girl skipped forward and tucked a cellophane-wrapped MD into Brandon's palm. "It's my latest single."

"I'm sure Sierra will love it."

Jasi gave the girl a nod. "Thanks for your time, Jessica."

"Agent McLellan!" the singer blurted. She gripped Jasi's arm tightly. "Don't let him get away!"

Jasi stiffened, then peered at Brandon. He had his back to her and was waiting at the bottom of the steps.

Don't let him get away?

Nervous, she glanced back at Jessica Taranko, about to ask the girl what she meant.

Then it hit her.

The singer was referring to the arsonist.

"Don't worry," Jasi assured her. "We'll get him."

The girl disappeared into the house, and the groan of locks engaging echoed loudly while Jasi made her way down the steps.

"You'll keep your promise," Brandon said quietly.

Jasi's eyes snared his. "Damn right I will!"

Brandon gawked at her, wanting to say something more. She froze when his heated gaze drifted to her mouth.

Neither of them said a word.

Then her data-com beeped.

Fumbling for it, Jasi stammered, "Y-yeah?"

"I've got nothing with the neighbors," Natassia's voice cut in. "One woman spotted a cable van but that checks out. Repairs on the opposite side of the street left the cable down."

"What about the installer?" Brandon interrupted. "He see anything?"

"Nothing. He was inside the house the entire time, according to the homeowners."

"Okay, Natassia," Jasi said. "Meet us in front of the house. I'm going in."

When she reached the sidewalk edging the Foreman house, Jasi took a hit of *OxyBlast* and waited patiently next to the *For Sale* sign on the lawn.

Natassia arrived five minutes later. "I ran. Didn't want you going in alone."

Jasi noticed Brandon's eyebrow wing up.

Natassia grinned, catching Brandon's eye.

"I know you're here, Chief Walsh, but Jasi doesn't go on scene without me."

Jasi saw Brandon shrug, then head for the backyard.

"Voice record on!" she barked, hurrying after him.

The Foreman's backyard was like everyone else's. Except it was devoid of life. In the shadows, a tire swing hung from a tree, motionless. Weedy flowerpots and a picnic table rested on a concrete base. In the far right corner an overgrown garden wilted in abandonment.

The left corner of the yard was a different story. An empty blackened pad, where the shed had been, reminded Jasi that two people had died here. Most of the loose wood had been cleared, but enough residue remained behind to trigger her brain.

"Let's do it."

Brandon hesitated. "Should I wait here?"

Jasi examined him thoughtfully, then released a slow breath and gestured for him to follow.

Natassia raised one eyebrow, surprised.

"It's okay," Jasi assured her, clipping on the nosepiece. Then she glanced at the shed pad. "It's *shake 'n bake* time."

Taking a few steps forward, she felt the irresistible draw of psychic energy beckoning her closer.

Within two minutes, she was in.

And *inside* the mind of a serial killer.

15

The pungent odor of death, of scorching flesh, hung heavily in the humid night air. Inhaling slowly, savoring every delicate nuance of human scent, I raised my hood-covered face to the stormy heavens, arms outstretched in glory. Turning slowly, I closed my eyes while thunderous clouds rolled and churned above me.

Death was such a release.

How could the old woman have been so blind, so easily manipulated?

I knew how. She had been arrogant, secure in her own little life. She had preyed upon the innocent, stalking them with her own evil. And all the while, I had carefully stalked her.

The hunter had become the hunted.

Peering through night-vision binoculars, I had recorded her movements, her every gesture and habit. I had witnessed her erratic behavior and seen her lash out violently at the children entrusted in her care.

Shrouded in darkness inside the musty utility shed, I waited patiently, calming my rapidly beating heart while I checked out my hiding place. Cobwebs hung from the corner of the door and a sliver of sunlight captured a bulbous black spider effortlessly spinning its web.

When my eyesight finally adjusted to the dark, I noticed an assortment of rusted garden tools scattered haphazardly across the surface of the wooden workbench. Along the plank-board wall behind my head, a variety of shovels, brooms and hedge clippers hung suspended from antique iron hooks. I shuddered when I saw the sharpened metal ends.

I wondered how long I would have to wait until I hooked her.

Blindly searching the shelves, I came across the large roll of yellow rope.

How long before she came for a piece of that?

I was answered by the sound of the screen door squeaking rebelliously. Then I heard her footsteps coming closer and I knew that my wait was over.

When the woman opened the door to the shed and stepped inside, I relished the startled expression on her face. Without a second thought, I smashed a heavy shovel into the side of her head. I watched her eyes flicker with shock while blood seeped from her scalp.

Then I waited in silence while she collapsed to the floor.

"Please!" the old woman begged pitifully when she regained consciousness.

With one hand raised to protect her bloodied face, she scrambled along the floor of the shed, searching for escape, clawing at the rough cedar planks below her.

"Please, let me go! I've done nothing!"

Crouching down with a piece of yellow rope grasped firmly between my hands, I stared at her. She reminded me of a deer, caught in the headlights of an oncoming car.

Removing the hood from my head, I smiled.

Her eyes widened with recognition and terror.

I carefully tied her feet together and pushed her to a sitting position. Then I wrapped the stiff rope around her neck. Yanking *her toward the wooden workbench, I heard her gasping for air, her short legs jerking spasmodically beneath her.*

I leaned down and asked her one important question.

With a glimmer of hope in her terrified eyes, she whispered the answer in a small voice.

"No...man. No...man wash—"

"Nana?" a child's voice called from outside the utility shed.

I held my breath and prayed that the child would go away, but when the door opened and a small face peered inside, I knew that I had no other choice.

Grabbing the little girl's arm, I hauled her into the shed.

"You should have stayed inside the house. Now look what you're making me do, you naughty girl."

The child whimpered softly while I tied her tightly to the semi-conscious woman. And then I left them, trussed up like animals, while I made the final preparations.

Outside in the dark stormy night, I inhaled the seductive scent of gasoline and watched the flames creep slowly over the small shed, encompassing it in scorching heat. A crack of thunder echoed overhead and a spear of lightning streaked across the sky.

"Just a bit longer," I murmured.

It was the perfect end...and the perfect beginning.

I glanced at my watch. It was getting late.

Time to get the show on the road.

For the old lady and child trapped within the confines of the burning shed, it was already too late. Nothing could save them. Their screams of terror and agony were lost in the howling of the storm. As the fiery heat and toxic smoke embraced them in death, their bodies were singed together—my masterpiece.

Finally, the storm clouds released their pent-up energy, drenching the land. I watched as the small building collapsed in ruin. Bright furious flames crept higher for a moment, fingers of fire leaping into the sky, and then they diminished quickly, extinguished by fat raindrops. Ten minutes later, the rain subsided into a rhythmic pitter-patter of droplets, pulling soft sizzles of smoke from the wreckage.

Sauntering over to the pile of rubble, I watched the final flame die a silent, sooty death. I breathed in the smoky night air, rubbing my tongue along the roof of my mouth. A cloudy haze lingered thickly, and I drew my hooded jacket over my head, breathing slowly.

Surveying the result of my revenge, I nodded. Kicking aside a smoldering plank of wood, I saw the blackened remains of two hands clenched in death, one with tiny, innocent fingers.

"I release you from your hell," I whispered, my teeth clenched in determination.

I reached into my pocket and withdrew a small item.

Flipping it between my fingers, I examined it carefully...lovingly. Searching the ground, I found the perfect place and dropped the item gently in the grass at my feet.

Then I shoved my hands deep into my pockets and strolled through the opened gate. Heading in the direction of the trees, I followed an invisible path and whistled softly...satisfied.

It is time.

It has finally begun.

Jasi flinched sharply when someone touched her. Her eyes flicked open.

Brandon was hovering over her.

"I can't believe he killed that child," she said in a choked voice. "Poor Samantha. She was in the wrong place at the wrong time."

"Let's get outta here," Natassia suggested, leading Jasi to the front of the house. "We've got everything on record."

"Is this far enough away," Brandon asked.

Jasi nodded, detached the nosepiece and then strode over to a small metal patio table near the *For Sale* sign.

"Give me a second."

Resting her head, she closed her eyes and listened to the rhythmic sound of her own breathing—exhausted beyond comprehension.

Without warning her head jerked up and her eyes flew open.

"Damn!"

"What?" Brandon and Natassia asked in unison.

Jasi tapped a finger on the table. "The arsonist asked the woman something. What did she say?"

She studied Natassia expectantly.

"She said something like 'no man washes'," Natassia joked, grinning to relieve the tension. "Well, something like that. I'd have to replay it."

"No...man. No...man wash—"

Jasi sensed a sharp mind-tug, and then she slipped into a thick fog.

"She's back in," she heard Natassia say. "This happens sometimes...when she's overtired."

A minute later, Jasi emerged from the vision. She saw fear gleaming in Brandon's eyes.

Damn! Brandon Walsh actually cared about her.

Her thoughts made an abrupt detour, steering her toward the vision of Charlotte Foreman.

No...man.

The old woman's words became suddenly clear.

"Wait!" Jasi gasped. "She wasn't saying *'no man'*. Charlotte Foreman was saying *'Norman'*. Norman Washburn!"

Natassia slapped her forehead with the palm of her hand. "Crap! Of course!"

"But what does that mean?" Brandon asked.

Jasi's voice was cool, clipped. "It means, Chief Walsh, that if the CFBI had been notified of this first murder the day it had been committed, we probably could have prevented Norman Washburn's death."

She leaned her elbow on the table and rested her head in her hand, wincing at the flicker of pain that sliced through her forehead. Her headaches were becoming increasingly frequent.

Especially when Walsh is around.

She scowled at Brandon's back as he turned away to talk to Natassia. Maybe he *was* the cause of her headaches. The man was certainly stress provoking.

She tried to resist the urge to stick her tongue out at him. A childish habit, she realized, but who cares?

She did it anyway.

Somewhat vindicated, Jasi closed her mouth and slumped further into the chair. Tucking her head into her arms, she allowed her body to relax. Exhaustion crept through her muscles and bones, and lulled her into a half-sleep.

"Is she okay? I mean, she seems a bit out of it."

Brandon's voice seemed miles away.

"She's just tired," Natassia replied.

"Jasi told me she could control her visions."

Natassia murmured a response that Jasi couldn't hear.

"So?" Brandon asked. "What the heck is going on?"

Jasi heard Natassia sigh. "I'm not sure. It could be residue from the Okanagan fires. It's like she's operating at half her power. I haven't seen her like this before."

Jasi lifted her head, frowned at them.

Then she pinned her eyes on Brandon. "You guys done talking about me?"

"We're just concerned," he admitted.

"I'm much better now," she lied.

His ice blue eyes told her that he didn't believe her.

Natassia's gaze was intense, suspicious. "Jas—"

"Listen—both of you!" Jasi snapped, cutting her off. "All I need is a good night's sleep."

"I think you should let Dr. Evans look at you," Natassia suggested.

"As soon as we get back," Brandon advised.

Jasi watched them both, her eyes narrowing. She wasn't accustomed to all this fuss and bother. It made her squirm.

"Well?" Brandon asked, waiting for her reply.

Jasi released an indignant sigh.

"We'll see."

Brandon watched her, annoyed and frustrated.

Damn, the woman was pigheaded!

He suspected that Jasi would see the case to the end before spending one minute in a doctor's office. The woman was being unreasonable. She'd drive herself into the ground at this pace.

"Call the helicopter," he told Natassia. "We need to get back to Kelowna."

"Not yet," Jasi argued. "We still have one more thing to check out here."

She stood up shakily and took a few steps.

"When I was in his mind, I walked the path the arsonist took. Victoria PD never checked the woods that far in. We'll go back to Kelowna *after* we check it out."

When Brandon caught her eye, she added, "I promise."

Cursing beneath his breath, he watched her move away from the house.

Why did she have to be so damned stubborn?

He recalled her vision. He had seen and heard firsthand her descent into the mind of a killer. The expression on her face earlier had chilled him to the bone. For a moment, he could have sworn that he was with the arsonist. Someone insane—twisted and extremely deadly. In a voice that was hoarse and unrecognizable, she had said, *"Now it begins."*

Jasi's voice, he reminded himself.

But the words and thoughts of a killer.

"You coming, Walsh?" she hollered.

He accompanied her down an overgrown trail that ran alongside the house. The trail ended where the woods began, about six yards from the back fence. The towering trees, like leafy sentinels, clustered close together, with no obvious path through them.

But Jasi saw a path—the one a murderer had taken.

"This way."

Brandon was right behind Jasi as she led them into the brush. He held his breath as she slipped between the trees and slowly scanned the ground and bushes for clues.

Natassia trailed closely behind them.

"He stood here," Jasi said, pointing to a boot print in the dried earth.

Moving in for a closer inspection, Natassia scanned the print with her data-com. "It's the same as the one we found at Washburn's. Size 11 Thermogard Cruiser."

Brandon crouched down beside Jasi and surveyed the ground. "This confirms the connection between the two cases. There's no room for doubt now. Do you need a cast?"

"No," Jasi replied. "The one we took from Washburn's will do." She glanced over at Natassia. "Can you get some photos?"

Natassia immediately brought out her data-com and a flexible ruler. She placed the ruler beside the print and took a few photographs.

While Natassia was busy, Brandon watched Jasi carefully. He noticed that her face had regained some color and that she appeared more rested.

He steered her a few feet away from her partner.

"You feeling better?"

Startled, Jasi's eyes flickered toward his. Swallowing hard, she mumbled, "I'm fine, Walsh."

His eyes grazed hers and held her captive. Then he swept a hand in front, indicating for her to go on ahead.

"I'll follow."

He heard her snicker and wondered what was so funny.

When Jasi reached a fallen cedar tree, she stopped suddenly. "He wanted to go around but the ground was too boggy."

Brandon held his breath as Jasi slowly climbed up onto the tree. The girth of the trunk was too wide for her to straddle so her long legs curled underneath her. She started to part the tree limbs in front of her, ducking her head through a small opening.

Suddenly Jasi stopped.

"Natassia! Have you got an evidence container?"

"What have you got?" Brandon asked.

"Our killer left behind some trace." She pointed to a small piece of shiny yellow fabric snagged on a branch.

Using a long pair of tweezers, Jasi picked up the fabric and gently slid it into a clear evidence tube. Then she held it up to the sun.

"There's some thread on it," she said, handing the tube back to Natassia.

"I'll get it to Ops," Natassia promised, carefully pocketing the sealed container.

"Data-com on!" Jasi commanded. "Phone Ben."

When Brandon heard Roberts' voice on the speaker, he thought it sounded tired.

"What's up?" Ben Roberts asked.

Jasi caught Brandon's eye, blushed and turned away. "We found something, Ben. A piece of plastic cloth. Yellow—bright yellow. It could be from a hat, a gym bag...or a yellow jacket."

"Just like my vision," Natassia murmured.

"Okay," Roberts said. "I'm going to the Paloma now. I'll check Baker's room for anything yellow. Divine has a team searching his home in Vancouver too."

When the transmission ended, Jasi looked at Brandon. "Do you believe in me now?"

He dragged in a breath. He knew his answer was important. To both of them. Strangely, he didn't want to let her down.

"I'm starting to," he admitted softly.

"Okay," she nodded. "Let's keep going."

He followed her through the trees until they reached the edge of the woods. The river loomed close by, its surface broken by rocks and whitewater foam. In a few areas near the shore, the water was glassy calm.

Deceptively calm, he thought.

Ahead, Jasi came to an abrupt stop.

Watching her stare out over the river, Brandon wondered what she was thinking. He stepped forward, about to ask her, when Natassia's arm reached out and restrained him.

"He stopped here," Jasi whispered after a moment. "He felt powerful and in control. One person off his list. Charlotte was the first to die...but she wouldn't be the last."

Brandon couldn't control the sudden chill that racked his spine. What was it like to be linked to a killer's mind? He had to admit that there was more to Jasi's special *gift* than some hocus-pocus nonsense.

Victoria PD had missed a vital piece of evidence.

He shook his head, trying to clear the cobwebs from his mind. He realized that he was beginning to believe in the unthinkable—that Jasi had psychic abilities and could reach into the mind of a psychopath. That possibility terrified him more than he wanted to admit.

"There's nothing more for us here," Jasi murmured softly.

"Are you all right?" Natassia asked, concerned.

Without answering, Jasi headed back toward the chopper.

Brandon was relieved. With a shiver, he glanced back at Charlotte Foreman's house. A house of empty shadows.

Aboard the helicopter, he nudged Jasi. "Why don't you get some sleep? Natassia and I'll take care of the reports."

Jasi's eyes flashed angrily while she jerked on her safety belt. "Don't baby me, Walsh! I'm fully capable of pulling my own weight around here."

Brandon realized that Jasi was desperate to prove herself, to validate her abilities. But why did she push herself so hard? She needed to surrender her stubborn pride. Maybe then Jasi wouldn't walk around acting so angry all the time.

But, damn she was sexy when she was angry!

"Just have a quick nap—"

"I can't afford to rest," she glared, cutting him off. "I have a report to file. And I have to call Cameron and give her an update. I'll get her to do some research."

Brandon heaved a sigh of frustration.

Jasmine McLellan, you're infuriating!

"Cameron?" he heard her say into her data-com receiver. "I'm uploading a file to you. What's your email address?"

A few minutes later, she disconnected and Brandon watched while she filled out a report.

Sleep is what you need, he thought.

He smiled slyly when he caught her yawning. Rather than accept his suggestion, she fought to stay awake by making notes on her data-com. He relaxed as her eyes closed after five minutes. When the data-com slipped from her hands and fell to the floor, he chuckled softly.

Jasi slept for the remainder of the flight as though she hadn't slept in days. Even the occasional air turbulence didn't stir her.

Her partner, Natassia Prushenko, on the other hand, remained wide awake. Natassia spent the entire flight to Kelowna watching him. When she caught him staring at Jasi, she grinned and gave him a knowing look.

Brandon gritted his teeth, his eyes resting on Jasi.

Women!

16

~ *Kelowna, BC*

I smiled while I read the newspaper.
There was a picture of the good old doctor on the front page, along with a report on his untimely death.

"You deserved it, you bastard!"

Reading the reporter's column I was surprised to discover that AI agent Brandon Walsh was on the case. That made me nervous. The man was good—the best in his field.

Flinging the paper to the floor, I cursed under my breath. It was bad enough that the CFBI had been called in. I could almost feel their breath on my neck. They were getting close...too close. But I had myself to blame for that.

I never should have sent them the first lighter.

"Are you new?" a voice said behind me.

Glancing back at one of my co-workers, I nodded. "Yeah, I transferred from Vancouver. A month ago."

I hoped that would end his questions.

"Must've been busy in Van." He eyed me strangely and I wondered if he suspected something. "I know some of the guys down there. You know Ryan Wilson?"

Trapped, I shrugged. "I wasn't there very long. I probably bumped into him somewhere along the line."

Hurrying, I grabbed my jacket and boots from the locker and made for the door.

"You off?" the man hollered after me.

Irritated, I gritted my teeth, turned to him and smiled. "I have the next two days off."

The man suddenly grinned. "You gotta hot date?"

I chuckled softly. "Oh, yeah. Definitely a hot one."

The man's laughter pursued me down the hallway while I rushed from the building. My boots felt heavy, like concrete blocks. My heart thumped so loudly in my chest I wondered if anyone else could hear it.

When I reached my car, I jumped inside and locked the doors. I looked in the rear view mirror. No one had followed me out. I was safe. If anyone I worked with found out that I was responsible for three deaths...

The thought made me laugh.

How stupid my co-workers were! No one had even checked to ensure that my transfer papers were legitimate. It was so easy to get in, so easy to fool them all.

I forced myself to go back to my original list.

Pulling a folded piece of paper from the glove compartment, I read it slowly. Each person on my list had sworn to protect me. Yet, all had done irreparable damage to me.

Charlotte Foreman had been incinerated for her betrayal. Too bad about the kid. Dr. Norman Washburn had been easy. He had finally paid for his crimes.

I smiled at the next name on the list.

Here was someone responsible for my endless torture. Torture...hmmm. Yes, that was how this person would pay.

I jammed the key into the ignition, eager to start.

But first I needed to make a call. And pick up some diesel, I reminded myself. I couldn't get it from work this time. Too dangerous. Someone might notice.

Driving a few kilometers out of town, I pulled over at a truck stop. From the trunk I removed a large gas can and walked over to the pumps.

"Can I help you?" a young attendant asked.

"I need some diesel for my truck back home," I lied.

The boy's complexion was bad. Acne and red patches marred his face. I felt sorry for him. When I looked at him, he stared back, unblinking.

He gave me a strange look, then took the can I offered and filled it. "Will that be all?" He shifted nervously from side to side.

I nodded and paid him quickly.

Securing the gas lid, I threw the can in the trunk and sped off toward Kelowna. When I reached downtown, I took a detour toward a mall.

I needed a phone—one that couldn't be traced to me.

Shoving my hands in my pockets, I quickly made my way through the shoppers and teenagers in the parking lot. Just inside the mall doors, a row of phone booths lined the wall. Selecting an empty booth, I stepped inside and after consulting the phonebook, I made a call. I used a piece of paper towel to hold the receiver, to hide my prints.

A few minutes later I smiled and hung up. Now all I had to do was make sure the area was empty. No innocents this time. I had one more call to make, but I'd do that much later.

Glancing at my watch, I realized it was already after six o'clock. I felt a sense of urgency mixed with excitement. Tonight's fire was going to be the last. Part of me felt relieved. Part of me wondered whether I would be able to stop.

I thought about the CFBI's involvement. After reading about Agent Jasmine McLellan and the Parliament Murders, I had challenged her by sending a Gemini lighter to CFBI headquarters. I always wondered what she had thought when she received the small package.

There was something strange about the woman. I couldn't put my finger on it. Watching her on TV and reading about her gave me the impression that she was solely responsible for solving the Parliament case.

Walking quickly, I scoffed at the idea that Agent McLellan could be that intelligent. How good could she really be? She had stood next to me, talked to me…and not even suspected a thing.

I laughed aloud. She hadn't caught me yet.

Catching my reflection in a shop mirror, I paused. For a moment, it was like someone else— a monster—was staring back at me through my own eyes.

How could this monster be me?

Shaking my head nervously, I backed away and knocked over an old woman. She glared at me and whacked my leg with her cane. She reminded me of Charlotte Foreman and I aimed a deadly look in her direction.

When the woman saw my face, she panicked and stumbled away in fear.

I strolled from the mall, feeling confident in my plan. Reaching my car, I climbed in and headed for my apartment. On the radio, the weather forecasters were predicting a mild night with calm skies.

I glanced at my list.

Reading the third name, I smiled.

Calm skies? How wrong they were.

Tonight was going to be a night to remember.

A storm was coming.

And it was going to be a scorcher.

17

~ *Penticton, BC*

While Jasi, Natassia and Brandon Walsh worked the Foreman crime scene in Victoria, Ben flew to Penticton where he watched endless disks of security footage from the Paloma Springs Hotel. Each floor had surveillance in the hallways while separate cameras monitored every elevator.

That meant twelve disks had to be scanned.

He had entered the security room of the hotel with a flash of a warrant and his ID. The hotel manager was eager to assist in the investigation, hoping either for some free publicity or for a quick resolution.

Ben wasn't sure which.

"Wait!" he ordered suddenly. "Stop there."

A security technician pushed the *pause* button.

Premier Allan Baker's image was captured on the monitor. He was following a woman down the hallway. The woman turned and smiled seductively at the Premier, then crooked a finger in his direction.

Lifting her chin, Lydia Gibney unknowingly smiled straight into the lens of a security camera. She wore a sheer black dress with a silver scarf trailing elegantly over one shoulder. Her jet-black hair was swirled into an elaborate up-do. A couple of wisps had escaped and curled next to her diamond-studded ears. Her dark eyes were shadowed in sultry shades and her blood-red lips pouted innocently.

"Want me to play it from here?" the security tech asked.

Ben nodded.

The technician pushed *play* and the images began to move.

They watched while Baker pressed a slightly intoxicated Lydia against the wall next to his hotel door. The Premier quickly glanced down the hall, then leaned forward and kissed Martin Gibney's wife…slowly.

Ben shifted uncomfortably.

The naked passion in the woman's eyes made him feel like a voyeur. He watched while Baker tugged her into his hotel room and closed the door behind them.

The computer screen showed a time counter in the bottom right hand corner.

"Can you fast forward until there's some activity in the hall?" Ben asked.

Just as Alyssa Bines had recalled, there was no one in the hall for almost half an hour. Then the Premier's door opened and an upset Lydia stumbled into the hallway. She grabbed onto the Premier's arm but Baker callously pushed her away.

Ben swore softly.

The tech zoomed in on Lydia's image.

The woman looked at Baker with a wounded expression in her eyes. She pleaded with him but he shook his head angrily. She shouted something and stormed down the hall toward the elevator while Baker hovered in the doorway. Then the door to his room slammed shut.

Ben watched the clock on the screen tick by slowly.

Then he saw Baker reappear. The man exited his hotel room and went into an elevator. He was talking to someone on his cell phone. Baker had sworn that he had remained at the party, that he hadn't left the hotel.

Yet, Ben had sensed the man wasn't being honest.

"Can you set up the disk for that elevator?"

After five minutes, he found what he was searching for. The security camera had caught Premier Allan Baker leaving the elevator at the basement level. Before the elevator doors closed, Ben spotted Baker sneaking out a door marked *Housekeeping*.

"Stop there."

The camera froze on the closing door.

"Where does that go to?"

The technician eyed Ben, then jerked his head toward the screen. "That's housekeeping. Where we keep supplies, do laundry—that sort of stuff."

"Can you access the outside from there?"

"Yeah. There's a door to the back parking lot."

Ben felt a ripple of excitement.

Baker *had* left the hotel.

But where the heck had the bastard gone? And what vehicle had he driven?

"Do you have a camera for the back parking lot?"

The technician navigated through the camera listings, then brought up the disk with the parking lot surveillance.

"There's your man."

Baker was getting into the passenger side of a black car.

"Can you enlarge it?" Ben asked.

The picture grew distorted as the tech zoomed in, but Ben identified the vehicle—a black BMW sedan.

Probably a 7 Series, he thought. A high-end vehicle for someone with money.

The license plate number was obscured by the angle of the camera. The moving shadows inside the car indicated the presence of one other person besides Premier Baker.

The driver. But the windows of the car were so heavily tinted that Ben couldn't identify him.

Disappointed, he watched while Baker and the mystery driver sped away into the night.

"I'll need the disks we looked at," he stated firmly.

Obediently, the security tech handed him the three disks.

"Thanks. I'm ready to see Premier Baker's room now."

"Okay," the tech agreed, pressing a button on his desk. "I'll get Kathy to let you in."

Ben was about to ask who *Kathy* was, when a security guard barged into the office, breathless and red-faced. The woman was of native heritage. Her almond eyes were framed by cropped black hair. Her skin was weathered.

From roasting in the sun, he mused.

"Kathy Fairmont," the woman grunted.

Her voice was low and gruff, like someone who had smoked two packs a day since birth. She was a woman trapped in a man's body. A body that probably weighed over three hundred pounds.

Ben introduced himself, ensuring that his gloves were on securely. There was no way he wanted to pick up anything from Kathy Fairmont's mind.

"CFBI agent, huh?" the woman mumbled.

She peered down her flat nose, huffing in disdain. Her three chins, one of which sprouted a large brown mole, mesmerized him.

Battleaxe. That's what came to Ben's mind.

"This way," Battleaxe said coolly.

She marched down the hall toward the elevator and waited inside, tapping her foot. He remained silent during the quick ride up to the fourth floor where Kathy led him down a hallway, the rolls of her uniform-clad buttocks swinging from side to side.

The woman walks like she has a bug up her ass, Ben thought with a snort.

Kathy's eyes aimed poisoned darts at him. "Yeah?"

"Something wrong?" he asked innocently.

Battleaxe stopped sharply and turned to face him. Her eyes sparked with animosity, her voice was arctic ice.

"Premier Baker's a good man. He's done lots for us. Don't know why ya guys have to bother 'im."

Damn! Another fan of Baker's. How did the guy do it?

Shaking his head in amazement, Ben massaged his temple. "We're just here to conduct an investigation, ma'am. This is for his protection too. You know, rule him out."

Battleaxe's eyes narrowed.

Ben could hear her labored breathing as she hefted her weight down the hall. A picture came to mind of her trying to climb up eight flights of stairs. He wondered what the woman would do if she had to chase someone through the hotel. He wouldn't want to run into *her* in a dark alley. With her attitude, she'd probably shoot first and ask questions later.

He snickered at the thought.

The woman shot an angry scowl in his direction before stopping at room 418. Swiping a security card, she opened the door and stepped inside the room.

He whistled appreciatively. The word *room* was an understatement. 418 was a luxury suite of spacious rooms—complete with sitting room, dining room, kitchen, bedroom and a large Jacuzzi in one corner. An empty bottle of champagne lay beside the Jacuzzi.

Someone had been celebrating.

"Don't make a mess!" Kathy warned. "Premier Baker's still using this room and he likes everything nice and tidy. He's got lots on his plate, that man. Specially now that his dad's dead."

Ben ignored her and extracted an object from his tote bag. The X-Disc Pro was a small computerized hovercraft that could scan for evidence. If there were trace elements such as illicit drug residue, skin samples, blood, semen or vaginal fluids, the X-Disc would find them.

Battleaxe locked her hands behind her, a soldier at ease.

"Thank you for showing me to the room," Ben said pointedly, hoping the woman would get the message.

Kathy eyed him rudely. "I can't leave you alone in the Premier's room."

"Actually, you *can't* be here while I conduct the search," he stated bluntly. "It's against CFBI regulations. Should I call your supervisor to explain this to you?"

The security guard's jaw dropped in outrage.

Ben jerked his head toward the open door. "Now, if you don't mind…"

Kathy Fairmont stomped out of the room, giving the door a final slam behind her.

"Make sure you put everything back!" he heard her yell.

Heavy footsteps thumped down the hall, away from room 418, and Ben groaned with relief.

"Jesus!" he muttered. "Is there anybody here who *doesn't* like Baker? Besides me?"

The empty room ignored him.

Ben pushed a small white button on the X-Disc Pro, activating its *search* mode. *Search and Destroy*, he called it. *Search* for evidence in a controlled area and then *destroy* any hope a defense attorney had of getting his or her client off on a technicality.

The X-Disc beeped softly and Ben set it down on the floor. About the size of his hand, the X-Disc quickly stored the measurements of Baker's suite and then with a soft hum, it lifted off the floor. Hovering about five feet in the air, it moved back and forth slowly, scanning the room and making peculiar clicking sounds. When it was finished, the X-Disc settled on the floor and a green light flashed.

Ben took out his data-com and scrolled to the satellite transmission page. Entering his ID and password, he downloaded the data from the X-Disc. The data was specifically categorized to make it easy to find evidence.

The first category Ben checked was *Prints*. Bypassing the fingerprint category, he scrolled down to *Shoe/Boot Prints*. The X-Disc had captured a number of footwear prints and had matched them to various manufacturers.

Thermogard wasn't anywhere on the list.

Next, he checked the list of fingerprints. Some matched the hotel employee database and belonged to housekeeping staff. A few were unidentifiable. Baker had entertained in his room. Perhaps he had entertained women other than Lydia Gibney.

The data-com beeped, indicating a hit.

Two prints found in the room matched the CFBI's international fingerprint database. The first one belonged to Premier Allan Baker who had been printed when he first stepped into a political position, as was standard protocol. The second print was a positive match to Martin Gibney. Gibney's prints were on file because he was on the board of administration at Kelowna General.

Ben grabbed his tote bag and stepped back into the living room. Placing the bag on a coffee table, he knelt in front of the sofa. He removed the cushions carefully, one at a time, and searched beneath them.

Nothing.

Sinking into the sofa, he rubbed his temple and checked his data-com. Then he scrolled over the other stats the X-Disc had picked up.

There were no hits.

Allan Baker couldn't be directly linked to either case.

Ben proceeded efficiently through each room, opening closet doors and checking clothing. He was hunting for something made of yellow plastic, perhaps a raincoat.

But yellow was not Premier Baker's choice of color.

When Ben reached the bedroom closet, he recorded Baker's shoe—size ten. Next, he ruffled through the pockets of the numerous suit jackets. He found a couple of gas receipts, but nothing for the night of Washburn's murder. And none of them were for diesel.

The X-Disc had mapped out where traces of hair, fibers, and paper were positioned in the room. Ben grabbed some evidence containers from his bag and consulted the map. Then he took a couple of samples from the bed sheets and tweezed some hairs from the pillows.

Disappointed that he hadn't found anything conclusive, he groaned aloud.

Then he recalled Natassia's vision.

The young man wearing a yellow jacket, smoking a cigarette. The incubators exploding all around him. His arm was in a sling...broken.

Was this man the arsonist?

Ben thought of Premier Allan Baker. Everything pointed to the man. If he was the young man in Natassia's vision then they only had to confirm that Baker had broken or injured his arm when he was younger.

"Data-com on! Personal file—Allan Baker."

Scrolling through the records, he found the one marked *Medical*. His heart pounded with anticipation. Reading the hospital reports, he discovered that while Baker lived with his mother, he had been relatively healthy child. There was nothing unusual in his medical records—no broken bones.

Then Ben came across a report filed during the time Baker had lived with Charlotte Foreman. The foster mother had brought Baker to the hospital after being attacked by a gang of boys outside her home. The boys had burned Baker's hands on a hot pipe.

There was no mention of any broken bones.

Ben chewed his bottom lip thoughtfully, remembering the scars on Baker's palms.

Perhaps Natassia's vision was symbolic. Maybe all they needed to know was that Baker had been hurt.

Scanning the hospital reports, Ben noticed that there were no other incidents. However, he did notice one thing that made him do a double take.

The doctor who had examined little Allan Baker had been none other than…Martin Gibney, M.D.

Small world, Ben thought.

Washburn's illegitimate son had ended up in Gibney's office. Had Martin Gibney known who the boy was back then?

Ben closed his eyes and a baby's face flashed before him. Natassia had seen babies in her vision. And a pregnant woman. Maybe Washburn had fallen into the seedy business of black-market baby sales, or abortions.

But how did that connect?

In Jasi's vision, the arsonist had said that Washburn had *'burned'* him once. An arsonist usually acted out of passion or rage. Or both. Fire was a method of cleansing. It destroyed the guilty by punishing or torturing them.

They were searching for someone with a hit list, Ben realized. A serial arsonist blamed more than one person for his situation. And he wouldn't be satisfied until they all paid the ultimate price—with their lives.

"Abuse," Ben muttered to himself.

That was the key.

Yet, he could find no indication that Baker's mother abused him. In fact, by all accounts, Sarah Baker had owned up to her addiction problem, sought help and recovered without incident.

Norman Washburn certainly hadn't been in the picture, so he couldn't have abused Baker.

That left one other person.

Charlotte Foreman!

Ben searched for listings of all children placed with foster mother. While the data-com downloaded the information, he experienced a tingling sensation down the back of his neck. It would take awhile for the satellite to transmit everything on Charlotte Foreman but he knew he was on the right track.

Picking up his tote bag, he examined the room once more before moving toward the door. One sofa cushion remained on the floor. Shrugging, he left it there.

Ben wanted Baker to know his room had been fully searched.

He opened the door and stepped into the hallway, half expecting Battleaxe to be skulking nearby. Relieved that the woman was nowhere in sight, he strolled toward the elevator and waited.

When the elevator doors parted, Ben stepped aside to allow the passengers out.

"Agent Roberts!"

Ben snapped his head toward the voice.

Allan Baker glared at him with an openly hostile expression on his face.

"I'm not sure what exactly you were looking for in my room, but I know you didn't find anything," Baker growled.

Ben fingered the security disks in his pocket, then stepped inside the empty elevator.

"Don't be too sure about that."

When the doors closed, he let out a slow stream of air. He had enjoyed the startled uneasiness on Baker's face.

Perhaps enjoyed it a bit too much.

Ben's data-com chirped loudly.

"Data-com on."

Natassia's voice greeted him cheerfully. "Hey! We just got back. We're on our way to the Prestige Inn."

"How's Jasi?"

"Sleeping." There was a hint of anxiety in her voice.

"What about Walsh?"

He heard Natassia laugh softly.

"He's watching Jasi sleep," she answered. "I think he's just what she needs."

Walsh?

Ben wondered what Brandon Walsh could offer Jasi—besides heartache. Walsh wasn't like them. He didn't understand Jasi or her gift. She deserved someone who accepted her in every way, someone who believed in her.

"Ben?"

"Yeah, Natassia?"

"I checked Baker's financial statements. There's no indication that he paid Gibney blood money. No evidence of a murder conspiracy that I could find."

"Okay. I'll be at the hotel in about two hours," he told her.

Natassia's voice was faint. "That long?"

"Sorry, I have a stop to make first."

18

~ *Kelowna, BC*

Ben flew back to Kelowna in the Ops chopper.
Then he hopped in a taxi and gave the driver an address. Fifteen minutes later, the taxi rolled up next to 103 Dremner Boulevard. Remaining in the back seat, Ben flipped open his data-com.

"I need to make a call first," he told the cabby.

The phone was picked up on the fourth ring. The voice on the other end was small and timid.

"Yes?"

"Is Martin Gibney there?"

"No, Mister is out."

Ben recognized the voice. It belonged to the Asian housekeeper, Su-Lin.

"What about Mrs. Gibney?" he asked.

"Yes, yes!" Su-Lin said excitedly. "Mrs. Gi-ney right here. You want speak to her?"

"No. That's okay." He hung up.

Speaking to Lydia Gibney over the phone was not what Ben had in mind.

He paid the driver to wait for him, and then headed for the mansion. A soft, feminine voice answered the *H-SECS* intercom.

"*Si?* Can I help you?"

"Uh, CFBI, Mrs. Gibney. I need to speak with you." Ben held his badge up to the camera lens.

When the door opened, Gibney's wife stood in the entrance wearing a pair of faded jeans and a t-shirt. Her long coal-black hair was clipped back away from her face.

The woman looked like she was eighteen.

Not quite the high society wife, Ben thought.

He showed her his ID again. "Agent Benjamin Roberts. I spoke with your husband yesterday."

"*Si.* Yes, I know. Martin mentioned that someone had stopped by. This is about Dr. Washburn's death. Is that correct?"

Her voice was soft, with a slight Spanish accent.

Ben accompanied Lydia Gibney through the house, past the sitting room where he and Gibney had sat the day before. Incense wafted from somewhere in the house and its sensual fragrance trailed after them. Sultry jazz filtered through hidden speakers in the ceiling.

Something caught Ben's attention.

A mood wall. The wall shifted gradually from peaceful aqua tones into shades of crimson as Lydia walked by.

Red, he knew, was the color of fear or extreme nervousness.

What was Lydia so afraid of? What did she know?

Ben followed her outside into the garden.

"Close deck door," she ordered loudly.

The door whispered behind them and closed.

She gave him an apologetic shrug. "I hope you don't mind, but I prefer being outdoors on a day like this."

Then she smiled and took the seat across from him.

Ben flicked on the data-com and clipped it to his jacket.

"No problem, Mrs. Gibney. I just have a few questions and, uh, some are of a rather sensitive nature."

The color drained from Lydia Gibney's face.

"What do you mean, a sensitive nature?"

He scooted forward, his voice calm. "We have the security disks from the Paloma. There are cameras everywhere."

He waited for his words to sink in.

When they did, the woman took a steadying breath, but it didn't stop the tremble in her voice.

"What exactly did the cameras see?"

Ben could sense her fear. He didn't envy her position. Having an affair was one thing. Getting caught was another. Her husband held a prominent position.

Lydia Gibney could lose everything.

"We know that you and Premier Allan Baker were having an affair," he remarked gently. "The cameras show you going into his hotel room the night of the party. We also have a witness who's seen the two of you together at other functions."

Lydia began to shake. Her dark eyes blinked back tears and she tossed a hasty glance over her shoulder.

"If Martin finds out—"

"Mrs. Gibney, I can't promise that we'll keep your name out of this, but if you can help us, give us some information…"

Lydia nodded slowly. "Allan and I have been, uh, seeing each other for the past year. Martin…doesn't know."

"When you left his room that night, what were you arguing about?"

"Martin had called while I was in Allan's room. He told Allan that they were going to fire Allan's father. Allan was very upset. He tried to get Martin to influence the board members, to keep his father on."

"Because he didn't want a scandal?"

"Allan was afraid that if the press caught wind of this, they would dredge up his past," Lydia answered, a distraught look in her eyes.

"How close were your husband and Dr. Washburn?"

"You mean, why would Martin cover for Dr. Washburn for so many years?" Her voice was tinged with disgust. "My husband met Dr. Washburn years ago. Martin was still trying to pay off his university loans."

The woman hesitated, guilt engraved across her face. "I-I really shouldn't say anymore."

Ben cleared his throat, then said, "Mrs. Gibney, if you know something, you need to tell me. Or I'll be forced to go to your husband with the security disks."

Lydia released a long sigh. "Dr. Washburn came to Martin with a proposition. A month later they were operating an abortion clinic. Underground, of course. Most of their clientele had money—real money. That's how Martin paid off his debts."

Just as Ben had suspected. Abortion was the key.

Terminating a pregnancy was legal and had been for years, but Washburn and Gibney had been doing it on the sly—and charging big bucks.

"Why would your husband jeopardize his career?"

Lydia shrugged, then shook her head.

"Martin was easily influenced back then. Dr. Washburn held my husband's career in his hands. Another reason why Martin was forced to influence the board to keep him on. If Dr. Washburn had told the board what they had done, my husband would lose his job too. And probably end up in prison."

"Did Allan Baker know what his father had done?"

"I'm not sure. Allan never mentioned it. He rarely talked about the past…or his father. Allan was always afraid of his past. He used to say ghosts were chasing him."

"Did he say who or what those ghosts were?"

"Ghosts from his past." Her black eyes examined him intensely. "He was placed in foster care as a child. Did you know that?"

Ben nodded.

"Allan was placed with a woman who abused him terribly."

"Charlotte Foreman?" he asked, shocked.

"Yes, that was her name. She had four other foster children living with her during the time Allan was placed there. She was an animal, that woman. She would burn the children with cigarettes or on the stovetop when they refused to do what she asked them. She'd lock them in the shed for hours."

Lydia stood up, agitated and shaky.

When she finally spoke, her voice was hoarse and filled with emotion. "Can you imagine what that would do to a child, Agent Roberts?"

It could turn a kid into a cold-blooded murderer, Ben realized.

Aloud, he asked, "Was she responsible for burning Allan's hands?"

Lydia froze and her gaze drifted.

"His foster mother held them down on the stove burner. She accused him of stealing money from her emergency jar. Allan swears he never took a cent from that woman."

Ben tapped the arm of his chair, restlessly.

"On the night of the party what exactly were you and Baker arguing about?"

For a moment, Lydia said nothing. Her eyes pooled and she slumped back into the chair.

"Allan demanded that I get a quiet divorce—leave Martin. He wanted me to tell my husband about our affair but I told him that I couldn't do that to Martin."

Her voice wavered and her smile softened.

"My husband is a good man. He took me away from a dangerous world and gave me all this." She waved a hand in the air. "How could I possibly leave him after everything he has done for me?"

"What about Allan Baker?"

Ben knew that his question was inappropriate and unnecessary to his investigation, but he was curious.

The woman smiled sadly. "I love my husband, Agent Roberts. But Allan is…well…Allan."

Clasping her hands in her lap, she bent forward and asked, "Haven't you ever felt the excitement of being with someone you know you should stay away from? Someone forbidden to you?"

Lydia didn't wait for an answer.

Instead, she smiled calmly. "That's what it's like for me and Allan. It's strictly passion. Sex, if you like. Martin has, well, *problems* in that area."

Ben shifted uncomfortably in his chair. "So you left the hotel and came home to your husband?"

Lydia's gaze was incredulous, shocked.

"No," she admitted. "I didn't come straight home. Allan called me on his cell phone and apologized. I thought you knew that already."

That was the cell call the security camera recorded, he realized.

Ben glanced at her sharply. "After your call to Baker, he left the hotel in a black BMW."

Lydia smiled mysteriously.

"Follow me, Agent Roberts."

She led him to a door on the side of the house. When she entered a security code the door opened, revealing a three-car garage. Parked in the middle stall, a Series 7 black BMW sedan gleamed expensively.

Ben drew a deep breath.

Baker, you son-of-a-bitch!

The man *had* left the hotel and he had lied about it.

They had him!

Lydia's voice grew quiet, solemn. "Allan and I met in the back of the hotel."

"So where did you drop him off?" Ben asked, concealing his excitement.

She glanced up, confused. "I didn't drop him anywhere. I picked him up and we went back to the Golden Sands Motel on Lakeshore Drive. I wasn't comfortable going back to his hotel room. There were too many of Martin's friends at the gala."

Damn!

Baker had an alibi.

And, Ben realized miserably, it would be easy to verify it with the manager at the Golden Sands Motel.

"How long did Baker stay with you at the Golden Sands?" he asked, a final shot in the dark.

Lydia turned away, ashamed. "Until almost three in the morning."

That let Baker off the hook completely.

Son-of-a-bitch! Allan Baker was innocent.

Ben clicked off his data-com, signaling that the interview was over.

"Here's my card," he said, scribbling his cell number on the back. "If you think of anything else, please get in touch with me. Thank you for your time, Mrs. Gibney."

Lydia Gibney escorted him to a garden gate, clutching the business card in her hand.

"Thank you, Agent Roberts—for your discretion."

He knew that the woman wanted nothing more than a guarantee that he wouldn't expose her affair with Allan Baker.

"You realize that the press will probably get wind of all this," he apologized. "I cant—"

"I know," she interrupted, holding up one hand. "Martin will find out. The house is wired with security cameras. He'll know you were here again."

Lydia swallowed hard. "I think I'll tell him tomorrow—before he hears about it on the news."

Ben smiled grimly, unsure of what to say.

"That's probably a good idea, Mrs. Gibney."

Without a word, the woman accompanied him down the sidewalk to the front yard. She waved goodbye, one hand shading her eyes from the sun.

Heading for the street, Ben was relieved to see that the taxi driver had waited. The driver was asleep. His baseball cap was pulled over his face to shade him from the hot sun.

Waking the man, he asked the cabby to drop him off at the Prestige Inn. As the taxi drove away from the house, he glanced back.

Near the waterfall, Martin Gibney's wife stood stone-still and peered up at her home with a despondent look on her face.

Shaking his head, Ben realized that he would never understand women. He couldn't understand why Lydia Gibney would put her marriage, her security—*everything*, at risk.

Especially for a man like Allan Baker.

Activating his data-com, he called Jasi.

When she answered, Ben uttered three grim words.

"Baker is innocent."

19

"Ben says that Baker isn't the arsonist," Jasi mumbled in shock. "Said he'd tell us everything after he gets here."

She was dumbfounded. And a bit pissed off that Baker had turned out to be innocent. The guy deserved a public humiliation—not a sympathetic pat on the back.

Jasi groaned aloud. Their investigation was hitting one brick wall after another, and she was ready to pull out the dynamite. She itched to get moving again. The hotel room was cramped. Too many people, too many frustrations. She wondered whether Brandon and Natassia were feeling it too.

The chair next to Brandon was vacant so she parked herself in it and allowed her thoughts to drift. Then she glared down at her data-com, positive that it had malfunctioned. How could Ben say that their number one suspect was in the clear?

"I must have misunderstood him," she muttered.

Brandon was watching her like a hawk circling its prey.

"What?" she demanded. "Everything pointed to Baker."

"I know," he said. "I thought the bastard was guilty too."
Magnetic attraction tugged at her heart. She
experienced it more often, now that Brandon Walsh was
involved in the investigation. Watching him from the
corner of her eye, she realized that she was inexplicably
drawn to him—the proverbial *'moth to a flame'*.

When she was close to him, a searing heat invaded her
body and a tight breathlessness clamped around her lungs.
It had been a long time since a man had made her feel
anything.

But why the hell had it been *this* man?

The thought made her angry. She was furious with
herself for being so weak. Why did she have to fall for an
Arson Investigator?

Aware of his every move, she peeked at him again and
was captured in his pale eyes. Yeah, she was attracted to
him, she admitted to herself. But falling for Brandon Walsh
was like…like—

She instantly had visions of small furry animals lined
up at a cliff's edge. What were they called?

Lemmings!

She was a lemming throwing herself off a cliff, plunging
to her doom. Voluntarily.

She shook her head to rid herself of the image.

"Now what? Where do we go from here?"

Brandon reached across, resting his arm casually over
the back of her chair. "We go over all the files until Ben
gets here. Then we figure this out…together."

His hand unconsciously kneaded her shoulder. His
touch was gentle, caring.

Quivering inside, she lost her concentration—until she
caught Natassia's wink. Stifling the urge to swear at
someone, Jasi pushed her chair back and stood quickly,
knocking Brandon's arm away.

"Vid-wall on!" She grabbed a pop from the fridge and
chugged it back.

For the next half-hour they rechecked every piece of data, scrutinized every file. Somewhere between the evidence reports and their visions, lay a clue.

The soil sample revealed minute traces of industrial car wash chemicals. It was a dead end. The chemicals could have been picked up on the arsonist's boots anywhere.

The boot print was a bust. Anyone could purchase a pair of Thermogard Cruisers, including campers, search and rescue, firefighters, paramedics, oil field workers and farmers. None of their suspects had footwear that size. Of course, one of them could be smart enough to wear larger boots to throw the CFBI off course.

As for the diesel and the lighter, the Super Clean diesel could have been purchased by anyone with an empty gas can. And not one fingerprint was lifted from the Gemini lighter.

The yellow fabric Jasi had discovered in the woods was the only solid clue left.

"Where's that report on the fabric?" she demanded.

Natassia gave her a sheepish look. "Uh...it's been misplaced."

"Misplaced? How the hell did Ops *misplace* a vital piece of evidence?"

"I sent it to Ops via the helicopter. The pilot was new and—"

"And he was probably concentrating on other things," Jasi added, eyeing Natassia's chest pointedly.

"Sorry."

"It's not your fault. I just wish we'd get a damned break."

A few minutes later, Jasi brought up the files on Washburn and Charlotte Foreman, placing them side by side.

"Natassia, give me a quick rundown on your vision."

"Okay. Dr. Washburn was an alcoholic. The board wanted him out of Kelowna General because he was drinking on the job and using drugs to keep himself going. His wife, Freda, knew that he slept—" Natassia's head snapped up and her eyes widened.

"What?" Jasi asked.

"He had an affair with a prostitute and wondered if his wife knew."

Washburn probably kept poor Freda in the dark about a lot of things, Jasi thought. The man had certainly done his fair share of sleeping around.

From the bar fridge, she fisted a pack of salted cashews.

"What about the woman giving birth and the boy in the back of the room?" she asked, ripping the bag open.

Natassia bit her lip. "I think the woman was someone Washburn knew. But it wasn't Sarah Baker or Freda."

"And the boy with his arm in a sling?" Brandon asked. "Who was he—Baker?"

"I'm not sure," Natassia admitted. "I don't really get the sense that Washburn knows this boy that well. I'd have to say *no*. The boy isn't Allan Baker."

"Can't you go back to Washburn's body, try again?"

Jasi shook her head, surprised that Brandon would even suggest such a thing. "She can't do it again."

"One reading. That's all I get," Natassia explained. "Then the psychic imprint or energy dissipates. There's nothing left of Dr. Norman Washburn to read."

Jasi's eyes wandered over Brandon, settling on his sensuous mouth. "We have to focus on our visions, Natassia. There's a connection there somewhere. We just have to find it." She popped a cashew in her mouth.

"I think the connection is the woman in Natassia's vision," Brandon interjected.

She realized that he was right. They needed to uncover the identity of the woman in Natassia's vision.

"If Washburn was involved in something illeg—"

"There's no 'if' about it," Ben said from the doorway. "I just talked to Lydia Gibney. Her husband and Norman

Washburn were involved in an underground abortion clinic from about 1975 to 2001."

He strode into the room, plunking his data-com on the table.

"They started in Victoria then continued here. Gibney convinced Washburn to give it up a few years ago. Then Washburn blackmailed him, swearing Gibney to secrecy."

"That's how Washburn forced Gibney to talk the board into keeping him on for so long," Natassia said, moving the empty chair beside her.

Ben dropped into the chair, stretching his long legs.

"Yeah. He knew that Gibney would do whatever it took to ensure that the board never discovered the abortion business."

The possibility that Gibney had killed Washburn had already crossed Jasi's mind. Washburn used him to keep his position. Martin Gibney would have been terrified that Washburn would screw up again, maybe inadvertently leak something to the press.

Or to his son, Jasi thought.

"And Baker?" she asked, emptying the bag of nuts into her mouth.

Ben shook his head. "He's got an alibi. He was at the Golden Sands Motel with Lydia Gibney. Baker used his credit card and the manager remembers seeing them leave. I think Martin Gibney warrants a closer look."

"Do you think Gibney was desperate enough to murder Washburn? To keep him quiet and get him out of the way?"

"Let's find out."

Ben called up Gibney's home number.

A minute later he hung up.

"He's in a meeting, according to his wife. We can catch him at the hospital if we hurry."

Jasi jumped to her feet and shoved her arms into the sleeves of her jacket. "Let's go."

Brandon started to rise but she blocked him.

"Not you, Walsh." She gave him an apologetic look. "Sorry. CFBI has jurisdiction over this arrest. And there's no need for all of us to go. Ben and I can handle Gibney."

From the corner of her eye, she caught Ben watching her. He winged one brow, questioning her decision. She prayed that he would keep his mouth shut.

When Jasi looked back at Brandon, his pale eyes flashed and his jaw clenched. He was pissed off but she couldn't allow his ego to interfere. She didn't want him with her. His close proximity clouded her judgement.

His slightest touch made her forget where she was.

How do I explain this to him?

To Natassia she said, "Check to see if they found the fabric yet. Okay?"

"So what am I supposed to do?" Brandon growled in her ear.

His mouth hovered inches from hers.

Jasi swallowed hard. "Wait for us. We won't be long."

Closing the door firmly behind her, she tried to ignore the twinge of guilt. Leaving Brandon Walsh out in the cold did not sit too well with her.

"Walsh isn't so bad, Jasi."

She was sitting with Ben in the back of a Speedy taxi while it wound its way through the heavy traffic. The driver had been enticed with a fifty-dollar bill to get them to the hospital within ten minutes. Of course, Ben never specified that they had to arrive in one piece, so the driver zipped through the lanes, passing everything in sight.

"Jesus!" she shouted, gritting her teeth as the taxi veered around a corner and swiped the curb.

She gripped the door handle, promising herself she'd never take a taxi in Kelowna again.

Her eyes held Ben's. "Did you read him?"

Ben nodded.

"And?"

"Brandon Walsh really cares about you."

She snorted in disbelief.

"Jasi, he's a good man. He won't betray you."

She turned and stared out the window at the flash of cars that passed by. They were in the middle of rush hour traffic. Everyone was in a hurry to get home.

"I know," she said finally. "But you know what happens if I get too involved, when I care about someone. It's just so hard to trust anyone."

Her partner's face grew dark, clouded. "Brandon Walsh is not like—"

Jasi grabbed his arm. "I don't want to talk about *him*."

"Here's the hospital," the taxi driver cut in. "Eight minutes, twenty two seconds. If you give me twenty more, I'll wait for you."

The dark-skinned man swiveled in his seat and grinned at Jasi.

It was Ahmed.

The driver who had ditched her outside City Hall.

Ben reached into his wallet, counting out fifty dollars, but Jasi shook her head.

Peeling thirty dollars from his hand, she shoved it toward Ahmed.

"Hey!" the driver whined. "You promised fifty."

Jasi's deadly look made the man gasp.

Leaning forward, she gripped the back of Ahmed's seat. Then she locked eyes with the man. "I gave you an extra twenty the other day to wait for me by City Hall. Remember, Ahmed?"

The tone of her voice was threatening and dark.

Ahmed squinted.

She could tell the moment he recognized her.

The man's eyes bulged with dismay. His jaw dropped and he probably would have argued with her, except that he spotted the 9-millimeter semiautomatic Jasi had strapped inside her jacket.

His beady black eyes flicked from her to Ben.

Raising his hands in surrender, he whimpered in fear.

"Okay, lady. No problem."

When they stepped from the taxi, Ben raised one brow, questioning her tactics.

"What? I hate being ditched!" Jasi snapped, stomping furiously toward the hospital doors.

Inside the crowded hospital, an old man hobbled past them wearing only a pale blue hospital gown. Jasi choked back a hoot of laughter when she noticed that the man had forgotten to fasten the back of the gown. The ties dangled to the ground behind him as his bare wrinkled bottom wobbled down the hall.

"Gibney's on the third floor, Boardroom A," Ben said, returning from the information desk.

Stepping into the elevator, Jasi zipped her jacket halfway, concealing her gun from curious eyes.

"How do you want to handle this?" she asked Ben when they reached the third floor.

"Boardroom A is to the left." He pointed to a hospital directory hanging on the wall. "We don't know if there's an alternate escape, so we'll just have to push our way in."

In front of the door to the boardroom, a receptionist's desk stood unmanned. The waiting area was empty too.

"We're in luck, Ben."

Jasi unzipped her jacket.

Gripping the gun firmly, she kept her hand tucked inside. No need to alarm everyone in the meeting. If they could take Gibney quietly…

Ben barged into the room.

She followed on his heels, taking long, brisk strides.

"Martin Gibney?" Ben demanded.

Jasi scoured the startled faces of the board members.

"There!" she hissed.

Gibney was bent over a stack of legal documents.

"A-Agent Roberts?" he stuttered. "What are you doing here?"

Bewildered, he straightened slightly.

Jasi detected fear in Gibney's eyes.

He knows *something*, she realized. But was he a serial arsonist?

Ben strode over to the cowering man and grabbed his arm. "Martin Gibney, we have a few questions for you. If you'll come with us, please."

"Is there somewhere private we can talk?" Jasi asked the man.

"There's a private lounge, two doors down."

A terrified Gibney motioned them to follow while fifteen shocked board members sat mutely.

"We're just questioning him," Jasi assured one woman on her way out the door.

"For now," she heard Ben mutter, annoyed.

When they were safely ensconced in the lounge, Ben ordered three hospital workers out, then locked the door behind them and told Gibney to sit.

"Voice record on!" Jasi commanded, placing her data-com on the conference table.

Taking the seat across from the doctor, Ben leaned forward, placed his elbows on the table between them and clasped both hands firmly.

"We need to know *exactly* what was going on with you and Dr. Washburn. We have proof that you were both involved in illegal abortion activities."

Gibney's mouth hung open. "I'm not saying anything."

"This is your last opportunity to talk to us."

"I want my lawyer," Gibney argued, staring at the wall.

"That's up to you," Jasi shrugged. "But then we'd have to bring you in for questioning. And we might have to find you some cellmates to teach you how to play nice."

She smiled acidly and perched on the edge of the table.

Jasi suspected that Gibney wouldn't like being dragged out in handcuffs, or the countless hours of processing and waiting around a police station. She also suspected that making new friends in a Kelowna jail cell wasn't Gibney's idea of a good time either.

"I'll lose my job, my house—everything," Gibney whined, desperation carved into his face.

"Then tell us what you know," she warned. "It's in your best interest to talk to us. If you answer our questions, then we may not have to bring you in. Right, Ben?"

"Maybe," her partner agreed.

Finally the doctor let out a long, unsteady breath and began talking. "Norman Washburn didn't just handle the occasional abortion, he also delivered his own kids."

Jasi was shocked. "What?"

"Norman brought in a prostitute one night," Gibney said flatly. "In August of 1979. The woman was in labor, full-term. I overheard her threatening to expose Norman."

"Expose him for what?" Ben asked bluntly.

"Norman had paid for her services—more than once. *He* was the father."

Jasi stood up suddenly and paced the room.

"Washburn couldn't deal with another scandal," she said. "So what did he do—deliver the baby?"

"Ba-*bies*," Gibney corrected.

Babies?

Jasi was stunned.

Somewhere out there, Washburn had more children.

Allan Baker had siblings.

"How many?" she asked.

Martin Gibney held up two fingers.

Ben leaned forward, pulled off a glove and grabbed the man's arm. "So let me get this straight. Norman Washburn slept with a prostitute, got her pregnant and delivered his own kids in the basement of the hospital?"

Gibney nodded. "He didn't want anyone to find out. Especially the board or his wife."

"So what happened to the mother and the babies?" Jasi asked.

"Norman took care of them," Gibney mumbled grimly.

"Wait a minute." Motioning Ben aside, she whispered, "In Natassia's vision, she saw the mother's eyes."

"Yeah?"

"Were they open or closed?"

"I don't know," Ben admitted.

Jasi punched in Natassia's data-com link.

"Wide open," Natassia replied. "But unmoving."

Jasi broke communication. "Ben? The mother's eyes were wide open. I think she was dead."

Gibney groaned loudly, then rested his head in his hands. "Norman killed her."

"Why would you think that?" Jasi demanded, lingering beside the man.

"Right after the twins were born, Norman told me to get a bag of AB blood for the mother. When I returned about fifteen minutes later, the woman was dead." Gibney's voice was flat and lifeless.

"I don't see—"

"I saw something wrapped in a towel," he interrupted. "The placenta. Norman refused to let me examine it."

Ben glided around the side of the table. "So, what exactly are you saying?"

Gibney dragged in a deep breath. "I'm saying that Norman ripped the placenta out of the mother. He knew what he was doing. He knew his actions would result in a postpartum hemorrhage."

"And he didn't want you to see what he had done," Ben guessed. "That's why he wouldn't show you the placenta. You would know that he had committed murder. But you already knew. You guessed, didn't you?"

Martin Gibney cowered guiltily.

Jasi bent over him, bracing herself on the arms of his chair. "Washburn intentionally made the mother bleed to death so that she wouldn't expose him. What happened to her body?"

The man looked up apprehensively. "I don't know. Norman got rid of it."

"We need to find out who this woman was," Jasi said to Ben. "Someone is out to avenge her death. Maybe her pimp, a boyfriend—someone."

Gibney shook his head grimly. "Norman refused to have any record of her existence. By the time I realized what had happened, I was in way over my head. It was too late to do anything about the mother...or the babies."

Ben cleared his throat. "We need to search hospital records and newspapers. The babies would have needed medical attention."

"Unless Washburn killed them too," Jasi murmured.

Martin Gibney looked like he was going to vomit.

"No, Norman found them a home," he argued.

Ben's eyes lit up suddenly. "Charlotte Foreman got them somehow."

Gibney nodded slowly. "Norman insisted that Charlotte Foreman get those kids...the twins. He wanted her to keep them out of his way—make sure they never went looking for him. Norman wrote her a glowing recommendation."

Jasi was appalled. "Why would he do that? She abused those kids."

The man's head jerked up sharply. "What?"

"How do you think Allan Baker's hands were scarred?"

"He told me a gang of boys burned him on a pipe," Gibney said nervously.

Ben glared contemptuously. "Actually his foster mother held them on the stove burner."

"My God!" Gibney sputtered. "I thought those boys were just accident prone. You know, boys being boys and all that."

"Boys?" Jasi questioned sharply.

"Yeah. Allan and the twin. Mrs. Foreman brought them in at different times. I treated them both for minor burns and broken bones."

"Jesus!" she whispered in disbelief.

"Tell us about the other boy," Ben demanded, his eyes snapping with barely controlled fury.

"Well," Gibney began slowly. "Uh, TJ, I think his name was, he came in with a few broken bones. He broke his arm twice in one summer. Climbing trees, he told me."

The man's eyes grew hazy with guilt. "One time, I treated Ronnie, the sister, for burns to her arm. She told me it was from a curling iron but I admit, I did wonder what a six-year-old was doing curling her hair with a hot iron."

Jasi glared at him coldly. "So two boys and a girl were brutally abused by Charlotte Foreman, and you didn't report it."

She leaned closer so that her face was inches from his. "My, aren't you a hero!"

Gibney recoiled as her sarcasm sliced through the room.

"But I didn't know for sure," he moaned.

"Yeah," Ben scoffed dryly. "A trained professional had no clue."

"I swear to God! The foster mother and the kids told the same stories. Even if I suspected something—"

"It was your duty to report *anything* suspicious," Jasi seethed. "Why the hell wouldn't you have done that much for those kids?" She stared at him for a long time.

Gibney slumped in his chair, deflated. His bloodshot eyes flooded with guilt and a shameful tear trickled down one cheek.

In a small voice he said, "I didn't want my own past to be exposed. She would have told everyone what we had done to her."

Ben bolted from his seat. "What do you mean?"

"She came to us, before she was married. Said she was too young to have a baby."

Jasi gasped. "Charlotte Foreman's medical file stated she couldn't have children. There was extreme scarring of her uterus—a botched abortion."

"We performed the abortion on her," Gibney confessed. "But something went wrong. Norman had been drinking and when we were done, we realized she'd never be able to conceive. She had us both by the balls, after that."

Jasi fervently wished that she could grab those balls and—

"So you didn't report her abuse because you knew she'd report yours?" Ben hissed. "Instead, you allowed her to continuously abuse those kids. So much for your Hippocratic oath to do no harm."

Gibney dropped his head. He rocked slowly in his chair, both hands covering his face.

"It's over," he moaned.

"It's not over until we find the sick son-of-a-bitch who's responsible for three deaths," Jasi reminded him. "Oh, and Gibney? Don't go anywhere."

Martin Gibney's eyes widened with shock. "Agent McLellan! I did not kill anyone! I never wanted this to come out. I wanted Norman to resign…step down."

Jasi glared at the man. "You know anyone else who wanted Dr. Washburn dead?"

"I've told you everything—everything I know. I may be…many things, but I-I am not a murderer. I swear to you, both of you. I did not kill Mrs. Foreman and that little girl. And I did not kill Norman Washburn."

"You're free to go," she said scornfully to Gibney. "Just don't go far. We'll be checking out your story."

The man stumbled from the lounge with a nervous twitch over his shoulder. Red-faced, he lifted his chin proudly and made for his office.

Motioning Ben to follow, Jasi hurried from the hospital.

"What did you get from him?" she asked.

Ben's lip curled in disgust.

"He's telling the truth, Jasi. He feels immense guilt and shame. But the only blood on his hands comes from his involvement with the underground abortion clinic. Martin Gibney's no serial killer."

Stepping outside the hospital doors, they passed a young mother and father smiling proudly at their newborn son.

"Tell that to the Pro-Lifers," Jasi muttered.

It was after eight o'clock when she opened the door to her hotel room. Ben hovered outside the doorway. He was finishing a report on Gibney.

"I'll send it to Ops right away," he stated, remaining in the hall.

Jasi nodded and then entered the room.

Brandon and Natassia were still sifting through the crime scene files. Brandon looked up from the table and she could see the relief in his eyes. He had been worried about her. How strange.

She recalled Ben's words.

He's a good man. He won't betray you.

"Well?" Brandon asked, his voice tinged with hope.

"Washburn killed a prostitute after she gave birth to twins—*his*!" Jasi said abruptly. "He and Gibney were also responsible for Charlotte Foreman's botched abortion. She blackmailed them and used Gibney for her family GP. That way, she could hide the child abuse and neither doctor could report her."

Brandon's pale eyes searched hers. "Maybe Gibney's who we're after?"

Jasi shook her head. "He wanted Washburn to disappear, but he wanted him to go quietly."

"Plus Gibney's got an alibi. A room full of board members," Ben added, stepping into the room behind her.

The tension in the hotel room mounted. Thick and pervasive, it brought the entire investigation to a crashing halt. The four of them stood there, staring at each other.

Their list of suspects had just self-destructed.

The case was ice cold.

"Damn!" Jasi muttered, frustrated.

She grabbed a pop from the bar fridge and dropped into a chair. Then she stretched her head over the chair back.

"Natassia!" she called. "Got anything on the yellow fabric yet?"

Her partner's face beamed. "They just found it under the pilot's seat. It's been logged in and scheduled for testing. The ev-tech on duty promised we'd have the report first thing in the morning."

Jasi ordered up Washburn's file on the vid-wall.

Her vision at the cabin had proved that the doctor somehow knew the killer. *Or the killer knew him…*

"We've been acting on the assumption that Washburn *knew* his killer but didn't recognize him because of the mask," she said as a trickle of excitement slithered up her spine. "What if Washburn didn't really *know* him?"

Ben twisted a chair in one hand then straddled it, backward. "I'm not sure I understand."

"I think the killer is someone from Washburn's past. Someone Washburn hadn't seen in years. In your dream, Natassia, the abortion was key. And the babies in the incubators."

Jasi beckoned to Brandon with one hand. "Give me some ideas."

Brandon stretched his legs in front of him, crossed them at the ankles. "What if Natassia was seeing the *birth* of the twins? Not an abortion. Maybe the boy from Natassia's vision is related to the mother, the woman Washburn killed."

"Then the boy would be one of the twins," Natassia exclaimed.

Jasi tried to focus on their conversation but something kept bothering her. What was there about this whole mess that seemed so damned familiar?

"Data-com on!" she barked.

When the familiar welcome screen popped up, she said, "Newspaper search, Kelowna. August 1979, births."

She glanced at Natassia. "I need you to search the birth registries in the area."

While her partner busily hunted through the birth records, Jasi scrolled the headlines. Discovering that there were a substantial amount of listings, she decided to narrow down the field.

What could she add?

Two babies.

"Same parameters, *twins*," she commanded.

There were two newspaper headlines.

One read, *Oil Tycoon Strikes Oil with the Birth of Twins.* She quickly read the report but realized that the twins were safe and accounted for. The mother was a well-known lawyer, not a prostitute. And the twins were female.

When Jasi's eyes fell on the second headline, she gasped in shock. The alarm that had been persistently ringing in the back of her mind was now an earth shattering 10.5 on the Richter scale.

Oh, shit!

20

The headline read:

Newborn Twins Found Alive in Dumpster!

August 21, 1979 ~ Victoria, BC
Early this morning, an elderly transient woman discovered two newborn babies in a back alley Dumpster. The twins, a boy and a girl, are alive but severely dehydrated.

Gina McNeil, a homeless woman in her mid-eighties, was walking with two other women near the Ross Bay Cemetery at St. Charles Street and Fairfield Road when she heard the cries.

"She pulled them out of the garbage and wouldn't let anyone near them," one witness stated.

A local storeowner, Sharif Kabar, called the Victoria Police Department after seeing the two infants in McNeil's shopping cart.

"I did not believe my eyes," Kabar said. "The old lady with babies? I knew it was a mistake."

When emergency response teams arrived, the twins were barely conscious, unresponsive and lethargic. Victoria PD confronted McNeil and she handed over the twins, stating that she was on her way to the hospital.

"Gina McNeil climbed into a filthy Dumpster," Officer Dan Wilkins, first officer on the scene, told reporters. "She saved those babies. That makes her a hero in my eyes."

McNeil, the hero of the day, has led police authorities to the Dumpster, where a thin, bloody blanket was recovered. A thorough search of the Dumpster has revealed no other clues at this time. The identification of the newborns remains a mystery.

"We're hoping that the mother will come forward and claim them," Officer Wilkins stated.

The twins have been airlifted to the Children's Neonatal Intensive Care Unit at the Children's Hospital in Vancouver, where they remain in critical condition.

"Hypothermic and hypotonic," ER Dr. James Doucette confirmed. "After being exposed to the elements for about five hours, both babies are suffering from a multitude of symptoms— including decreased heart rate and circulation, dehydration, and they're overwhelmingly septic."

Dr. Doucette went on to say that it would be "miraculous if they survived without brain damage. The babies' prognosis is uncertain but, because of Miss McNeil's valiant and quick response, there is hope for the twins."

Victoria PD is requesting the public's help in locating the mother. She may also require medical attention.

If anyone knows her whereabouts…

Jasi's mind worked quickly, putting together pieces of the puzzle.

Twins in a Dumpster.

Cameron Prescott had told her a similar story. The reporter had also mentioned that she was a Leo. *August!* There was no doubt in Jasi's mind that Cameron and her brother were the very same twins that Washburn had tried to get rid of.

"I know who the babies are," she mumbled.

Three heads snapped in her direction.

She transferred the newspaper clipping to the vid-wall, then straddled the chair beside Ben. Indicating the screen, she repeated Cameron's story about being abandoned at birth.

"All this time we were focusing on Natassia's vision, we forgot about the money she saw in her hands. And Natassia heard a woman's voice say '*I'll take care of everything*'."

She paused, gathering her thoughts. "Washburn tried to get rid of Cameron and her brother by tossing them in the Dumpster. If the Dumpster had made it to the dump, the babies would have died. That's what the good old doctor wanted. To kill them. Dispose of his infidelity."

"But someone found them," Brandon pointed out. "Washburn was afraid the police would get wind of his involvement so he paid Charlotte Foreman to keep his *bastards* hidden from the public."

"Yeah, but Norman Washburn was the real bastard," Jasi seethed.

Reading the file on the wall, she smiled bitterly. "He paid the foster mother to keep Cameron and her brother away from some other well-meaning foster parent, someone who might try to discover the identity of the birth parents."

"But Jasi, no one else knew they were Washburn's," Brandon stated.

"Except Gibney," Ben reminded him.

Brandon's head dipped in a nod. "So Gibney obviously knew that Washburn had dumped them and left them to die. He would have read that in the papers. So why didn't Gibney tell you?"

"He's petrified," Ben frowned. "Gibney's already looking at charges of accessory to murder in the death of the prostitute. He didn't want to add two counts accessory to attempted murder for the twins."

Folding her arms across her chest, Jasi listened while pacing the room. Furious, she muttered, "Martin Gibney is just as guilty as Washburn."

"*And* Charlotte Foreman," she heard Natassia say behind her.

Brandon's blue eyes followed her. "Maybe the brother, Ronald, did it."

Jasi shook her head. "No, Ronald Jones drowned when he was a kid. An accidental death. In the river behind the house."

"What else do we have?"

"We have the twins," she acknowledged. "They're the main connection in both cases. But who would want to kill for them?"

Brandon stared at her, hard. "Ronald is dead, Jasi. That only leaves one other person with motive, means...and opportunity."

Stunned, her head jerked toward him.

"Cameron Prescott?"

"She could be the one we're after," he suggested softly.

"But I sensed a male mind, not female," she protested, dropping onto the bed. "And Natassia saw a young man in a yellow jacket."

Natassia raised her hands, then dropped them in her lap. "I don't know, Jasi."

"She doesn't fit your profile, Ben," she argued, rolling over on her side, one hand propped beneath her head.

Ben shrugged. "Theoretically, Cameron is the *perfect* suspect. Washburn abandoned her, Foreman abused her and her twin brother drowned while in Charlotte Foreman's care. And the low voice you heard in your vision? You said yourself that her throat had been damaged. Revenge is a deadly thing, Jasi. We can't rule her out."

"But, Ben—"

He gave her an apologetic look. "My profile is based on commonalities. Arsonists *are* predominantly male but not always."

Brandon settled beside her on the edge of the bed.

"Ben's right," he remarked softly. "Women commit about ten to eighteen percent of all arson crimes, Jasi. I've apprehended a few myself. And most of them reported abusive adult relationships or childhood abuse."

Jasi frowned, remembering the scars on the reporter's arms. "Cameron had cigarette burns on her arms...a childhood injury, she told me."

Brandon lowered his voice. "The evidence is all there."

She shook her head. "It can't be her. I would have sensed something."

"Hey, Jasi?" Natassia interrupted softly. "I know what happened to her brother."

Jasi sat up hastily. "What?"

"Ronald Jones went swimming with a foster brother in the river out back. The brother told police that Ronald went too far into the water and was swept downstream by the current. Search and Rescue found some of Ronald's clothing covered in blood, and a running shoe, but they couldn't recover his body."

Brandon turned to Natassia. "How'd you come up with all that?"

"I'm psychic. Remember?" Natassia grinned. "Actually, while you were all talking I ran a search through the newspapers. After the twins' arrival at Vancouver General, they were placed into Child Protective Services. I just followed the trail from there."

"But how'd you get into the CPS records?" Brandon asked, surprised.

Jasi locked her eyes on his. "She hacked in, Brandon. Natassia's good at that." She smiled at Natassia and was rewarded with a wide, proud grin.

"The kid who went swimming with Ronald. I think that was Baker," Jasi suggested. "Maybe he can tell us something about Cameron."

Ben connected with Baker's message system. "Baker's not picking up. I'll leave him a message." He left an urgent message telling Baker to call right away, and then he hung up.

Jasi flopped in the chair beside Natassia and mulled over the sudden change of direction their investigation had taken. How could she have known that when she sat at *Bits & Bytes* drinking coffee with Cameron Prescott, she had been sitting across from a serial killer?

I should have known!

Shit!

How was she supposed to bring Cameron in? Yeah, some of the evidence pointed to her, but some of it just didn't add up. How did a woman her size drag a heavy man like Washburn across the cabin floor? How could she have watched while three people burned to death?

How could she have murdered a little girl?

Jasi leaned forward in her chair, her hands clasped tightly between her knees.

"When I read the crime scene at Washburn's cabin, I experienced the killer's rage. But at Charlotte Foreman's I sensed remorse—regret. The killer knew that the child was being released from something worse than death."

A horrible thought flickered in her mind. Cameron would have seen the death of Samantha Davis as a mercy killing.

When Jasi raised her eyes, she realized Ben had had the same thought.

"We'll have to bring her in, Jasi," he warned pensively.

"I know," she whispered softly. "Just remember, innocent until proven guilty, Ben. I need some air."

I need to escape…to think.

She stepped outside on the balcony deck and abandoned herself to the night sky. Dusk was settling over Kelowna. And with the dimming light, Jasi sensed that they were running out of time. She knew in her heart that the killer would strike again.

The killer…Cameron.

Staring out over the city rooftops, Jasi tried to make sense of it all. If Ben and Brandon were right then Cameron Prescott was a violent murderer. The woman she had met had hardly seemed capable of murder. Jasi had liked Cameron. Now all the evidence linked Cameron Prescott to three murders.

Was she a cold-blooded killer?

"Can we place her at or near the Foreman scene?" she called out from the doorway.

"Yes," Natassia answered. "She was in Victoria the day of Foreman's murder covering the backlash from the Parliament case."

Jasi kneaded her pounding forehead. A headache had developed, tiny pinpricks stabbing her eyes. She leaned forward and rested her head against the cold glass, closing her eyes for a moment.

"Cameron Prescott was also here in Kelowna the night of Washburn's murder," she heard herself say. "She was covering Baker's campaign."

Her own gullibility enraged her. She prided herself on being able to read people. Not in a psychic way, just purely intuition. And usually her intuition was correct. Although it had let her down before on at least one occasion.

How could I have been so wrong about you, Cameron?

Jasi flopped on the bed. Raising one arm, she covered her eyes, grateful for the cool darkness. The last thing she needed was a migraine.

She thought about Cameron Prescott. The evidence against her was convincing. The reporter had been near both crime scenes. Fire could have been a way to purge herself of past demons.

Jasi sighed. It seemed impossible to believe. But she had been fooled before, tricked into believing someone was a friend. That mistake had almost resulted in Ben's death.

She glanced at Brandon.

Perhaps her intuition had been blocked by other emotions—like desire. Her face burned at the thought. She needed to concentrate on the case and forget about Brandon Walsh. Time to focus on the evidence that was pointing to Cameron Prescott. If they rushed this and Cameron was innocent, her career as a reporter would be over. But if she was guilty…

"I'm not thoroughly convinced it's Cameron," Jasi admitted. "Let me tie up a few loose ends, Ben. Not everything fits her. I find it hard to believe she carried Washburn's dead weight into the cabin. And what about the boot prints we found?"

Ben said nothing.

"Just give me until the morning," she sighed.

"Okay," he agreed. "Cameron doesn't know we're on to her. Tomorrow I'll contact Divine and have him issue an arrest warrant for her first thing in the morning. Right now, we all need some food and a good night's rest."

Natassia agreed readily but Jasi shook her head. "I'm not hungry. I'm staying here to review the files."

Ben opened his mouth to argue.

"It's okay," she assured him. "I'm fine."

She opened the door to the hallway and waited expectantly. Natassia followed Ben through the doorway, while Brandon hung back.

"Go!" Jasi snapped. "I don't need you here, Walsh."

Without waiting for a reply, she turned and disappeared into the bathroom. Catching her reflection in the mirror, she made a face.

"Liar!"

21

Brandon felt like a bug trapped under a microscope.

In the hallway, Agent Roberts examined him with a strange, penetrating look. One hand held the door ajar while Natassia waited at the far end, casting curious glances in their direction.

Roberts grabbed him. "Hold on a minute, Walsh."

Suspiciously eyeing the ungloved hand that detained him, Brandon sucked in a breath. "What?"

The man grinned. "You're all right, Walsh."

"Yeah, I know," Brandon grinned back, releasing the air trapped in his lungs. "You reading me again, Agent Roberts?"

Roberts quickly took his hand from Brandon's arm.

"I'm not sure what's up with Jasi," he admitted, nudging his head toward the closed door. "But she needs someone to keep an eye on her."

Brandon agreed, bewildered that Roberts was encouraging him. "Maybe I'll stay behind, order up some room service."

"If you don't mind," Roberts replied wryly.

He released the door and Brandon grabbed it quickly.

"Not at all."

"I didn't think so," Roberts chuckled, and with a nod, he headed for the elevator. "Natassia won't be back tonight."

When Brandon entered Jasi's hotel room, he felt awkward—like a teenager sneaking into the girl's dorm. His heart skipped a beat at the thought that he would be alone with Jasi.

Finally.

Locking the door behind him, he took a deep breath and squinted into the darkness. The lights had been dimmed. Probably to ease Jasi's headache, he reasoned.

He allowed his eyes to adjust, then scoured the room.

It was empty.

Feeling a slight breeze, he strode over to the balcony. The doors were open and the sheers billowed softly.

When he peered outside, he spotted her.

Jasi stood on the balcony, wearing a thick aqua-colored robe. She had her back to him. She was lost in thought, watching the sun slowly dip over the horizon. The sky was flame-red, and the sun's rays painted her hair with streaks of fire.

For a moment, Brandon couldn't breathe. He stepped up behind her, about to call her name, when she spoke.

"Why did you come back, Brandon?"

Her voice was weary.

"Sorry," he said ruefully, although he was unsure of why he was apologizing.

He leaned against the sliding door. "You okay?"

She turned slowly, her green eyes drifting over him, nervous and afraid.

"What are you doing here? I thought you were going for supper with Natassia and Ben."

He shrugged, folding his arms across his chest. "I'm not that hungry either. And I thought you could use some company."

Jasi raised one brow, eyeing him disdainfully.

"Okay, I know," he chuckled softly. "I'm not your favorite company. But damn it, lady, I'm all you've got."

She released a ragged breath. "I guess you'll have to do then."

Brandon was surprised. He had expected more of a fight from her.

"This thing with Cameron Prescott has really thrown you, hasn't it?" he asked, stepping closer.

He couldn't resist sliding his hands along her arms.

Jasi froze at his touch, then lowered her head and sighed.

When he lifted her chin, she twisted away.

"You don't understand, Brandon! I was in the killer's mind. *Cameron's* mind! I saw everything she did. I felt every ounce of hatred. Every evil…murderous…thought."

Turning her back on him, Jasi gripped the rails of the balcony, her voice bitingly soft. "And then I had coffee with her. I never suspected she could be a killer."

"Why do you think that is?"

"I'll tell you why," Jasi muttered bitterly. "Because I was too busy thinking about you! I wasn't focussed. Instead, I told her things—things I don't normally tell people I've just met."

She seemed so fragile and lost that he barely registered what she had said about him.

"You told her you were a PSI?"

"No, not that," Jasi huffed, spinning around to face him. "Other things. About my family—personal things. I saw her as a…friend."

Confused, Brandon looked at her, reached for her. "But that's normal, isn't it, to confide in a friend?"

She pushed his hand away. "It's not normal for me. I'm not like everyone else. I can't have *normal* relationships."

Instinctively he wrapped his arms around her. He could feel her resistance as she struggled against him.

"It's okay, Jasi," he murmured in her ear. "Relax."

Brandon knew the moment she gave up fighting him. He savored the rapid beating of her heart echoing against his hand. Holding her tightly reminded him of the night before. Too much wine had resulted in Jasi sliding up to him, whispering suggestively in his ear.

Then she had passed out.

He deserved a medal for his control. Any other man would have taken what she had so willingly offered, but Brandon didn't want her that way.

But I want her now. Right here, right now.

"Jasi?" he whispered hoarsely, staring into the depths of her emerald eyes.

He smiled wickedly as she anxiously peered down over her shoulder. Jasi's back was against the rail of the balcony, trapped. There was nowhere to go.

Except down. And it was too far to jump.

He shifted closer. "What are you so afraid of?"

"Lemmings," she murmured softly, her eyes capturing his.

Her moist lips parted slightly and he knew he had to taste her. He almost lost control when her tongue slid nervously across her lips.

Damn!

Brandon slid his hands beneath her hair, caressing her face with his fingers. His thumbs gently traced her soft lips and his body leaned in toward hers.

And then he lowered his head.

"I want you," he groaned, before his mouth clamped down on hers.

There was a moment of shock when Jasi responded to his kiss. Her soft mouth slowly opened and invited him in.

The heat was searing and raw, and it was all he could do to restrain himself and not take her right there on the balcony.

"I'm not going to let you jump off any cliff," he promised against her lips.

His arms circled her, tightening. Then he devoured her face, her eyelids, and the long line of her sensuous throat. His tongue traced a salty path along the inside of her neck, down across her shoulder where he bit gently into her skin.

He slowly nudged her robe aside, his fingers grazing over smooth, delicate warm skin. She was naked, shivering beneath the robe. He caressed her, his fingers spanning under her breasts, lifting them, while soft moans erupted from the back of her throat.

An aching hunger arose and he felt its gnawing urgency.

Brandon was lost, starved for her touch.

When he felt Jasi trembling, he deepened his kiss, entwining his tongue with hers. He gasped when her hands fluttered against his chest and the buttons of his shirt began opening, one by one. Seconds later, his feverish flesh made contact with hers, and he choked back a groan as a jolt of electricity sizzled along his stomach, down into his groin.

"I want you, Jasi," he groaned, intrigued by her, intoxicated with wanting her.

His mouth crushed down, hard and ravenous, and he dragged her back into the room. He held her tightly, unwilling to let her go.

"I want you now."

Lost in her eyes, he recognized desire.

And fear.

Brandon kissed her again—soft, tender nibbles.

Without taking his lips from hers, he stumbled backward into the room, pulling her with him until they bumped into the wall near the door to the hallway.

Sliding his hands to the collar of her robe, he peeled it back over her shoulders, baring her breasts, and pinned her against the door. Then he plunged into the depths of her awaiting mouth, half-mad from wanting her.

"This is heaven," he whispered.

"Brandon, this is...crazy."

Her lips contradicted her as they sought his.

"I'm crazy," he muttered. "About you."

"Wait!" she begged breathlessly, pulling back.

He didn't want to wait.

She watched him with eyes so green that he was reminded of the sea. A man could drown in those eyes, he thought.

I'm drowning.

He roughly stretched her hands above her head and held her there, captive. His other hand had a mind of its own. It skimmed down the side of her body, lightly touching every hot, trembling curve.

"I'm on fire, Jasi," he groaned, his fingers stroking her ribs, her waist...lower.

Then he fastened on her eager and willing mouth.

"We can't," she gasped against his lips.

"Yes, we can," Brandon whispered. "We've got all night, Jasi. We can take our time, go slow. We've got all the time in the world."

When she abruptly pulled away, he realized too late, that he had said the wrong thing.

"No!" she panted, ducking under his arm. "*Jesus!* We can't do this, Brandon!"

She stared at him, motionless and wide-eyed. "Oh my God! What was I thinking?" Her voice was breathless, filled with panic.

Confused, he stepped toward her. "What do you mean, Jasi? You want this as much as I do."

"It doesn't matter what I want," she answered harshly. "You and I? All we are is *business*. Don't you—"

His lips seared hers, stealing the oxygen from her, halting her angry words.

Jasi let out a ragged cry. *"Stop…"*

His eyes found hers. "Then you'd better say *please*, Agent McLellan."

Brandon dropped his head and his hungry mouth branded her.

Lost in the heat of passion, Jasi fought to regain a grip on reality. It was a fragile thread that held her sanity intact. With her past history, she knew it was inevitable—the thread would break…eventually.

"Please, Brandon."

She heard him under his breath. Then his hands immediately dropped to his side.

She exhaled slowly, relieved.

Hauling the robe up around her shoulders, she remained silent, uncertain of what to say. She knew she was being unfair to him. But hell! Life was unfair.

Self-loathing made her turn away.

"I'm sorry. It's late. You have to leave."

Before I do something we will both regret.

Frustrated, Brandon grabbed her arm and spun her around. "Why won't you trust me?"

"Trust?" she hissed. "How can I trust you, Brandon? I don't really know you."

"Then get to know me," he said bluntly.

Jasi wanted to tell him what had happened to the last man she had gotten to *know*. But it was too dangerous—for both of them.

You have to end it, Jasi!

"Listen, Brandon. After this case is over, you're going to go back to your job and I'm going to go back to mine. We won't see each other again. I don't need that in my life."

"You're afraid, Jasi. Our jobs? Those are just complications and—"

"And I don't *need* complications," she interrupted, bitterness and a trace of regret edging her voice.

"We could make this work," Brandon insisted, running a hand through her hair.

For a moment, she almost believed him.

Then, shaking her head, she said, "No, we can't. *I* can't."

He stepped away from her, giving her a hard, penetrating look.

"So you want to ignore what just happened between us?" His voice was sharp, bitter.

"Brandon! There's *nothing* between us! There can't be! Don't you get it?"

Jasi felt her annoyance mounting. Why wouldn't he listen to her? She had to make him see that nothing could happen between them.

Even if she wanted it to.

She watched him clench his teeth.

"We're still working this case together, Jasi. I won't leave until it's over."

"I know," she replied softly.

She watched him walk to the door. Her heart was pounding rapidly, but this time not from sexual passion.

What was it about Brandon Walsh that made her blood boil with frustration…and desire? What was there about the man that made her lungs ache to scream his name? That made other parts of her body ache?

"What did you say to me after I kissed you the first time?" he asked suddenly, pausing at the door.

She went still.

"When I promised that I wouldn't let you jump off a cliff," he prodded. "You whispered something in my ear."

She shivered slightly and when she spoke her voice was dull, dead. "I said *'too late'*."

Too late. Those two words strangled her.

Brandon gave her a piercing stare.

A second later he was gone.

Alone, Jasi felt like someone had kicked her in the stomach. Her eyes blurred with unshed tears.

Were they for Brandon—or for her?

Her past history with men and relationships in general gripped her like a noose around her neck, strangling every breath of hope, every sign of life that kept her human. But worse than that was her acceptance of that noose. It was almost as if she had carefully woven each strand, braided each rope—created the noose from her very existence.

A trail of tears escaped down her cheek and she batted at them angrily.

"Stop wanting something you can't have, Jasmine McLellan!" she moaned.

Caring for Brandon Walsh would only prove to be dangerous to her. She knew that. It was her curse! The one she carried with her everywhere she went. The last man she loved was lying at the bottom of the ocean somewhere. Her job had killed him.

No! She was better off alone, focussing her attention on capturing serial killers. And living with the dead.

But how do I turn off these emotions?

Push them away and solve the case, came the answer.

Gathering her inner strength, she took a deep breath, meditating on her heartbeat. Confident that she could maintain her composure, she hailed Ben on his data-com.

"I'll meet you downstairs tomorrow at eight," she said firmly. "Tell Natassia I'm going to bed."

"Jasi, are you okay?" Ben's voice sounded hesitant, worried.

"I'm fine. I'll see you in the morning."

"Uh, okay then. Is Brandon still—"

Click.

Jasi abruptly ended the call.

She perched on the edge of the bed, staring at the silent data-com in her hands. She didn't want to answer Ben's questions. Or talk about Brandon.

What she wanted was to find the serial arsonist. And if that turned out to be Cameron...

I am a professional. Nothing will stand in my way.

Not even Cameron Prescott.

Or Brandon Walsh.

Taking a deep breath, she activated his number.

"Hey, it's me," she said hastily. "We're meeting downstairs tomorrow. Eight o'clock sharp."

"Fine," came his cool reply.

"Brandon? I-I'm sorry," she whispered.

There was an unbearable silence on the other end.

For a moment, Jasi thought he had hung up. When he finally spoke, his voice sounded tired, beaten.

"So am I, Jasi."

Then the data-com died—and a part of her died with it.

22

Someone called to her, plucking her from a thick fog of sleep. Jasi raised her head from the pillow—disoriented. All she wanted to do was sink back into the warmth of her bed but the voice kept nattering at her, invading her pleasant dreams.

"Jasi! Wake up!"

"Natassia?" she groaned, opening her eyes cautiously.

The shadowed blackness of the room wavered suddenly, a shift in time and space. Her hand crept from beneath the blankets, reaching for the Beretta she had tucked between the mattresses.

"Natassia, is that you?" she called out, immediately alert.

From the dark, she heard Brandon's voice, dry and full of sarcasm. "Do I sound like Natassia?"

She heard a whisper of footsteps as he moved closer. Then the mattress dipped suddenly.

"Iziot!" she heard him mutter in irritation.

She wasn't sure if he was referring to her or himself.

Rolling over, she caught the vague shape of Brandon's arm stretching past her head. Suddenly the lamp beside the bed flashed, blinding her. She squinted and blinked until her vision cleared.

He was sitting on the edge of her bed.

She glanced at her watch.

It was just after midnight. She had only been asleep for an hour.

"Shit!" she muttered. "What are you doing here? And why are you whispering?"

He flicked his head at Natassia's empty bed. "I thought she was here and I didn't want either of you to clobber me."

Jasi eyed him suspiciously, shifting her position.

"How'd you get in?"

He threw her a leering grin. "Someone from housekeeping was in the hall checking the ice machine. I told him that I locked myself out and that a gorgeous redhead waited in bed for me...naked."

"I was asleep," she muttered dryly.

She sat up quickly and the blanket fell to her hips, exposing a thin t-shirt. "And as you can see, I'm not naked."

His searing eyes drifted slowly, leisurely, down her body. Then he caught sight of the pistol barrel pointed in his direction.

"Jasi, for crying out loud!" he hissed. "Put that thing away before it goes off!"

She gave a muffled snort, and then her gaze rested on the gun that was leveled at his groin.

"I *do* know how to use this thing, you know. I'm a highly trained CFBI agent, in case you've forgotten. This is an M9 Beretta. Fifteen rounds, double-action semiautomatic. It's lightweight."

She paused, admiring the gun in her hands and stroking it lovingly. Then she looked him dead in the eye.

"And lethal. I can take out a rat at fifty meters."

She held his gaze, unwavering.

"Fine, but I'm not a rat," he mumbled resentfully.

Her brow arched in skepticism and she pursed her lips.

He chuckled nervously. "Come on, Jasi. Point it somewhere else. I'd like to keep what you're aiming at."

"Then you'd better say *please*." She smiled mockingly.

"Please," he said between clenched teeth.

Jasi noticed Brandon began to breathe again when she lowered the Beretta and placed it on the nightstand.

"Are you going to tell me why you're sneaking around my room in the middle of the night?"

She glared at him, uneasy and distrustful. "And you better not tell me you're here to finish what you started."

"What *we* started," he grumbled belligerently.

"What?" She spared him a look, then reached for the robe she had dropped on the floor.

Brandon stood and paced nervously. "Nothing."

Unfolding herself from the tangle of sheets, she elbowed past him and flicked on the lamp at the table.

"Well? Why are you here, Walsh?"

"I couldn't sleep," he began. "I've been thinking about the case—about Cameron Prescott."

"You could have discussed your thoughts with Ben instead of—"

"I couldn't get through to Ben," he cut in. "His data-com is on privacy mode."

They both turned toward Natassia's empty bed.

Then Brandon faced her.

His expression was serious. "I don't think Cameron's finished. And I think I know who her next target is."

"Brandon," she said, straightening. "I still have doubts about Cameron's involvement."

Brandon reached for her hand.

"Don't," she warned him, pulling away.

Grabbing her hand, he forced something smooth and sleek into her palm.

"What's this?"

She opened her hand slowly.

In her palm was a Gemini lighter. "Gemini…the sign of the twins." Her head jerked upward. "Oh, shit. It was there all along. The goddamn clue was right in front of me!"

"You received one in the mail almost two months ago, didn't you?" he prodded.

"Yes."

Brandon gripped her shoulders lightly. "*Before* Charlotte Foreman was murdered. Jasi, each lighter is a *warning*. She drops the lighter to indicate that someone is next on her list. She's warning us that there's another victim."

Jasi gaped at him blankly.

"Martin Gibney," he explained.

"Gibney?"

"Cameron Prescott wants revenge. Gibney allowed the child abuse to continue and he was directly involved in her mother's death."

Jasi realized he made sense. There was something *right* about what he was saying.

Martin Gibney and Norman Washburn were the two doctors responsible for the death of the prostitute. Cameron and Ronald's mother. Cameron would be relentless in her pursuit for justice. Revenge for her mother's death, retaliation for the constant abuse both she and her brother had suffered at the hands of Charlotte Foreman, and retribution for her brother's subsequent drowning.

Jasi remembered her vision.

The killer had crossed off a name…the *middle* name.

Martin Gibney *was* next.

"We have to stop her, Brandon." She scurried toward the dresser and started to remove her robe before realizing that he still watched her.

Flicking her head, she ordered him to turn away.

"You sure?" he asked with a devilish smile.

Annoyed, she waited impatiently with her hands on her hips. As soon as he turned around, Jasi peeled off the robe and stripped naked. Then she slipped into fresh panties and a pair of jeans.

"Have you warned him?" she asked.

"I, uh, called his house," Brandon stammered, still facing the balcony.

Bending over to reach into a drawer for a clean t-shirt, she heard a sharp hissing sound. She spun around, holding the t-shirt tightly in front of her, and eyed him suspiciously.

Brandon stood motionless, his back still turned to her. Her eyes were drawn to his well-defined arms and the tight black jeans. She sucked in a breath and her heart skipped a beat. There was something about Brandon Walsh that was just so damned sexy.

This is insane, she thought, mentally slapping herself.

"Give me another minute!" she blurted.

Brandon cleared his throat nervously.

Realizing that he could turn around any moment, Jasi quickly fastened her bra and slipped into the t-shirt. Over it, she strapped on a lightweight Kevlar vest. It was black with fluorescent orange letters stenciled across the front and back. *CFBI.*

"Okay, you can turn around now."

Brandon hesitantly faced her, watching her every move. There was admiration in his eyes…and something else. Desire.

"D-did you talk to Gibney?" she stuttered.

He nodded. "His wife answered the phone. She said Allan Baker called an hour ago and asked to speak to him."

"And?" she prompted anxiously.

"*And*...about ten minutes ago, Gibney took off. To meet Baker. His wife has no idea where he went, or why. But Lydia did say one thing."

"What?"

"She said Allan Baker didn't sound like himself. He was impersonal, distant. She thinks he sounded scared."

Jasi locked onto Brandon's pale blue eyes. "I think Cameron wants to kill two birds with one stone, so to speak. She's after Baker too."

"You think she's jealous of him?" he asked her.

"Cameron interviewed Baker on many occasions. She knows that he would never be a loving half-brother. He's too much like his father. Maybe she holds him responsible. After all, Baker has the life she deserved. And Gibney helped take it from her."

"And now she has them both," Brandon murmured.

Jasi cursed. Where would Cameron take Baker and Gibney at this time of night?

She caught sight of the moonlit sky through the glass door, and she gasped. Moving purposefully toward the balcony, she stopped dead in her tracks. With the two lamps casting a golden light across the room behind her, she could see Brandon's reflection in the glass of the door—perfectly. In fact, she could see everything.

Everything!

Mortified, she whirled around, crossing her arms defensively over her chest. She gaped at him, indignant and pissed off at his brashness.

At least he had the decency to look guilty. He reminded Jasi of a boy caught with his hand in the cookie jar.

But damn it, these were her cookies!

"Nice view, Walsh?" she sneered, her eyes narrowing.

"Very nice," he quipped smoothly.

Ignoring him, she grabbed her data-com from the nightstand and activated it. "License plate search, Martin Gibney, 103 Dremner Boulevard, Kelowna."

When a list of Gibney's license plates showed up on the monitor, she noticed one was in motion. "GPS search, license 1DOC739."

The green light on the monitor flickered while the satellite circuits busily navigated through the city. A few seconds later the GPS locked on its target.

"He's heading north on Highway 97," she stated.

"Loon Lake is up there."

She groaned. "So is Washburn's cabin. Or what's left of it. Did you try Baker or Gibney on their cell phones?"

"Yeah, they're not answering. If we hurry, we might be able to catch up to Gibney. He's only got maybe fifteen on us."

She leaned over, grabbed her hair and pulled it into a ponytail. Securing it with a black elastic band, she said, "Maybe we'll get lucky and he'll have to stop for gas."

"Maybe he'll run out of gas," Brandon replied wryly. "That would be lucky for him."

Jasi strode over to the closet, then strapped on a shoulder harness for her gun. Then she pulled a short black jacket over top, zipped it halfway and tucked her data-com into a pocket.

"Why do you think Ben isn't answering his 'com?" she mused.

Brandon eyed her candidly, then flicked his head toward Natassia's bed.

"Oh," Jasi blushed, tucking the Beretta into her holster.

When she looked up again, his eyes pulsed with worry.

"I never realized you carried a weapon," he admitted.

She shrugged. "There's a lot about me you don't know."

Ignoring Brandon's wicked grin and leering eyes, Jasi let out an indignant hiss. "I'm a CFBI agent, for Christ's sake! I can work other cases—not just arsons. As a PSI, I don't just read fires and let someone else bring the bastards in. I bring in my own."

He grinned slyly. "So you always get your man?"

She resented his attitude and scowled. "Almost always."

There was a moment of silence, and then she opened the door. "Come on! Let's get Natassia and Ben."

Crossing the hallway, she rapped loudly on Ben's room. No answer. Brandon nudged her aside and began pounding on the door, hollering Ben's name.

Suddenly a bald, sweaty man in a dirty tank top poked his head out from a room across the hall. "Hey! Shut the hell up!" The man's eyes were inflamed—bloodshot.

Jasi mumbled an apology, barely looking at him.

"She's CFBI," Brandon explained with a flick of his head in Jasi's direction.

The man took an unsteady step forward, jabbing a beefy finger threateningly in the air. "I don't give a shit *who* she—"

He broke off, then stammered, "CFBI, d-did you s-say?"

Jasi growled when she recognized Albert Hawkins, the manager of Kel-Cabs. When she marched toward him, Hawkins swore and slammed the door.

Brandon flicked his head. "Maybe I should—"

"Come on, Walsh," she ordered, intercepting him. "We don't have time for him now. I have to go back to my room, pick up a few things."

Long strides took her back to her hotel room. She wrenched the closet door open, reached inside and seized a black tote bag. Opening it, she yanked out two extra clips for the Beretta, dropping them into a pocket on the front of her jacket. Then she grabbed two mini-cans of *OxyBlast* and her nosepiece.

"I never know what I'll need," she explained when she caught him studying her. "We definitely need a ride though."

Brandon grinned. "A rental is waiting downstairs for us."

She flashed him a surprised look. "Hmmm, a man who thinks ahead." She glanced at her watch. "Shit! It's after midnight. Where the hell are Ben and Natassia? And why aren't they answering their 'coms?"

"What do you want to do?" Brandon asked hesitantly.

Frustrated, she chewed her bottom lip. "I have no idea how long they'll be. We have to get to Gibney and Baker—before Cameron does."

Stepping out into the hallway, they made their way toward the elevator. Inside, Jasi recorded messages for both Ben and Natassia. She wanted to contact Divine, maybe have him pick up the arrest warrant for Cameron Prescott. But then she'd have to explain how two of his best agents were currently unavailable.

Glancing at Brandon, Jasi was relieved. He may not be a gun-toting CFBI agent, but he was strong and intelligent. He also knew arsonists.

Five minutes later, they were seated in a spacious Infiniti FX75 SUV.

"When you said *rental* I was thinking more along the lines of a nice little compact," Jasi complained as they screeched out of the hotel parking lot.

"Bigger is better," he winked, then grinned.

Clenching her hands in her lap, Jasi stared straight ahead, determined to ignore his innuendo. Her imagination, however, had other plans.

"Jesus, Walsh!" she snapped. "I'd like to get there in one piece, thank you."

Brandon laughed lightly as he wove the silver SUV in and out of traffic. "Relax, Jasi. I know what I'm doing."

It wasn't so much what he was doing that had her all hot and bothered. It was what the man was *capable* of doing. Being in close confinement with him made her palms sweat. Watching his strong hands shifting gears with ease brought dangerous thoughts to her mind.

Gripping the door handle tightly, her heart stopped beating when they took an off-ramp and headed for the highway. Somewhere between the vans and trucks loaded with camping gear, she felt the familiar pitter-patter of her heartbeat, kicking itself into high gear. While they dodged through unusually heavy traffic, she wondered whether everyone in Kelowna was escaping something.

Maybe they knew something she didn't.

Jasi pressed the glow-light on her watch. They were making good time. Perhaps there was a chance that they would catch Gibney after all—before he made it to Washburn's property.

Peeking from beneath her lashes, she examined Brandon's profile. Part of her was desperate to take the plunge, dive right into a relationship with him. But the controlled agent in her told her it wouldn't work out. Long distance relationships never did.

Neither did relationships for a Pyro-Psychic.

At least not *this* Pyro-Psychic, she thought resentfully.

Fully alert and running on adrenaline, Jasi thought of Cameron Prescott. Child abuse left scars and often they were permanent. But some scars were below the surface, invisible to the human eye.

Jasi thought Cameron had been lucky. The reporter had escaped while her twin brother had been forced to endure more abuse, until he died. But perhaps Ronald Jones' death hadn't been accidental. For all anyone knew, Charlotte Foreman could have murdered him. Maybe she had gone too far.

Leaning her elbow against the window, Jasi rested her chin in her hand and watched the passing shadows. The headlights of the SUV bounced off the green board of a highway sign. Loon Lake was about twenty minutes away.

"There's no sign of Gibney's vehicle," she murmured uneasily.

"We're almost there," Brandon promised.

A few seconds later, he swore and the SUV lurched. In front of them, a line of twenty or so vehicles sat stationary. A chemical truck slanted sideways across the middle of the road. Nearing the truck, Jasi could see that one of its back tires had blown. Thankfully, it had not rolled over or spilled its load.

"Damn it!" she swore. "We've got to get through!"

Brandon's eyes drifted to hers. Then he winked. Shifting gears, he hauled on the steering wheel and the car slid precariously close to the right shoulder.

"Jesus, Walsh!" she shrieked, fisting her seat belt with both hands.

"Hold on," he grinned.

The SUV dipped, sending Jasi crashing into the door. Gripping the left side of the seat, she held on while her right hand white-knuckled the door handle.

"Sorry," he apologized contritely.

Sucking in a gasp, she examined the vehicles they passed while Brandon carefully navigated between stressed out travelers. One man, probably in his eighties, flipped them *the bird*. Jasi leaned across Brandon and flashed her badge at the old guy. The man's hand disappeared in a flash.

"We're gonna make it, Jasi."

They had made it by the tenth car—the halfway mark.

Brandon thumped on the horn when someone veered out too far on the right. A rusty station wagon rattled out of the way and they gathered speed as they passed the chemical truck.

When they finally cleared the stalled traffic, Jasi checked her watch again. It was after one in the morning. They had lost some time. Martin Gibney had been on his own for over forty-five minutes. Not alone, she reminded herself. Cameron and Baker would be there too. She was sure of it. Baker had probably been forced to call from the cabin.

"We have to hurry, Brandon," she urged. "I have a very bad feeling."

Brandon cranked the wheel and headed east on Beaver Lake Road, following it past Doreen Lake. A few minutes later, he geared down and turned south onto a loose gravel road, pitted with craters. Instantly they were plunged into a dense forest. Tall, looming trees blocked most of the moonlight and made it difficult to see the road ahead.

A minute later, they came to a large wooden post with a dull light on top. A black and white sign hung from raw rope chains.

Loon Lake.

With no street lamps to guide them, Brandon slowed the SUV. Just ahead, Jasi could make out the shadows of unlit chalets and a few log homes. Interspersed were cabins with warm lights glowing from inside.

Suddenly Jasi's data-com chirped insistently.

"Ben!" she chided, activating the speaker so Brandon could hear. "Where were you two?"

"Sorry, Jasi. We went dancing—"

"Dancing?" she sputtered. Natassia and Ben, two of the CFBI's most dedicated agents went dancing?

"I know," Ben said sheepishly. "But we're on our way. We're almost to Beaver Lake Road. We tried you earlier but there was too much interference. We couldn't get through."

"The reception here is bad," Brandon agreed. "By the way, we went past a chemical truck with a flat. Just before the turn-off to the lake. We had to take the shoulder."

"Okay. We're right behind you."

Relieved, Jasi ended the call.

Brandon slowed as they arrived at the fork in the road.

"Take a right here," she reminded him.

She pressed her face against the window, gazing up at the sliver of moon. The stars glittered in the clear black sky, thousands of tiny lights dancing above her—unlike

Vancouver where the brilliant city lights obliterated most of the night sky.

As Brandon edged the vehicle closer to the western side of the lake the trees parted, and Jasi recognized the area where the fire trucks and tents had been pitched. The SUV veered down the road toward Washburn's cabin. When they reached the edge of the doctor's property, Brandon slowed the SUV to a dead crawl.

Jasi pointed to an empty RV pad, half-buried by overgrown shrubs. "Pull over and park there. We'll walk the rest of the way."

Sniffing the humid night air, she reached into her pocket, found the nosepiece and slipped it on. Strange, she thought. Washburn's cabin had burned down four days ago and the air still reeked of smoke.

When the SUV stopped, Jasi jumped out, grabbed two flashlights and chucked one at Brandon. Then she started running. Rounding a corner, she stopped dead in her tracks.

A black BMW sedan had been abandoned on the side of the road.

"Gibney's car," she whispered.

"Yeah," Brandon nodded. "Baker's is over there."

Half-hidden in the shadows of a narrow lane sat Baker's Mitsubishi Zen. Walking toward it, Jasi put her hands to her eyes and peered through the driver's window.

The Zen was empty.

"We've got trouble, Jasi."

Rushing to Brandon's side, she was about to ask him what was wrong. That's when she noticed that the trees ahead of them were lit by a deadly fiery back-glow.

"Oh, hell!" she groaned.

23

Flames licked angrily at the large shed at the back of Washburn's property. Black smoke belched out of the tiny windows, thick and pungent.

Jasi swallowed hard as they raced for the building.

"Brandon! Baker and Gibney are inside."

"You stay here!" Brandon yelled.

She shook her head stubbornly. "No! There are two of them in there. You need me."

She watched while Brandon quickly tore off a strip of his shirt. Then he hissed in a breath, leaned down and roughly captured her lips. His kiss was brief, almost desperate.

"Okay, Jasi. You stay close to me. The smoke will be thick and it'll be hard to see in there. Stay low! Got it?"

He wrapped the cloth around her mouth and nose, securing it snugly behind her head.

"Got it?" he repeated.

"Yeah." She threw her pack on the ground.

Brandon kicked in the door to the shed and a thick curl of smoke erupted from the entrance. He quickly ducked within, taking swift, sure strides.

Jasi followed in his tracks.

Inside the shed, it was pitch-black. Except for the fire that engulfed a mound of what appeared to be old blankets. Frenzied flames leaped above, reaching toward the ceiling. But other than that, Jasi could barely make out her own two feet. Crouching low, she held one hand out in front and kept contact with Brandon's jacket.

After a few seconds, her eyes adjusted to the fiery infernal and she could make out bare shadows and shapes. It was difficult to breathe and the intense heat scorched her throat while sweat trickled down her face and into her eyes. The roar of the fire was deafening. Wood popped and hissed, a dragon spitting fire, and every now and then, Jasi heard a resounding *crack*, like a gunshot.

"We have to hurry," Brandon warned. "There might be chemicals in here."

Seeing something, she tugged on his arm and pointed to the corner behind the door. "Over there!"

Someone was tied to a chair.

The man's head slumped forward, lifeless. She couldn't make out whether it was Martin Gibney or Allan Baker. Choking on noxious smoke, she pushed ahead, ripping at the knots in the rope that bound him.

Then the man's head lolled backward.

"It's Baker!" she yelled hoarsely.

"We need a knife," Brandon shouted. "Stay here!"

He disappeared into the blaze.

Kneeling beside Baker, Jasi closed her eyes and wrestled blindly with the rope. She gagged on a thick cloud of fumes, coughing violently. The nosepiece couldn't block enough of the fumes and she could feel herself slipping. Her reality shifted and the irresistible lure of psychic energy threatened to drag her in.

"Jasi?"

Brandon shoved her fumbling hands aside and began slicing through the ropes with a fishing knife. Then he hoisted Baker over his shoulders while Jasi hastily pushed herself to a standing position.

"Brandon!" she yelled, swaying dizzily.

"What's wrong?" Brandon demanded, one arm grabbing her around the waist.

"Too much smoke. It's taking me…in…"

"Shit!" he swore. "Get outside!"

"Not yet! Where's Gib—"

"Now, Jasi!" Brandon shouted, grabbing her arm and shoving her ahead of him. "I'll come back for Gibney. You shouldn't be in here."

"I'll be fine in a few minutes," she lied. "Give me Baker. I'll take him outside."

Pulling both cans of *OxyBlast* from her pocket, Jasi passed him one. "I'm stronger than I look, Walsh! You need to find Gibney. He's in here somewhere."

Brandon adjusted Baker's limp body over her shoulders. "You sure you can carry his weight?" When she nodded, he eyed her suspiciously, then strode toward the burning blankets.

Jasi forced herself toward the open door, gripping Baker tightly. The heat from the fire singed her lungs and brought burning tears to her eyes. Staggering under Baker's dead weight, she struggled to bring the *OxyBlast* to her mouth.

She dropped it.

Shit!

Jasi couldn't pick up the can and hold onto Baker at the same time so, gathering her strength, she made a beeline for the door. She could feel Baker's limp body pressing her to the ground…and he began slipping from her shoulders.

Panicking, she urged herself into a trot, and when she finally reached the open air, she felt like she had reached an impenetrable wall. She pushed through the invisible wall and stumbled, almost losing her grip. She made it a few yards away before her strength finally gave out. She dumped Baker on the grass, gripped his arms, and then dragged him under a tree, away from the flames. Then she slumped to the ground, panting and gasping for oxygen.

"Hurry up...Brandon!" Jasi rasped loudly.

Please, God! Let Brandon get out of there in one piece.

"Jasi!" someone yelled.

Natassia and Ben dashed toward her. Their guns were drawn as they peered into the shadows.

"Are you okay?" Natassia asked.

"Brandon's...in there," Jasi replied, distraught and breathless. "Cameron... took off somewhere."

Ben glanced at the raging flames. "I'm going in. Jasi, move back a bit, as far as you can." He disappeared into the burning building.

Natassia eyed her with concern. "Jasi?"

"Baker's...over there," Jasi said sluggishly. "He's alive, I think. No burns...as far as I could...tell."

Worried, Natassia inspected her. "You need to get away from the smoke. Go! I'll call the paramedics and stay with Baker."

Jasi shifted to her feet, her eyes latching onto a patch of trees just north of the cabin. A strong wind was carrying the black smoke south, she realized. The air would be clearer by the trees.

"I lost my nosepiece in the fire. I think Baker...knocked it off me. When Brandon put him over...my shoulders." She spoke more to herself. Natassia was already a few feet away.

Jasi concentrated on moving her feet.

One foot in front of the other.

The ground was spongy and damp, and she leaned against a young sapling, its bark slightly damp and soothing. Her head felt woozy, thick with cotton.

The shed was not a massive fire, she told herself. In ten minutes, she'd be back to normal.

She watched Natassia lean over Baker's immobile body, checking for a pulse. Her partner raised a thumb in the air. Baker would live.

But damn it! Where were Brandon and Ben?

Something stirred in the dark behind her.

There!

Jasi turned, expecting to see a bird or small animal. What she saw instead was a flicker of yellow. Someone was cutting through the trees, heading for the road—someone wearing a yellow jacket.

Cameron.

Jasi pushed herself away from the tree, her feet pounding toward Natassia.

"Cameron's in the woods," Jasi rasped, grabbing her pack from the ground. "I'm going after her."

Natassia's head jerked up. "I'll send Ben after you when he comes out." She tossed Jasi the keys to Ben's rental.

With a hasty glance toward the burning shed, Jasi made a decision. Ben and Brandon would watch out for each other. Cameron Prescott, on the other hand, needed to be brought down.

Grabbing the Beretta from under her jacket, Jasi checked the clip. Praying that she wouldn't have to use it, she gripped the gun in her right hand. She inhaled deeply.

Then she began stalking Cameron through the woods.

Deep in the thick forest, rays of moonlight cast haunting shadows between the moss-covered trees. Fishing a flashlight from her pack, Jasi flicked it on. Her head twitched nervously from one leafy specter to the next. Still disoriented from the smoke, she thought of a movie she had seen years ago—*The Blair Witch Project.*

She shivered.

Crack, crack.

A wisp of yellow disappeared into the dense brush.

Adrenaline jumpstarted her heart and Jasi lengthened her pace. Trotting cautiously through the woods with only a thin stream of light from her flashlight to guide her, she realized that she couldn't afford to lose Cameron now. If the reporter reached a vehicle, she could vanish without a trace.

Losing her balance, Jasi stumbled clumsily against a rotted stump. One hand scraped over rough bark while the other aimed the thin light toward the trees, searching for signs of Cameron.

Where are you?

Shit!

Her sense of direction was compromised and she spun around, searching for a clue. Nothing.

What do I do now?

Turning in slow circles, Jasi squinted up through the thick canopy of branches, hoping to get her bearings. When she lowered her eyes, she glimpsed something glowing on the ground a few feet away.

Something florescent pink.

Moving cautiously, she crept forward.

A child's pink skipping rope lay on the ground.

Jasi's heart stopped.

"Follow it," a voice whispered behind her.

Terrified, Jasi whirled around, shining her light carelessly into the trees. Nothing moved in the dark.

"You're losing it, Jasmine McLellan," she muttered.

Warily eyeing the skipping rope, she followed it—all the while wondering how something from her nightmares could possibly be in the woods. Or *someone*.

Creeping forward, Jasi came to the end of the pink rope. The trees opened slightly, revealing the moon, and ahead of her, she recognized the same fallen cedar where they had found the piece of yellow fabric.

Jasi knew where she was now.

Snap!

Following the noise of snapping twigs, she prowled forward stealthily, guessing that they were near the road...near the vehicles. Cameron would have her choice of Baker's Zen or Gibney's BMW...if she had their keys. And if she took the Zen, Jasi would never catch her.

Yellow fabric...

Something teased her memory.

She plucked an earpiece from the bottom of the data-com and plugged it in one ear.

"Data-com on!" she ordered softly. "Natassia."

When she heard Natassia's voice, she whispered, "Contact Ops. Find out about that fabric and get back to me."

"Are you still following her, Jasi?"

"Yeah, she's almost to the road—by the vehicles. I'll get her."

"Okay, but be careful. Baker is conscious, by the way. Some minor injuries and smoke inhalation. Ben called Ops for an airlift and Brandon's on his way to you."

"What about Gibney?" Jasi asked.

There was a pause at the other end, then Natassia said, "Not good, Jasi."

Jasi broke communication, leaving the earpiece in place, and eased her way toward the road. With the Beretta clasped to her chest, she leaned against a tall pine and marked it with a swipe of the neon chalk. If she were lucky, Brandon would find it and determine her direction.

Tucking her flashlight in her pocket, she poked her head from behind the tree.

One, two, three!

Cameron was nowhere in sight.

The sweat trickled down her back, partly from her jaunt into the burning shed and partly from stalking Cameron through the forest. She suspected that the woman carried a gun. That would explain how she had been able to get Baker and Gibney into the shed.

Please don't make me shoot you, Cameron.

Sidestepping behind a bush, Jasi held her breath…waiting. Her eyes flicked back and forth, cautiously searching the bushes, but the only thing that stirred was the pile of leaves at her feet.

I can sense you, she thought. You're watching me.

I'm coming for you, Cameron.

Her heart pumped rapidly and she blinked to clear her vision. Sucking in a puff of air, she crept forward and darted between bushes and deadwood.

Whirrr…

Jasi jumped nervously as her data-com vibrated.

"Shit!" she swore softly, ordering it on.

"Jasi?" Natassia hissed. "I have the report in front of me now."

"Go ahead, but be quiet. I'm right on her heels."

Something crackled to Jasi's right. She ducked between some bushes, crouched low to the musty ground.

"The material is multi-layered," Natassia whispered. "It has, uh, a moisture barrier, thermal barrier and it's flame resistant."

Jasi flicked a watchful glance toward the road, barely listening to Natassia's report. Lowering her voice to a bare whisper she said, *"Anything else?"*

"Hold on. I'm still reading the report myself."

Jasi straightened and edged closer to the road. She was three feet away when she sensed someone close by. Ignoring Natassia's mutterings, she gripped the Beretta firmly in both hands and swept it slowly in front of her from left to right.

Cameron was close.

"Crap!" she heard Natassia exclaim. "Jasi, you're not going to believe this. That material you found? It's from a fire jack—"

Whack!

A solid mass ambushed her and connected with the back of Jasi's shoulder, forcing her to her knees. It happened so fast that she barely had time to register the importance of Natassia's words.

Her backpack went flying. The data-com that was clipped to her jacket was ripped away and thrown on the ground, while a strong arm clenched her tightly around the neck and a gloved hand effortlessly plucked the Beretta from her grip.

"Don't move!"

She felt the muzzle of a gun shoved into her back.

Shit! How could I have been so careless?

Jasi was dragged backward. Her muscles burned in retaliation. Stay calm, she reminded herself. Brandon was somewhere behind her.

As they reached the road, her captor chucked the Beretta into the grass. She was on her own—no weapon.

Things weren't looking good.

"You won't get away," she panted.

"I really didn't want to hurt you, Agent McLellan," a raspy voice cut her off. "You're as useless as tits on a bull."

Tits on a bull?

"Cameron, plea—"

Jasi was forcefully shoved to the ground.

She raised her hands defensively in front of her face and waited for the bullet.

Nothing happened.

"Did you call me *Cameron?*" a familiar voice asked shakily.

Slowly lifting her head, she recognized the face of her captor.

He wore a yellow firefighter's jacket with a shoulder patch that flapped loosely in the wind.

24

"R. J. Scott?" Jasi uttered in disbelief.

She stared in shock at the severely scarred face of the firefighter she had met the first time she had gone to Loon Lake. *Steroiz-man*, she recalled. She remembered that he was a rookie, recently transferred in from Vancouver.

If he *was* an actual firefighter.

Scott stood over her, a brutal expression on his face. He held a gun aimed directly at her head.

"Scott ain't my real name," he muttered.

Jasi eyed the gun uneasily as the man crouched close.

"Why'd you call me Cameron?"

"I thought you were someone else," she murmured, scanning the bushes for signs of Brandon's presence.

Jasi was perplexed. Nothing made sense! Why the hell had this man gone after Baker and Gibney? Why had R. J. Scott killed Washburn and Charlotte Foreman?

Branzon, where are you?

She shifted forward slightly, inching her hands behind her back. She needed a weapon. If she only had her Beretta.

Lost in thoughts of escape she almost missed what the man said next.

"Had a sister named Cameron once. We were twins. She's dead though."

Scott's arm twitched and the gun swayed slightly.

Jasi was stunned. "You're *Ronnie*—Ronald *Jones* Scott?"

"Was," he admitted, eyeing her nervously. "A long time ago. Changed my name when I lived on the streets. Wanted my own identity, I guess. Too many bad memories growing up as Ronnie Jones."

Scott's voice was hoarse and raspy. Like his sister's.

Jasi recalled what Cameron had told her about her injured vocal chords. It only made sense that Cameron's brother would have suffered similar damage.

"Why did you say your sister is dead?" Jasi asked softly.

The man lowered the gun a couple of inches. "Cameron died in a car crash when she was eleven. After she was adopted."

Jasi gasped. "Who told you that—Charlotte Foreman?"

The murderous look in Scott's eyes paralyzed her, and her brain shifted into overdrive.

Each sibling had believed the other was dead.

Before she could correct him, Scott mumbled, "Alan Baker was my foster brother. Now it turns out he's my half-brother too. How's that for irony?" Sneering cynically, he gestured with the gun. "Get up!"

"Cameron is alive!" Jasi blurted, rising unsteadily to her feet. "I've seen the scars on her arm…the cigarette burns."

"Liar!" Scott screamed.

Whack!

Sharp, penetrating pain coursed through her as the butt of the gun smashed down across her face. Faltering, she raised a trembling hand to her mouth. Blood trickled from a gash on her lower lip.

Peering into Scott's eyes, she recognized remorse, doubt…and certain death. She had to think fast. Cameron's brother was a time bomb ticking down, ready to explode.

"Your sister is Cameron *Prescott*," Jasi insisted, fighting back her fear. "The news reporter for *CTBC News*. You must have seen her on TV, Ronald. They told her *you* had drowned."

Scott's eyes flared angrily. "I faked my death. Allan and I went swimming and when he looked away, I took off down shore. Chucked one of my shoes by the water and threw in an old shirt. It had blood on it from morning—when she burned me."

He paused, a faraway look in his eyes. "I just kept walking. I knew that was the only way to get away from *her*."

"Ronald, did Charlotte Foreman do *that* to your face?" Jasi asked hesitantly.

Scott glared at her, his mouth sputtering angry words that were barely discernable.

Then he raised the gun, waving it in the air.

"That bitch! She pushed my face into the fireplace, held me down."

Oh my God!

"And when I passed out from the pain, do you think she'd take me to the doctor?" he demanded furiously, his voice rising. "Oh, no! Not Nana!"

Jasi knew that she had to get the gun away from him.

"Ronald! If you end this now—"

Her eyes caught something moving in the shadows of the bushes. *Brandon?* She licked her lips, desperately wondering what to say next.

"We know what Charlotte Foreman did to you, Ronald. To you and your sister. We know about Washburn, Gibney and your birth mother." She kept her voice steady and calm. "Cameron will know everything too—eventually."

Scott gulped in a breath then hesitantly lowered the gun to his hip. "Nana told me Cameron was dead."

His eyes searched hers. "Is she really alive?"

Jasi was about to answer his question when a black mass leapt from the shadows. Brandon launched his body into the air, screaming at her to move.

Everything grew hazy, and Jasi sensed the sluggish passing of time—like a movie on slow motion. She heard a deafening blast and felt a streak of heat singe past her. Shaking off a piercing pain in her arm, she watched as Brandon's knee connected with Scott's ribcage. Legs flew in all directions while fists smacked into clothing and skin.

And grunts echoed in the dusky woods.

Scott's beefy fist made contact with the corner of Brandon's eye and Jasi watched in horror as he crashed to the ground, doubled over with pain.

"Brandon!" she shouted, running to his side. "Are you okay?"

"I think so," he answered, clenching his head.

Then, from the corner of her eye, she saw Scott dart down the road. *Toward the vehicles.*

"Stay here!" she told Brandon, reaching for the Beretta lying in the grass.

Hot on Scott's heels, Jasi heard an engine roar to life, and she scanned the shadows for a ride of her own. To her left was Natassia and Ben's rental. The Zen was too far down the road. She grabbed the keys from her pocket, then jumped into Ben's car and jammed the key in the ignition. Pressing hard on the gas she gunned the engine and released the brake.

Following the streak of dust that trailed behind Martin Gibney's BMW, Jasi caught up to Scott and leaned on the horn. She rolled down her window and steered to the right of the sedan, forcing Scott to move over to the side of the gravel road. Then she eased forward until they were neck in neck.

Scott turned his head. His eyes were cool, determined.

"Pull over!" she yelled.

She held the Beretta in her right hand, crossing it in front of her while she gripped the steering wheel with her other hand.

"Pull the goddamn car over *now!*"

Ronald jerked the wheel and smashed into the side of the rental, and a high-pitched grating sound cut through the air. A second hit sent Jasi's vehicle flying forward.

Hovering her foot over the brake, she hesitated for a second. Then she slammed her foot down. Scott drove the BMW directly into the backend of her car, and the impact snapped the seatbelt against her, fracturing one of her ribs and knocking the air from her lungs.

From the corner of her eye, she caught a flash of metal behind her. With Scott trapped inside, Gibney's sedan flipped and sailed into the trees. Then it crashed to the ground with a horrendous thud and a screeching of metal.

Finally, there was blessed silence.

Jasi faded in and out of consciousness—until she smelled gasoline.

"Move it, Jasmine!" she groaned, dazed and lightheaded.

Wrestling with the seatbelt, she managed to crawl from the vehicle. When she staggered to her feet, she winced in agony. Her ankle ached with every step, her ribs were on fire and her arm throbbed mercilessly.

She leaned against a tree, surveying Ben's car in the moonlight. No gas leak, she thought.

Then she turned slowly.

Ronald Scott was slouched over the steering wheel of what remained of Martin Gibney's car. The airbag had exploded, sending white powder everywhere.

When she inched closer, Scott sat up. His eyes followed her unsteady progress.

Swallowing hard, she leveled her gun at him. "Get out of the car, Ronald!"

Scott shook his head. "It's gone too far. Don't you understand, Agent McLellan? Cameron and I were innocent children."

"Like Samantha Davis—the little girl you murdered?" Jasi asked in a deadly voice.

"That was an accident. She was in the wrong place at the—"

"Wrong time," Jasi finished for him.

"But I *freed* Samantha, from a childhood of pain!" he shouted defiantly. "You have no idea what that bitch did to her. To all of us! She'd starve us—chain us to the wall like animals, hang us like slabs of gutted beef. And if Nana was in a good mood, we'd play games. She had her own version of *Survivor*. But in her version? You didn't get booted off the island—you got burned! That's how Cameron got the scars on her arm. That's how I got this!"

Scott wrenched back the hair from his face, exposing the vicious-looking scar.

Then his eyes clashed with hers.

"I couldn't protect her! My own sister, my twin."

Jasi stood dead still.

The Beretta in her hand quivered slightly.

And then a waft of gas fumes assaulted her.

Wrenching a piece of metal away from the car door, she noticed a thin stream of gas pouring from the ruptured fuel tank of the sedan. And a puff of smoke trailed from the engine.

"Come on, Ronald! Get out!"

Remaining inside the battered car, a slow smile crossed the shadows of the man's scarred face. Scott's eyes locked onto hers, daring her to shoot. Daring her to put him out of his misery.

Jasi began to panic.

Smoke sizzled from somewhere underneath the car and she was afraid that her senses would be triggered. Her shoulder throbbed and a shooting pain sliced down her arm.

Brandon! Where are you? I need you!

"Do the time, Ronald," she begged, motioning him to get out of the car. "Then you can start over."

Scott laughed derisively. "Start over? With a face like *this*? I've been scarred for life, Agent McLellan."

In more ways than one, she thought.

Scott slowly raised a closed fist.

When he opened his hand, moonlight bounced off a small cylindrical shape in his palm.

Shivers of dread pulsated down Jasi's spine.

"Don't!" she whispered.

Scott flicked the lighter.

Raising her gun, she aimed between his eyes. She fingered the trigger but was unable to squeeze it. When she peered down the gun barrel, she saw an innocent, tortured little boy who had been tossed away—unloved.

Scott held up a folded piece of paper.

"I don't need my list anymore."

He twisted the paper and she froze, helpless, as he held it to the flame. Fire erupted and curled around the paper like a serpent, deadly and sly.

"No!" she screamed, taking a few steps forward.

"Stay back, Agent McLellan." Scott's eyes were glazed, lost. "Enough people have died. Justice has been served."

"Let me bring you in, Ronald. Please!"

"It's too late for me. Tell Cameron…tell her, I'm sorry."

He held the burning paper out the window.

Then he let it go.

Jasi whipped around and started to run when a massive blast shook the ground, drowning out her scream. The impact of the explosion propelled her forward—away from the car—and she hit the ground, face-first and hard.

Gasping for breath, she weakly pushed herself to her knees and flipped over on her back, her eyes drifting over the inferno. Smoke billowed from the burning wreck, pouring over her, coating her.

Stunned and battered, she faded in and out of consciousness, barely aware of the blazing car. Dark clouds sailed over the night sky, making it difficult for her to count the stars.

Frowning, she wondered why the universe was so hazy. How could she see a shooting star when there were so many clouds?

"Jasi..."

Someone called her name.

She knew she should recognize the voice, but the clouds were getting in the way. Smoke clung to her mouth, her nose. Every inch of her skin was painted with it. It sucked at her, its tentacles gripping her firmly and pulling.

Where am I?

Lost in the clouds, she searched blindly for a way out. Stumbling in the darkness of her vision, she jabbed her hands in the air, anxious to connect with something solid.

"She's over here!" a disembodied voice called from somewhere.

Lost in the dark. No escape.

Unresisting, Jasi connected with Ronald Scott and slipped into his mind...

I freed Samantha Davis from a childhood of suffering—the kind of pain that torments the body, the mind and spirit. Allan Baker got off easy. He was only there in that house of torture for a few weeks. Then he got out and started over.

No one knows what my sister and I went through. Our own father tried to kill us shortly after birth. He murdered our mother, then paid a sick, disgusting woman to abuse us...to keep us under control.

Nana was pure evil.

She'd drag my sister and I inside that shed, bind our wrists, and then hang us from iron hooks while she tortured our bodies with a lighter. Sometimes she'd take us to Dr. Gibney's, threatening to kill one of us if we told.

Dr. Gibney ignored our cries, our pain and our agony.

And then he'd send us back to her.

We were punished if Nana forgot something, punished if we ate too much, punished if we cried. And each time we were punished, she told us the same thing.

It was always our fault.

A child can only survive for so long, being made to feel worthless.

To Nana, we were nothing!

Cameron, my sister—my other half.

The good part of me.

I often sensed your presence. I think I always knew that you were still alive.

Somewhere.

I just couldn't find you.

So, I tried to find...myself.

Blinking back tears of grief, Jasi awoke and found herself cradled in Brandon's arms. They were sitting on the ground a few feet from the smoldering ruins of Gibney's car.

And Ronald Scott's body, she reminded herself.

Ben hovered anxiously nearby.

"Here," Brandon insisted, handing her a can of *OxyBlast*.

Putting the bottle to her mouth, she inhaled deeply.

"I'll be fine. Just give me a few minutes to clear my head."

Stubbornly, she tried to roll away from him and gasped when an excruciating pain raced through her left arm.

"Relax," Brandon told her, trapping her firmly against him. "Don't move."

"Jesus, Walsh!" she snarled sharply. "Will you stop babying me?" She elbowed him in the ribs and was rewarded with a sharp grunt.

"Just lie still and wait for the chopper," Ben ordered, hovering above her.

Jasi eyed both men suspiciously.

Brandon was holding her tightly, caressing her face. Ben paced in front of her while ripping a piece of cloth into strips.

Why are they acting so strange?

Angry, she flicked Brandon's hand away. "Where's Natassia?"

"She's with Baker and Gibney. Baker's okay, but Gibney..." Brandon paused, glanced at Ben, then said, "He might not make it."

"If you let me up, I'll go stay with them."

Brandon shook his head, reaching for the cloth strips.

"You've lost a lot of blood, Jasi."

"I'm okay," she scoffed. "Just a few scratch—"

"No, you're not okay," he growled fiercely, his eyes flashing darkly.

Brandon shone a flashlight on her arm and her eyes followed the path of light. Something dark and wet stained the sleeve. Then she saw something peculiar.

Uncomprehending, she stared at a bloody, gaping hole in the sleeve of her jacket.

Then it hit her.

Ronald Scott had shot her when Brandon had jumped him.

Judging from the position of the bullet hole, the slug had just missed the kevlar vest. But it hadn't missed her arm. She vaguely recalled the stinging sensation that had rippled through her arm. The residue from the fire had blocked her pain receptors.

But the pain was kicking in now—full force.

Brandon tightly secured the cloth around her arm, but within seconds, it was soaked with blood.

"It may have hit an artery," he explained grimly.

With those words, she realized that her injuries could be serious.

Or worse—fatal.

Jasi shivered, her body quivering with icy cold. She blinked, trying to focus as Brandon swayed dizzily in front of her.

She raised her aching arm. The cuff of her jacket was damp, and when she held up her hand, droplets of crimson fell to her lap. She watched her blood, mesmerized. Her hand was sticky, cold, and she couldn't feel her fingers.

Jasi drew in a ragged breath, her head shifting slowly from Ben to Brandon.

"Oh shit," she moaned.

And she promptly passed out.

25

"How's the patient doing today?" Natassia smiled, perching cautiously on the edge of the hospital bed.

"Not very patient," Jasi mumbled groggily. "Get me outta here."

There was no answer.

"Well?"

Natassia wagged her finger. "I don't think so, girl friend. You have to stay here for a couple of days. You lost so much blood it put Dracula to shame."

Jasi managed a grimace of a smile.

"Do you know how hard it was to get in here?" Natassia asked, outraged. "Nurse Hitler wouldn't let me in. I'm not _family_, she said. I had to flash her my badge. So how are you really feeling?"

"Two fractured ribs, a sprained ankle, a mild concussion and a bullet wound in my left arm. They removed the bullet. No permanent damage. All in all, I'd say a normal day at the office."

She saw Natassia roll her eyes toward the ceiling.

Jasi's left arm was bandaged, secured in a sling. It throbbed mercilessly.

"You lucky *be-atch*," Natassia grinned. "That means more downtime for you. And something new to add to your collection."

Jasi tried to bite back a smile.

Only Natassia would see the 'bright side' of being shot.

"So what happened after I passed out?"

Natassia told her that an Ops helicopter had flown her to Vancouver General Hospital. Jasi had arrived unconscious and bloody. She was immediately taken into surgery where the bullet from Scott's gun was tweezed out, half an inch from the radial artery. There was some minor damage to her nerve endings but that would heal.

"Did they save the bullet for me?" Jasi asked in a small voice.

The drugs were making her sleepy.

"Yeah. They found your note."

Jasi kept a note tucked behind her ID photo requesting that any foreign object taken from her body be put into a Ziploc bag. She possessed a bizarre collection of slugs and shrapnel. She kept them on a shelf in her spare room.

"How's Baker?"

Natassia flinched as she flopped into a chair beside the bed. "As obnoxious as ever in some ways."

"What's he up to now? Did he hit on you?"

"No, not me. But he hit on half the nurses on the floor."

"Some things never change."

There was a soft rap on the door.

When Jasi glanced up, Ben entered the room, carrying a huge bouquet of blue roses. Setting the flowers down on the small bedside table, he dragged a chair toward her.

"They're from everyone at Ops," he explained, indicating the flowers. "Do you need anything?"

"I'm fine, Ben. My memory is just…cloudy. Fill me in."

"You and Brandon got Baker and Gibney out of the shed just in time," Ben said. "Brandon told us how he followed your tree marks. He heard most of what Scott told you too."

"And Ronald Scott?" she asked.

"He's dead, Jasi" Natassia sighed. "He died before the paramedics arrived."

"What do you think set him off?" Jasi asked wearily.

Ben patted her hand.

"We think Scott tried to block his memories of the abuse. Approximately three months ago, he made some inquiries into his birth. He tried to find out the identity of his foster mother but the records were sealed. He probably couldn't remember the Foremans' names or address. He had no idea where Charlotte Foreman lived until he called out with the VFD to that earlier fire in their neighborhood. You remember? Jessica Marie told us about that fire."

The fence fire that the teenagers had set.

"He must have recognized the house or the neighborhood," Ben guessed. "He had his foster mother's death planned for months. That's why he purchased the Gemini lighters. For some reason, he sent the first lighter to Jasi. Then, once he knew where she lived, he went after Charlotte Foreman."

"And before he killed her, she told him that Washburn was his father," Jasi added.

Ben clenched his jaw. "Scott killed his foster mother in the shed where she had tortured him. And with Washburn, he stretched him out as if on a hospital table, then used the IV tubing to strangle him."

"How'd he get the tubing?"

"We figure he stole it from a paramedic's truck," he replied. "It would have been easy for Scott to jump inside an unattended truck, steal the tubing and then take off. If he was in uniform he could have easily disappeared into a group of firefighters—unnoticed."

Jasi looked at Natassia. "The boot print. It was a fire fighter's boot, right?"

Natassia nodded. "Ronald Jones Scott joined the fire department in Vancouver. Maybe it was his way of psychologically putting out fires. He knew the Foremans lived somewhere in Victoria so, when he was ready, he forged a transfer. That yellow fabric we found with the blue thread was a match with Scott's fire jacket."

Jasi remembered the first time she had met *R. J. Scott*. He had been wearing the standard yellow firefighter's jacket...with a loose patch.

"How'd he manage to get Baker and Gibney to Loon Lake?"

"Scott called Baker first and told him he had some information on Washburn," Ben said. "Once he had Baker tied up, Scott forced him to call Gibney and tell him he had proof that Gibney was involved in the prostitute's murder. Of course, that wasn't true. Once Gibney arrived, Ronald Scott knocked him out then poured gasoline on him. Made Gibney a human sacrifice. Baker witnessed it all before he passed out."

Jasi closed her eyes for a moment. "Ronald told me he faked the drowning, then lived on the streets."

Natassia nodded. "After ERT pulled him from the car, we found his wallet in the grass. Ops sent a team to his apartment and as near as we can tell, Ronald Scott spent most of his youth living on the street. When CPS couldn't locate him, they eventually forgot about him. And if he wasn't hiding on the streets, we figure he was in the woods. Ops found camping equipment in his room."

Jasi's head snapped anxiously toward Ben. "What about that pink skipping rope in the woods? Did you pick it up?"

Ben frowned. "What skipping rope?"

"There was a pink skipping rope on the ground. That's how I knew which way Scott went." Jasi gasped. *Now why would Scott have left a clue like that?*

Ben and Natassia exchanged startled looks.

Then Ben shook his head. "Jasi, there was nothing in that woods. Except the markings you made in the trees. We've already scoured it—thoroughly."

She was confused. The rope *had* been there. She was sure of it. She recalled touching it, following it.

"What about Scott?" Natassia prodded. "What did he have to say?"

Jasi explained how all the children in Charlotte Foreman's care had been mistreated—burned with cigarettes or lighters, and left in the shed. How his foster mother had scarred Ronald's face, permanently disfiguring him.

"Charlotte Foreman told him Cameron died in a car accident. Scott faked his death to escape the abuse. But there was no escape for him. He never had a hope in hell. He was molded into a killer from the moment he was born. From the second he was dumped into the garbage along with his sister."

Jasi's eyes drifted shut.

Ronald Scott was gone—dead.

She should be relieved. And part of her *was* relieved, but another part cried for a forgotten little boy, abused by his foster mother, abused by the system.

The people Scott had relied on the most had created a killer. Charlotte Foreman, Washburn, Gibney. They were all responsible. Even Allan Baker had his role.

"And so continues the cycle of abuse," Jasi murmured sadly.

No one spoke.

She thought of her visions, of Natassia's. She ached for the twin babies who were abandoned, left to die. She ached for the young boy whose face was forced into a scorching fire. She ached for Cameron who would have to live with what her brother had done.

Cameron *Prescott*.

Jasi blinked suddenly. "Cameron was adopted by a couple by the last name of Prescott. Around the same time, in a different town, her twin brother changed his last name to *Scott*."

"Coincidence?" Natassia asked.

"No, I don't think so. I think it was a twin thing. I wonder why neither of them *knew* the other was alive?"

Natassia and Ben gave her a blank look.

"Ben, what about Baker?" Jasi asked suddenly. "What's he going to do? He has a sister now. A half-sister at least."

"Premier Allan Baker? Now there's an enigma. I passed him at the nurse's station. He told me he'll stop by before he leaves."

"What do you mean *leaves*?" she demanded, her green eyes flashing dangerously. "How the hell—"

"He only had minor injuries," Ben interrupted. "Bruised ribs and a few cuts. They're sending him home."

Jasi eased herself into a sitting position. "Benjamin Roberts! You know there's only one thing I hate more than my goddamn birthday and that's—"

"Hospitals!" Ben and Natassia finished for her.

Jasi pouted. "That bastard gets to leave already?"

There was a muffled sound from the doorway.

Premier Allan Baker took two steps into the room, his feet shuffling restlessly. A thick white bandage was taped to his bruised forehead, just above his right eye. He was holding a plant in one hand and a small box in the other.

"Mind if this bastard comes in?" he asked ruefully.

Jasi gaped at him, open-mouthed.

Then she waved him in.

Baker took tentative steps, like an old man.

Wincing, he set the plant on the window ledge. Then he looked from Ben to Natassia, and finally to Jasi.

"I, uh, just wanted to thank you—all of you. For saving my life."

"Natassia and I had nothing to do with it," Ben said coolly. "It was Jas—uh...Agent McLellan."

Baker glanced awkwardly in Jasi's direction. "Brandon Walsh told me."

At the mention of Brandon's name, Jasi experienced a stab of sadness, an ache that could not be dulled with drugs. Brandon would be leaving soon. And she was not going to stop him.

It's better this way, she reminded herself.

Baker edged closer to her bed. "Chief Walsh told me that you're responsible for finding Gibney and me. That you carried me out of that fire, even though the smoke was deadly. I just wanted to say...thank you."

Jasi flicked her uninjured arm in the air. "No big deal, *Premier* Baker."

Baker flinched noticeably. "You won't have to call me that for long. I'm stepping down."

Jasi was speechless.

Ben and Natassia exchanged bewildered frowns.

When Baker finally spoke, his voice held a trace of bitterness. "There's just been too many secrets, too many lies. Everything's going to come out in the end. My father left me a legacy of death. He killed a woman, abandoned two babies in the garbage and he was involved in illegally operating an abortion clinic. Who's going to want a Prime Minister with a family history like that?"

He had a point, Jasi realized. The man would never be able to hold a public position again. Allan Baker's political career was over.

"Agent McLellan?" he asked. "I've been told that you usually use public transport or CFBI vehicles. Agent Roberts told me that your car was destroyed, during your last case. Some unfortunate accident?"

Jasi lifted a brow, twisted her head and glared at Ben.

"I had a visitor in my car," she mumbled dryly. "One that really *ticked* me off."

When Baker gave her a dull look, she rolled her eyes.

No one appreciated her warped sense of humor.

"A bomb," she explained with a hoarse chuckle.

He smiled nervously and then his scarred palms pressed the small box into her hands. "I hope you'll accept this then. As a token of my thanks."

Jasi carefully opened the box, watching Baker from beneath her lashes. She peeled aside a small piece of tissue. Underneath it was a silver key. Attached to the key was a small, rectangular black square with security buttons.

She choked back a gasp. "The key to your Mitsubishi Zen?"

"*Your* Zen," Baker replied.

Realizing the impact of his words, her head snapped up and she exclaimed, "Oh, no you don't! I can't accept this!"

"The Zen is yours, Agent McLellan."

"No, it's not! CFBI policy states that we cannot accept outside payment for doing our—"

"This isn't payment," Baker pressed. "It's a gift—for saving my life. I wouldn't be standing here if it wasn't for you."

"But this is too much!" she sputtered. "It's too, uh, too damned valuable!"

Jasi darted a quick glance at Natassia for support.

Natassia grinned at her. "We *can* accept gifts, Jasi. No matter *how* expensive they are. And Divine's already approved it."

She stood up, bent toward Jasi and whispered loudly in her ear. "Take the car, you stubborn mule."

Outnumbered and exhausted, Jasi glanced at Ben.

He shrugged, holding back a smile. "You do need a new car, Jasi. You'll still have to pay the insurance."

"The insurance is a bit high," Baker advised her. "But I have a few contacts. I'll get you a good deal."

Ever the politician, Jasi thought. Maybe the guy should go into car sales.

She wondered whether BC would suffer, losing a Premier who slept around so casually with other men's wives or girlfriends. She had to admit, though—she was seeing a different side to the man. Perhaps his father's death had changed Allan Baker after all.

She picked up the key, running her thumb over the fob.

Then she turned it in her hands and remembered Ronald Scott.

"Why do you think Scott didn't take your car? He could have bypassed the alarm and I wouldn't have been able to catch up to him."

Baker grinned. "I had an upgrade added to the door handle. A fingerprint security system. You can't open the door until the system checks the print. Don't worry. It's all ready for you to program your own prints."

Jasi was tempted—so very tempted.

What had her father always told her?

Don't look a gift-horse in the mouth?

"But don't you need your car?"

He smiled down at her. "Not where I'm going. I'm taking a long vacation, Agent McLellan. Probably to the Caribbean. At least until things die down. So I won't need a car for awhile."

Jasi spared a quick glance at Ben.

"Just take the damned thing!" he huffed.

Smiling, she thanked Baker. "A fingerprint security system, huh?"

"There are a few other perks too," Baker smirked as he limped to the door. "But I'll let you discover them yourself."

Natassia let out a loud sigh of relief after Baker had gone. "Jesus, Jasi! For a moment I thought you were going to give him back the key."

Ben laughed. "Me too." He gave Jasi a friendly peck on the cheek. "I almost buzzed the nurse for more drugs."

His data-com chirped insistently.

When Ben shifted away from the bed, Jasi heard only a few muffled words before he whispered something in Natassia's ear.

"I'll be back later, Jasi," he said, a serious expression on his face as he hurried out the door.

She studied Natassia. "Where's he going?"

Her partner's voice was somber. "To meet with Lydia Gibney. Her husband didn't make it. He had third-degree burns to most of his body. His nerve endings were completely destroyed, along with underlying muscles and tissues."

Jasi knew what that meant.

If he had lived, Gibney would have been scarred beyond recognition. Years of therapy and excruciating pain were what he would have had to look forward to.

Martin Gibney was better off dead.

Feeling drowsy, she was about to give in to the drugs when she remembered something. "Hey! On my birthday, you were going to tell me something. Some secret."

Natassia gave her a sly, wicked grin. Then her brow twitched up, twice.

Jasi giggled. "You and Ben?"

"Yeah, but don't say anything. Ben doesn't want anyone to know."

"Piss off! I'm not just anyone," Jasi grinned, closing her eyes. "Oh, and Natassia?"

"Yeah?"

"You *are* family."

The room was so quiet that Jasi had to pry one eye open to see if Natassia was still there.

Her friend sat in the chair, beaming widely and wiping tears from her eye.

Jasi scowled, then clenched her eyelids shut.

Damn!

This friendship business was a lot of work.

"Don't you want to know where a particular TDS firefighter has been the past two days?" she heard Natassia say hesitantly.

Brandon...

When Jasi's eyes popped opened, Natassia leaned forward eagerly. "Brandon Walsh has been by your side the entire time. The nurses wanted to boot him out, but—"

"Let me guess," Jasi said dryly. "He charmed them into letting him stay."

"No," a male voice announced from the doorway. "I told them there was a beautiful woman waiting in here for me...naked."

Wearing a huge grin, Brandon sauntered into the room.

"For crying out loud, Walsh," Jasi snapped, flustered by his remark.

He held up both hands in defense and grinned. "Okay, I left out the naked part."

Jasi glanced uneasily in Natassia's direction while Brandon shifted forward, his pale eyes scanning her injuries.

"Don't leave me with him," Jasi hissed between clenched teeth.

Natassia patted her shoulder gently, clucked like a mother hen, and then vanished.

Jasi scowled after her.

Some family you are, Natassia!

Brandon waited while she adjusted her position and pushed herself back against the pillows. "How are you feeling?"

"Like I've been run over by a semi. Twice!"

"You look pretty damn good—for roadkill."

She flinched at the undertone in his voice.

He scooted the chair closer and reached for her hand. "Jas—"

"Don't!" she threatened, pulling away.

"I've been doing a lot of thinking while you've been lying in here. I think we can make this work between us."

Jasi groaned tiredly. "There's another reason why we can't get involved, Brandon."

She heard his soft intake of breath.

"When I get involved with someone it takes something from me. It can interfere with my skills. It blocks me, exhausts me...drains me."

"But what about Ben? Natassia?" he asked, rising to his feet. "You care about them?"

"I don't know why it's different with them. It just...is."

Brandon fiddled with the plant that Baker had placed near the window. "What if we take it slow, Jasi? We could see how I affect you, your gift. Maybe it'll be different with me. Maybe your psychic abilities won't—"

She shook her head.

"I'm not willing to take that chance, Brandon. I'm sorry but it's not just my career we're talking about. This is my life! Helping people. What I do can mean the difference between life and death for someone."

Jasi thought of the man lying at the bottom of the ocean.

"When I get...close to someone I lose something and that could cost a life. A victim's, mine...even yours."

Standing by the window, Brandon looked away.

When he finally spoke, his voice was cool. "You care about me then." It wasn't a question.

"Yes."

Her answer was bittersweet.

Neither of them uttered a word.

There was an endless silence—a void of emptiness. And in that emptiness, Jasi found herself. Alone.

In two swift steps, Brandon reached her side and leaned down. His mouth was hard, demanding. His kiss ravished her. It made her body tingle right down to her toes. Then he drew back until his face was inches from hers, and his ice blue eyes devoured hers.

"I'm not giving up on us."

She wasn't expecting that. His comment shook her.

Brandon strode to the door, then halted.

"Can I ask you something, Jasi?"

Too tired to resist him, she nodded.

"This job you do—it's dangerous. You almost died on this case." His voice cracked slightly. "Why?"

Confused by the question, she stammered, "W-why, what?"

"Why did you choose this line of work?"

Her breath hung suspended in time.

Then she exhaled a long, ragged sigh. "Brandon...you don't understand."

His eyes blasted her with coolness...and a tinge of something else.

Regret.

Without a word, he walked out the door.

"I *didn't* choose it!" Jasi shouted after him. "Walsh!"

But the door had already closed.

Her heart was tearing.

She could almost envision it—shredded and useless, lying on the floor.

"I didn't choose it, Brandon," she whispered hoarsely, her eyelids fluttering shut.

It chose me.

The sedatives in her IV lured her toward a safe, painless unconsciousness.

And then Agent Jasi McLellan slept.

The sleep of the dead.

Epilogue

She floated in and out of consciousness, like a wave lapping restlessly against the shore. She was oblivious to the sounds and faces that floated past her.

Where was she? Why was it so dark and cold?

Jasi's eyes wandered, taking in the long corridor before her and the door at the end of the hall. It seemed so far away. The bare floor gleamed, polished to a reflective shine. She could hear the patter of her black sandals as they clicked along the floor.

She leaned down, staring at her reflection—a face that she did not recognize. Blinking rapidly, she cried out in terror when the face became two. Her head whipped around. A scream became trapped in her throat.

The dead girl from her closet was coming for her.

The girl's eyes were hollowed and black. Her face was a ghastly pale shade of gray. The pink skipping rope noose cut deeply into her lolling neck.

"Why can't you leave me alone?" Jasi pleaded.

The dead girl's gray, blistered face moved. "I can't leave. You need me. And I need you."

Her accent was soft—southern.

"He keeps callin' me," the girl whispered, her eyes wide and full of fear.

"Who?" Jasi demanded.

The girl began to sob.

Jasi reached out to touch her blistered shoulder but snatched her hand back when it encountered skin that was colder than ice.

"Who are you?"

The hallway closed in around them, pulsating like a snake's belly digesting its prey. A bright light at one end of the hallway made Jasi turn away.

"Emily," came the soft reply.

"What do you want, Emily?"

The girl's next words chilled Jasi to the bone.

"I want you to find me."

Jasi shook her head, confused, and took a few steps back toward the light. "What do you mean? You're right...here."

The girl said nothing.

"I've seen you ever since I was a child," Jasi remarked. "You've never spoken to me before. Why now?"

She took two steps toward the light, then waited.

Emily lowered her head. "You jes never heard me before. Now you're open. Now you're hearin' me fine."

Jasi glanced behind her. The light flickered once. The brilliance beckoned her closer, enveloping her in its warmth—a cocoon of safety. She paused and looked back at the dead girl with the pink skipping rope around her throat.

"It's okay, Jasmine," Emily smiled weakly. "Go."

The girl drifted backward into the shadows of a closet.

"Emily, wait!" Jasi cried out. "How do I find you?"

The girl's smile brightened and her lifeless body flared with color for a second. "When you're ready, I'll find you."

As Jasi drifted off into a peaceful healing sleep, she made a solemn vow to the dead girl in her closet.

I'll find you, Emily.

I promise...

Divine
Justice

~ the second novel in a new 'psi-fi' suspense thriller series by Cheryl Kaye Tardif.

CFBI agent Jasi McLellan battles a serious infection that threatens to claim her life. Slipping in and out of consciousness, she relives the Parliament Murders.

One by one, members of Parliament are disappearing, only to be found days later—disoriented and drugged. Two have washed up on the shore…*dead*.

In this extreme case of identity theft, Jasi and her PSI team head for Ottawa. Accompanied by longtime partner, Ben Roberts, and the new VE, Natassia Prushenko, Jasi uncovers a plot so devious that Canada's national security is put at risk.

And to make matters worse, Jasi bumps into an old flame, Zane Underhill, who wants to pick up where they had left off three years ago. It doesn't take long before Jasi realizes that Zane isn't the person she once knew.

In the end, Jasi is forced to make a decision—one that will cost the life of a friend.

Divine Justice ~ Watch for it soon!

Check out Cheryl Kaye Tardif's
terrifying new techno-thriller...

THE RIVER

How far do we go until we've gone too far?

The South Nahanni River has a history of mysterious deaths, disappearances and headless corpses, but it may also hold the key to humanity's survival—or its destruction.

Seven years ago, Del Hawthorne's father and three of his friends disappeared near the Nahanni River and were presumed dead. When one of the missing men stumbles onto the University grounds, alive but barely recognizable and aging before her eyes, Del is shocked. Especially when the man tells her something inconceivable. Her father is still alive!

Gathering a group of volunteers, Del travels to the Nahanni River to rescue her father. There, she finds a secret underground river that plunges her into a technologically advanced world of nanobots and painful serums. Del uncovers a conspiracy of unimaginable horror, a plot that threatens to destroy us all. Will humanity be sacrificed for the taste of eternal life?

And at what point have we become...God?

"Tardif specializes in mile-a-minute potboiler mysteries."
—*Edmonton Sun*

ISBN: 1412062292

And Cheryl Kaye Tardif's
bestselling novel,

Whale Song

In Cheryl Kaye Tardif's tragic **Whale Song**, *haunting native legends
merge with the modern world as a young woman struggles with long-
forgotten memories of her mother's suicide.*

A timeless story of love, tragedy and transformation.

Thirteen years ago, Sarah Richardson's life was shattered
when her mother committed suicide. The shocking tragedy
left a grief-stricken teen-aged Sarah with partial amnesia.

Some things are easier to forget.

But now a familiar voice from her past sends Sarah, a
talented mid-twenties ad exec, back to her past. A past that
she had thought was long buried.

Some things are meant to be buried.

Torn by nightmares and visions of a yellow-eyed wolf, yet
aided by the creatures of the Earth and by the killer whales
that call to her in the night, Sarah must face her fears and
uncover the truth—even if it destroys her.

Some things are meant to be remembered—at all cost.

ISBN: 978-1-60164-007-9 or 1-60164-007-2
Available at your favorite bookstore or online.

Cheryl Kaye Tardif is the author of *Whale Song*, a novel that has become a hit with adult and young adult readers. She also wrote a public service announcement for a racial harmony campaign. Her PSA script, *One Voice ~ One World* placed third and aired on cable channels in Alberta.

Ms. Tardif has published numerous works of poetry in small Canadian newspapers, and was the author of two regular newspaper columns in BC. She also published a work of poetry in an American anthology, and currently maintains a website.

Born in BC, Cheryl Kaye Tardif was a 'military brat' and then a 'military wife', and has lived all across Canada. She currently resides in Alberta with her husband, Marc, her daughter, Jessica, the current Japanese exchange student, and the family dog/reincarnated spoiled child, Royale.

Ms. Tardif is already working on her next novel, *The River*, a gripping techno-thriller that is both thought-provoking and terrifying. And she has started *Divine Justice*, the second in the *Divine* 'psi-fi' suspense thriller series.

**For more information about the author,
please visit her website at:
www.cherylktardif.com**

You can e-mail Ms. Tardif at:
cherylktardif@shaw.ca

Lightning Source UK Ltd.
Milton Keynes UK
19 October 2009

145137UK00001B/297/P